P9-EED-679

200

DEAD RINGER

A JACOB ASCH MYSTERY

DEAD RINGER

ARTHUR LYONS

An Owl Book

HOLT, RINEHART AND WINSTON
New York

Copyright © 1977 by Arthur Lyons, Jr.
All rights reserved, including the right to reproduce this
book or portions thereof in any form.

Published by Holt, Rinehart and Winston,
383 Madison Avenue, New York, New York 10017.
Published simultaneously in Canada by Holt, Rinehart and
Winston of Canada, Limited.

Library of Congress Cataloging in Publication Data
Lyons, Arthur.
Dead ringer.
(A Jacob Asch mystery)
"An Owl book."
I. Title.   II. Series: Lyons, Arthur. Jacob
Asch mystery.
PS3562.Y446D44   1983   813'.54   83-104
ISBN 0-03-060396-X

First published in hardcover
by Mason/Charter in 1977
First Owl Book Edition—1983
Printed in the United States of America
1 3 5 6 7 9 10 8 6 4 2

ISBN 0-03-060396-X

For
KENNY NORTON
a banger with heart
and
BOB GOODMAN
who told me what
a banger with heart is
and
DAVE HARRIS
who made this
book a dead ringer

1

Carlos Realango had a picture-book left hook. That was about the only thing he had that was picture-book.

He was strictly a brawler, a swarmer, a club fighter. Where a master boxer might fight a strategic fight, geared to capitalize on the weaknesses of his opponent's style, Realango waged wars of attrition, relying solely on guts and brute strength and a seemingly endless ability to absorb punishment to wear his man down.

Two years ago, when he had been in his prime, that had been enough to take out all but the very best of them. But two years ago was two years ago and now he was up there in the ring, looking like an ad for Haley's M.O.

The kid in with him was a tall, lanky black nobody had ever heard of named Billy Majors and he couldn't have been more than twenty-one or two. He had a sizable advantage over Realango in reach and a sizable disadvantage in everything else. He was strictly an opponent, a payday, and nobody had expected him to be vertical at the end of four, never mind nine. He had been on the canvas twice—once in the second and once in the fourth—but he had managed to beat the count both times and keep that long left in Realango's face long enough to shake out the cobwebs and now it was going into the tenth and he was still on his feet and seemingly in full control of his faculties. And because of that fact, the sympathy of the crowd had taken an abrupt shift.

Nine rounds ago, the half-empty arena had erupted in cheers when Realango stepped into the ring. He had just recently come out of retirement and they had wanted to see him make it all the way back. Now the only place they wanted to see him make it back to was Argentina.

1

The seat beside me in the fifth row was empty, but then it wasn't anymore. The man who slipped into it was short and chubby and he might have been thirty-five or even a boyish forty, but not much more than that. He had sandy-colored hair that hung over the back of his collar in a shag-cut and a moist, pink, lineless face on which were arranged a small nose, a wide mouth and blue eyes that were set far apart and slightly bugged. He had on an expensive gray checked sports jacket which was too tight under the arms and too short in the sleeves, an open-necked navy blue Ban-Lon shirt, gray slacks, and maroon patent leather Pierre Cardin shoes. One side of his shirt collar overlapped the lapel of his jacket, the other was tucked somewhere out of sight, as if he had thrown the coat on in a hurry. I had a feeling he could take two hours to get dressed and still look as if he'd thrown his coat on in a hurry.

"Excuse me," he said, tapping me on the arm. "Is your name Asch?"

"Yes."

He smiled amiably and stuck out his hand. "Jack Schwartz."

The hand was plump and red and hairless, with thick, blunt fingers that were squared-off on the ends, as if they had been lopped off a little short. "Sorry you had to come all the way down here," he said, "but we couldn't get to L.A. and I didn't want to talk about it on the phone."

I tried to place his accent. Middle New Jersey somewhere. "That's all right. I'm enjoying myself. I haven't been to a good heavyweight fight in years."

The smile disappeared as he looked up at the ring. "You still haven't been to one."

Realango was in his corner, slumped forward on his stool. Sweat poured off his back as if someone had dumped a bucket of water over him and his chest was heaving like a bellows. He had a small egg over his right eye that was nothing serious, but you wouldn't have been able to tell that from the expression on his trainer's face. The trainer, a wiry, gray-haired man with cotton swabs stuck behind both ears, chattered away nervously as he wiped Vaseline

2

above and below Realango's eyes to keep the skin moist so it wouldn't cut. I couldn't hear what he was saying, but he looked anything but pleased.

Majors, by contrast, was in much worse shape—his right eye was nearly swollen shut and he'd been bleeding from the mouth for the last five rounds—but everyone in his corner looked happier than pigs in shit. The tall black nodded attentively as his trainer punctuated his instructions with clandestine movements in the air with his fists.

"I *have* seen him look better," I admitted.

Schwartz grimaced as if he were suffering from an acute gas attack. *"Better?* Shit. He's making the kid look like a fucking ballerina. He's just lucky Majors hasn't got anything to hurt him with."

The bell rang and the arena went black, leaving only the ring bathed in the stark light of the overhead spots. Majors shot out of his corner and danced into the center of the ring, moving with what seemed to be a lot of confidence. Realango plodded steadily forward, ignoring the jabs Majors kept flicking in his face. He threw a couple of tentative jabs of his own and then a right uppercut that missed Majors' head by a yard.

"Want some No-Doz, Realango?" someone shouted behind me.

"I think he's *got* a doz!" someone else yelled a few rows away. That brought a few chuckles from the crowd.

Majors was sticking and backpedaling and even though his punches were floating now, without any snap to them at all, he was still managing to keep Realango off.

"They're gonna send your ass back to the carwash, Realango, if you don't win this fight!"

Realango suddenly sidestepped and cut off the ring and Majors looked worried as he found himself boxed into a corner. He tried to step out of the trap, but Realango anticipated his move and slammed the door shut.

Realango waded in and threw a wild overhand right, but Majors slipped it and rebounded off the ropes with a desperate flurry of

3

punches, one of which landed flush on Realango's chin and turned his head into a silvery halo of sweat. A jubilant roar went up from the crowd as the black kid danced past him and into the center of the ring.

"Jesus," Schwartz said, his voice thick with disgust.

"What's the *matter* with him?" a woman's voice cried out in vexation.

The answer came back loud and clear: "He got a head job last night, lady! He's tired!"

Across the ring, a gaunt, auburn-haired model type with a huge pair of sunglasses on top of her head stood up in the fourth row and cupped her hands over her mouth. "Two more minutes! Hang in there, Billy!"

The crowd took up the cry. "Two more minutes! Hang in there!"

Realango was not paying attention to the crowd. He was shuffling forward, stalking his man like some relentless predatory animal, his eyes yellow and malevolent in the overhead lights. Once more he sidestepped and cut off the ring, catching Majors on the ropes, but this time, he ripped into the lean body with three tremendous shots that seemed hard enough to snap the spine. Majors fell on Realango's neck and tried to hold on, but the ref stepped in and broke them and Realango came back fast, digging into the body again and again.

"I don't believe it," Schwartz said, waving his hands at the ring. "He headhunts for nine fucking rounds and *now* he decides to go downstairs."

Majors took a hook to the right kidney and he grimaced in pain and dropped his elbow reflexively just as Realango was coming up with the left hook. The hook landed high on the jaw, but there was enough of Realango's 225 pounds behind it to turn Majors' legs into Jello Instant Pudding.

The crowd came to its feet, shrieking and screaming for Majors to hold on. Realango was throwing a lot of leather, but Majors was leaning far back on the ropes, his gloves glued to his chin, rolling with the punches like a seasick sailor, and not many of the shots

4

were connecting with anything but elbows and arms. Then, suddenly, Realango seemed to run out of steam. He was pawing and pushing more than punching.

Still Majors wasn't answering with any punches, and after ten more seconds of shoving and pawing, Realango stepped back and made a helpless gesture to the referee, as if to say: "Aren't you going to stop it?"

Responding to the cue, the ref stepped between the two men and pushed them apart, signalling it was over, and the arena was immediately filled with a deafening din of boos. Majors' handlers leaped into the ring, screaming at the referee, who was busy dodging the shower of paper cups full of beer and soft drinks that began to rain down on the ring. Schwartz and I were the only ones who were still seated in our row. Everyone else was on his feet, making a megaphone out of his hands, booing for all he was worth.

"Let's get the fuck out of here, while we still can," Schwartz said.

We stood up and shouldered our way through the crowd and Schwartz waved to a uniformed security guard who was trying to clear a passageway for the fighters. We made it to the edge of the sea of bodies and got the nod from the two security men guarding the hallway that led to the dressing rooms.

Our footsteps reverberated in lonely echoes against the brick walls of the corridor.

"I had him all lined up for a shot at Foster," he said, throwing up his arms. "Foster's people were ready to go, CBS was ready to negotiate for it and the whole fucking works, and he blows it. I should've known this was going to happen. The biggest goddamn mistake I made was taking him up to Reno."

"What happened in Reno?"

His lips were pursed into a tight line. "That's where all this shit started."

"You mean the calls?"

"The calls and the broads and the booze and everything else that got him into the shape he was in tonight."

5

We turned a corner and he stopped at the second dressing room door and opened it. The room had bare brick walls painted in a high-gloss white enamel. It was barely large enough for the massage table, three chairs, and the dressing table that constituted its furniture. Above the dressing table was a large mirror. Some men's clothes—presumably Realango's—were hanging from a hook on one wall and on the massage table lay a box of adhesive tape and a pair of scissors. The bright light from the fluorescent fixtures in the ceiling stripped the room of its shadows and the glare from the white walls gave the place a sterile, almost boiled appearance.

Schwartz sat down on one of the chairs and I half-stood, half-sat on the edge of the dressing table. He took out a pack of Marlboro 100's, snapped one from the pack with an abrupt flick of the wrist and put it between his teeth. He held the pack out to me.

"I don't smoke."

He shrugged and lit the one in his mouth with a gold lighter, dropped the lighter back into his coat pocket, and blew smoke through his nose. His motions were all precise, economical, flawless, what you would expect from an actor or a gigolo, someone who watches himself in the mirror a lot, not a pudgy man whose clothes did not fit too well.

"Tell me about the calls," I said. "Anybody have any idea who's making them?"

"We *know* who's making them," he said. "The problem is getting him to stop."

"Who is 'him'?"

"Sal Mezzano."

"Who's Sal Mezzano?"

"Ever hear of Moonfire Ranch?"

"The whorehouse near Reno?"

He nodded. "Mezzano owns it."

"Why would he threaten Realango?"

He crossed his legs and leaned back in the chair. "Because his

6

wife is down here with Carlos. She owns Carlos' contract. She's his manager."

"I take it the arrangement involves more than just business."

"It'd better," he said with a sneer, "because if things keep going like they did tonight, the business part of it isn't going to be worth shit." He raised one eyebrow and grinned. "It's funny, I never thought of it before, but Sal and Susan's marriage is the arrangement that's really the business one. The whole situation is ass-backwards."

"What do you mean?"

"The Mezzanos' marriage has been *drek* for ten years. Everybody knows it. It's strictly a business arrangement. She runs Moonfire while Sal runs around screwing every whore in the place. Sal is the horniest guy I know. If there was a crack in the wall, he'd suck it. They've only stayed together because it's been profitable. A hell of a lot more profitable than if they'd start splitting everything up."

"Then what's he getting all upset about?"

He shrugged helplessly. "Who the hell knows? These fucking Sicilians are all nuts anyway. All those Latins are. To them, women are all either saints or whores, nothing in between. All I know is that the whole thing is screwing Carlos' head up. He says he's out of retirement to make another run at the title, but the way things are going, he's just jerking himself and everybody else off. I mean, Susan is a nice woman, I've got nothing but good feelings for her, but Carlos had no business signing her as a manager. She knows about as much about handling a fighter as I do about running whores."

"He must know that."

"Sure he knows it."

"Then why did he sell her his contract?"

"He didn't exactly. It's a long story," he sighed. Carlos isn't the easiest guy in the world to handle. Sometimes I wonder why the hell I've bothered all these years."

"How many years has it been?"

He counted back in his mind. "Nine. I've been making most of his matches for about nine years."

"That's a long time," I said. "You must have some rapport with him if he's as hard to handle as you say he is."

"We have," he said, nodding, then pointed the two fingers holding his cigarette at me. "But I'm telling you, if he doesn't straighten his act out, this is gonna be it. I love Carlos like a brother, but I'm not gonna wind up jerking myself off for anybody."

His buggy blue eyes searched the place for an ashtray. When they didn't find one, he shrugged and dropped the cigarette on the floor and mashed it out with his foot.

"How did he get hooked up with Mezzano's wife in the first place?"

"Through Sal," he said. "Up until a month ago, Sal owned Carlos' contract. She bought it from him."

I was starting to get confused. "How did he get it?"

He sighed. "Actually, it was my fault. That's why I feel guilty about this whole goddamn mess. See, I've known Sal for a few years. I put together a couple of fights in L.A. and Reno for a local kid he had a piece of. When Carlos came out of retirement, he asked me to look around for a manager for him. I approached Sal to see if he'd be interested. I figured he'd be good because Carlos is so goddamn independent, he needs someone with a strong hand to keep him in line. I should've known Sal would come on too damn strong."

"What happened?"

He shrugged with his face. "I matched Carlos with a stiff named Jerry Cavanaugh at the Centennial Coliseum in Reno. Comes fight time, Carlos and Sal got into a big beef about money. Carlos didn't think he was getting enough. Anyway, he went through with the fight, but after that, Sal had soured on him. That was when Susan stepped in. She'd been hanging around all the time while Carlos had been training for the fight. The next thing I know, she owns his contract and then Sal throws them both off the Ranch and then the phone calls start."

"When was that?"

"About three weeks ago."

"Has she been getting calls, too?"

"Not yet. Just Carlos."

I nodded. "The cops know about it?"

He rubbed his forehead with three short, stubby fingers. "Sure they know. They won't do a fucking thing. All they keep saying is, 'Try to record the calls.' They say Carlos and Susan are moving around too much for them to hook up bugging equipment. That's why I called you. Art Matuzsak recommended you. He said you'd know what the hell to do about it."

I remembered Art Matuzsak. He was the general manager of a large electrical supply house who had hired me a year or so back to gather proof that his wife was carrying on an illicit affair with their daughter's fifteen-year-old boyfriend. He had needed the evidence to make sure the court awarded him custody of their two children when the divorce was settled. I had gotten him his proof and he had given me a check for half the amount of my bill, and, in a moment of emotion, a punch in the mouth. He gave me an apology later for the punch in the mouth, but not the other half of the bill. The last I heard, he had reconciled with his wife and they were as happy as clams.

I was going to ask Schwartz more about his conversations with the police, but the dressing room door opened and Realango came in, trailed by his trainer and a plump, platinum-haired woman in a shocking pink pants suit I took to be Susan Mezzano. Realango had on a red velour bathrobe and a white terrycloth towel was draped over his head. A few strands of dark hair hung over his forehead like wet string. He smiled at us and said: "Hi."

The platinum-haired woman said: "Hell of a fight, Jack," then looked questioningly at me.

"Susan, this is Jake Asch," Schwartz said. "The detective I mentioned yesterday."

"Glad to meet you, honey," she said, and offered her hand. The back of the hand was covered with liver spots and the fingers were slightly deformed by arthritis. From the generous apportionment of diamonds on them, I guessed Moonfire Ranch had a good-looking stable. "Glad you could make it down. Carlos and I appreciate it."

Her voice was not as old as she looked. It was firm and had a snap to it, a slight tinge of a country twang.

She had a pale, puffy face and a broad nose and her skin had a shiny, almost waxy sheen to it. She looked as if she had pushed well into her sixties, although she was not ready to admit just how far. Her platinum hair sat on her head like a swath of bleached cotton candy. She wore a lot of makeup, but none of it was having the effect she hoped. Her false eyelashes only made her brown eyes look smaller and narrower than they were; her plucked and repenciled eyebrows drew attention to her prominent brow and the bright-red lipstick only managed to make her thin lips look even thinner. But there was something underneath the makeup and the flamboyant pink pants suit that made it all something less than pathetic. Something in the way she stood or maybe the cool, cynical confidence in the shiny, indestructible eyes that straight-armed you and said: "Don't worry about it, buddy, I can *still* take care of the likes of you," and you knew she probably could.

"Carlos," she said, making a gesture with her hand. "This is Mr. Asch. He's come down here from Los Angeles. He's a detective."

A child-like smile spread across Realango's swollen lips. He pushed out a hand that looked like twenty pounds of spareribs. "How you do?"

In the ring, he looked ugly. Up close, he looked positively troglodytic. He had about a mile of forehead, an overlapping lower jaw and a huge expanse of chin. His nose looked as if it were trying to touch both ears, and right now both of his eyes were swollen into dark slits, giving him a slightly Oriental appearance. The Museum of Natural History might have used him as a model for Peking Man.

Realango sat down on the massage table. Susan Mezzano gazed lovingly at that Neolithic countenance, then took the ends of the towel covering his head and wiped the sweat out of his eyes. "My boy fought a hell of a fight," she said. "We're going to kick Foster's ass in March and then we're going to go for the title. Sometime this summer. Maybe at the Garden—"

"Foster's off," Schwartz cut her off.

She dropped the towel and looked sharply at Schwartz. "What the hell do you mean, Foster's off?"

"Just what I said. The deal turned to shit tonight. I'm cancelling it."

Realango's eyebrows knotted above his nose and he leaned forward on the massage table, gesturing frantically with his hand. "Why? Why you cancel Foster?"

Schwartz's jaw tightened against the question. "Why? Look in the mirror, for chrissakes."

Realango stood up and walked over to the mirror. He turned his head from side to side and shrugged. "What?"

"What? Your face is what."

"That kid no hurt me," Realango said in a scoffing voice.

Schwartz smiled. "Well that's good, Carlos. I'm glad that kid didn't hurt you, because that kid is a tomato can, Carlos, a fucking stiff. That kid is 10 and 5." He recited the numbers slowly, precisely, like an actor on "Sesame Street." "You know how many KO's he's had out of those ten wins, Carlos? *Two*. You know why that is? Because he can't punch his way out of a fucking paper bag, that's why that is. Foster ain't any Billy Majors. Foster is 42 and 5 and out of that 42, he's stopped 38. If Foster connected with one-tenth of the punches that kid landed on you tonight, you'd be in the fucking third-row seats."

Realango made a scoffing face and waved his hand at Schwartz. "Foster fight bums—"

Schwartz leaned forward. "Just what the hell do you think you've been fighting? Class opponents?"

Susan Mezzano stepped away from Realango, her waxy face flushed with color. "If Carlos looked as bad as you say he did, Jack, then you'd better start looking in your own backyard for somebody to blame. You set it up. You should've known Majors was a spoiler—"

"Majors is no spoiler," Schwartz said. His voice was calm and steady, but it seemed to be taking an effort for him to hold it that way. "Majors has been put away by a washed-up bum like Cookie Lewis. And not on a TKO in the last fucking minute, either. Carlos had him a dozen times and couldn't finish him."

"He got lucky that's all—"

"*We* were the ones who were lucky. Lucky we had a ref who'd make a great hypnotic subject for Pat Collins. Majors was in worse shape in the fourth than he was at the end. Why the hell do you think Carlos asked the ref to stop it? And don't tell me he was worried about giving the kid brain damage. I know him too well for that. He just ran out of steam, that's all. He knew he couldn't put him away and he wanted the KO. We're just damned lucky it worked. He looked bad enough without having a ten-round decision with Billy Majors on his record."

He paused and turned to Realango, who looked like he was starting to get mad. "Listen, Carlos, I'm talking as a friend as well as a business advisor. I'm telling you you're not ready for Foster. When you're in shape, you can take Foster, but I mean in *top* shape, not in the half-assed shape you're in now. You're thirty-two years old and you've been lying around for a year and a half. You can't fart around in training camp like you've been doing and survive with the likes of Foster. On top of everything, you've been going through too much mental aggravation with all these bullshit phone calls. Let's get all that out of the way—that's what Asch is here for—and let's get you into shape and then I'll set up Foster." He turned to the gray-haired trainer who was standing behind Realango, staring silently at the floor. The cotton swabs were still behind his ears. "How about it, Fred? Am I wrong, or were we just watching different fights tonight?"

The trainer rubbed his chin uncomfortably. "No. You're not wrong."

Susan Mezzano shot him a smoldering glance, but he would not look at her. Schwartz caught her look and said: "Look, Susan, you're Carlos' manager. You can do whatever you like. I'm just not going to set Carlos up to look like a fucking bum on national

12

TV. If you don't like it that way, you can always get somebody else to set up your matches."

Realango grinned and held up a hand. "No, no. You right, Jack. I no fight good tonight. I should have knock that kid out. You say wait, we wait. We a team, you and Carlos. I love you like you my brother. You say wait, we wait."

Susan Mezzano pursed her lips and said: "We'll talk about it later. Right now, we're going to talk to the press boys and then he's going to hit the showers. We'll see you at the hotel," she said to me.

I looked questioningly at Schwartz. "If that's where we're going."

He stood up and looked at his watch. It was one of those paper-thin gold jobs that cost a nice chunk of change and always run slow. "About what? An hour?"

"That sounds about right," she said.

In the hall outside the dressing room, half a dozen sportswriters milled around, waiting to see Realango. They didn't seem overly thrilled by their assignments. Schwartz told them to go on in.

One of them, a small, hawk-faced man in a garish maroon-and-green plaid sports jacket, piped up: "Hey, Schwartz, is Realango really going to fight Foster?"

Schwartz smiled easily and shrugged. "We'll have to wait and see. We've had some conversations with Foster's people, but nothing has been signed yet."

"Better not put your name on anything," the man said. "That'd make you an accessory to murder."

"You might be surprised, Harry."

The man sneered. "Why, is Foster going to take a dive?"

The smile lingered on Schwartz's lips, but it had a frozen quality to it. "Don't worry. If we sign with Foster, Carlos will be ready." He glanced down at his watch again, and said: "Look, I'd love to stand around and bullshit with you guys, but I gotta get going."

He waved at them and moved away. When we got out of hearing range, he said: "I hate that prick."

13

"Who is he?"

"Harry Atamian. A sportswriter for the *Union*. A real asshole. Always ready with some lippy remark. And there's always one of him around."

He sighed heavily with the burden of his existence, and we walked through the deserted hallway to the parking lot.

2

The Polynesia was a luxurious eighteen-story hotel on San Diego's Mission Bay, the grounds of which were lavish with tropical plants and wooden tiki gods. A tour group from East Jesus, Iowa, was milling around the lobby as we went through, doing its best to get into the spirit of the place. The women were all in their bathing suits or muumuus, the men in shorts and loud Hawaiian print shirts and black shoes and black stretch socks with the hair on their legs poking through. Schwartz's room was on the seventeenth floor. We rode the elevator up to the accompaniment of Musak ukuleles.

The room was large and airy, with dark green spreads on the twin beds and a thick lime-green carpet and groves of green-and-white bamboo on the walls. A sliding glass door led outside to a balcony, complete with a cocktail table and chairs. While Schwartz went around the room and turned on lights, I went out there. I could never resist a view.

The view was spectacular. Mission Bay spread out below and beyond it rose the green hills that ringed the city. The overcast daylight was rapidly thickening into dusk and lights were winking on in the hills. The slip lights on the boats moored at the docks below flickered like an arrangement of altar candles in the dark water. The beauty of the panorama lulled my senses and I was filled with a feeling of tranquility. I had to remind myself that the reason I was here had nothing to do with tranquility.

I stepped back inside. "Some view."

Schwartz was standing by the television, switching channels. "Um-hmm," he said in a bored tone. He stopped on Wide World of Sports, then went over to one of the beds and stretched out.

15

He propped his head up with a pillow and lit himself another cigarette. "They should be here pretty soon."

"They staying at this hotel?"

"Yeah. They've got two rooms on the next floor down."

Wide World was covering some stock car race. Schwartz seemed mesmerized by the drone of the motors and Jackie Stewart's unintelligible brogue as the cars went round and round the oval track. I took one of the straight-backed chairs that sat around the round breakfast table by the window and tried to get into it. I could not manage it. Finally, I said: "Is Sal Mezzano connected?"

He put a hand under his head to get an extra inch of elevation and looked over at me. "What do you mean, 'connected'? You mean Mafia-connected?"

"Yeah."

He turned back to the cars. "There's been talk," he said slowly, "but I don't believe any of it."

"Why not?"

"For one thing, because there's talk about everybody in Nevada. Most of the talk about Sal is being done by people who have an axe to grind or people who think that anybody with an Italian last name has a charter membership in the Mafia. For another, you got to know Sal. He could never handle it. His ego's too big for him to take orders from anybody. He could never be an organization man, I don't care what the organization was— Xerox or the Mafia."

I nodded and made another attempt to watch the race. From the emotional tone of Stewart's voice, I gathered he was excited about something one of the drivers had just done, but I couldn't for the life of me figure out what it was. I once went with a friend from Brazil to a Carmen Miranda Film Festival. He sat and roared through all her numbers while the rest of the audience, including me, just sat and stared. It seemed all her cute "Tico-tico-ta's" would have been banned in Rio. I found myself wishing that was what Jackie Stewart was doing, telling dirty Scotch jokes

16

and having a good laugh on all of us. I would have liked him better for it.

"How old is Susan Mezzano?" I asked.

"Fifty-eight."

"That's all?"

He caught the incredulity in my voice. "You think she looks old now, you should have seen her six months ago. She looked ten years older and she didn't care. Half the time she never bothered to put on any makeup. She was at least twenty pounds heavier and she was so crippled up she had to walk with a cane. Some drunk driver broadsided her a few years ago and she's been crippled ever since. Something to do with her spine. I guess they've done a couple of operations on her, but none of them did what Carlos did. She started to care about herself again. Carlos kept telling her she didn't need a cane, then he started hiding them so she'd have to walk without one. Every time she bought a new one, he'd rip it off. She gets around pretty good now."

I nodded. "I can see how an older woman could get hooked on the attentions of a younger man, but what's his attraction for her?"

His tone turned petulant. "Look, Carlos' private life is none of my business. My business is setting up fights. As long as his personal life doesn't interfere with that I don't care what he does or who he does it with or why."

"Obviously it is interfering, otherwise I wouldn't be here."

He didn't have a chance to comment on that. There was a knock at the door and he got up off the bed and went to answer it.

Susan Mezzano and Realango came in together. He was dressed in a white tennis sweater with a tan shirt, dark brown flared slacks, and brown imitation alligator shoes. His face was blotched with purple from the blows he had taken an hour ago. Maybe it was because Schwartz had mentioned it, but for the first time, I noticed Susan Mezzano walked with a slight limp. She beamed at us, seemingly in better spirits than she had been when

17

we had left her at the Sports Arena. "Why don't you call up room service, Jack, and get us a bottle of something up here? What do you drink, Mr. Asch?"

"Anything."

"My kind of man." She waved a hand at Schwartz. "Tell them to bring up a fifth of Wild Turkey and a fifth of Dewar's. And some ice."

Realango stretched out on the unoccupied twin bed, and without saying a word, stuffed a pillow behind his head and began watching the race. He seemed to understand what was going on. I wondered if Stewart was really speaking Spanish.

While Schwartz phoned down the booze order, Susan Mezzano sat down in the other chair around the table. She stared at me for a few seconds, smiling silently, then said:

"What's your first name, anyway? I don't believe I caught it."

"Jake."

"Okay, Jake. You can call me Susan. You know, I can't stand to call people by their last names. I just can't get used to it. Seems unnatural somehow. That's what happens when you live around whores from the time you're seventeen. No working girl ever uses her last name in a house. The only thing that can bring is trouble." She smiled, then squinted at me through her false eyelashes. "Jack here tells me you're supposed to be pretty good."

"That would depend on what the job was, I guess."

"Before we get into that," she said, "I'd like to get a few things straightened out, like for instance, what you charge for your services. See, Jake, I'm the kind of a woman who likes everybody's cards on the table at the beginning of the game, just so there's no misunderstandings later on. I mean, a guy comes in to my joint and wants to get laid, he wants to know up front how much it's going to cost him, right?"

"I normally get a hundred and fifty a day plus expenses. Plus fifteen cents a mile."

Her stare was unabashedly cynical. "Don't you think that's a little steep?"

"Let me ask you a question," I said. "That guy who comes into

18

your place and wants to get laid—how much is it going to cost him?"

"A straight lay? No extras?"

"Yeah."

"Fifteen bucks."

"And how many customers does one of your girls take on in a day?"

"That depends. I've had some girls who've handled more than a hundred. But that's on a real good day."

"Well, on a real good day, one of your girls makes ten times what I do on my best day and all she has to do is lie on a bed and pump her pelvis a few times. Don't you think that's a little steep?"

She broke into a grin. "Honey, there's a hell of a lot more to being a good whore than that. A good whore is an amateur psychologist and a wet nurse and a physical therapist all rolled into one. But I get your point." She paused thoughtfully and asked: "You think for that hundred and fifty dollars a day plus expenses you can take care of this situation we got?"

"I don't know. I'm not really all that clear as to exactly what your situation is. All I know is that you've been getting some threatening phone calls and that you think your husband is behind them. I'd have to have some of the details."

"What do you need to know?"

"How many calls have you gotten?"

She bounced the question to Realango, whose eyes were fixed on the television screen. "What? Six? Seven?"

He grunted and nodded.

"Exactly what does the caller say?"

"Carlos can't get all the words," she said. "He doesn't understand a lot of English, but he understands enough to get the message that the guy's threatening to kill him if he comes back up to Reno."

"Same caller every time?"

"Seems to be."

"How about the voice? Do you recognize it?"

"I've never heard it," she said. "If I answer, the asshole hangs

19

up without saying anything. Carlos says the voice sounds muffled, like the guy is covering the mouthpiece with a handkerchief or something. But I can tell you who it is. It's one of two people: Gene Merritt or Joe Battaglia."

At the mention of those names, Realango hissed some profanity in Spanish.

"Who are they?"

"Merritt is Sal's bodyguard and personal head-masher. Battaglia is an ex-private eye who's in charge of security at the ranch. They're both loyal as hell to Sal, but I'm not sure Battaglia would stick his neck out that far by making threats like that. Merritt would. Merritt would dive head-first into ten feet of cowshit if Sal told him to. He's worked for Sal for ten years, ever since he got out of the Nevada State Pen. That's where he met Sal, as a matter of fact, in the joint. Merritt was the one who burned all of Carlos's clothes."

I was starting to get confused. "What clothes?"

She waved a hand in the air. "I'm sorry, honey, I forgot you don't know about all that. Up until three weeks ago, Carlos was living in a trailer out at the ranch. One day we came back to find somebody had gone into the trailer and taken out all of Carlos' clothes, set them in a nice, neat pile outside and set them on fire. I found out later it was Merritt. While he was doing it, the bastard also threw Carlos' passport in the fire. We had to drive to the Argentine Consulate in San Francisco to get him a new one. Carlos wanted to go back there and rip Merritt's head off, but I talked him out of it."

"Did you report that to the police?"

She smiled. "Sure. I drove into Silverville and told Frank Dierdorf about it. He's the sheriff of Evans County."

"What did he do about it?"

"Just what he was supposed to do. Nothing."

I looked at her questioningly.

"Evans County has exactly seven hundred and fifty registered voters and the incomes of at least half of those voters are directly or indirectly dependent on Moonfire Ranch. That's why Sal picked that site for Moonfire in the first place. Without Sal's endorsement, it'd be goddamned hard for someone to get elected to a county office. *Any* county office, and that includes the sheriff. And if Sal didn't like you, it'd be impossible."

"You mentioned a second ago your husband has been in prison. What was he in for?"

"Extortion." She glanced over at Schwartz, who was lighting up another cigarette. "Pass one of those over here, will you, Jack? I'm dying for a smoke."

Realango hoisted himself onto one elbow and said: "Doctor says you no smoke."

"That doctor is a quack. He's had three heart attacks I know about and he still smokes like a chimney. One damn cigarette won't hurt."

"No," he said firmly. He turned to Schwartz and said: "She no smoke. Smoking no good for her."

Schwartz shrugged, obviously not wanting to get put into the middle of whatever was going on, and put the package of cigarettes back down on the nightstand.

Susan Mezzano grimaced and rolled her eyes. "It's enough to drive you crazy. He's always bugging me about something. He nags the shit out of me. I'm going to have to give the sonofabitch up for Lent." Her voice sounded vexed, but she was obviously pleased at Realango's concern and she made no move for the cigarettes. "Where were we? Oh yeah—Sal. What happened was he tried to get cute with a D.A. Only the D.A. was cuter. That's always been Sal's trouble. He's always thought he's the smartest fox in the woods. He still does. Three years in the joint didn't even teach him different."

"I thought he owned all the politicians in the county," I said.

"Carew wasn't from Evans County, he was from Washoe County. And that was in the fifties, before Evans County legalized prostitution. Carew's still D.A. in Reno, but in those days he had bigger plans. He wanted to be Senator and he planned to use the D.A.'s office as a stepping stone. Since there weren't that many sensational cases around for him to build his reputation on, he had to settle for us. He got the local papers all lathered up about the evils of prostitution and set himself up as the White Knight who was going to clean it all up. He dug up an old Nevada statute that said whoever habitually visited a house of prostitution would be legally considered a vagrant and he declared Sal and me undesirables. We couldn't even shop in Reno without getting permission first. Then, he started going around to all the restaurants and casinos in town where Sal used to like to go and told them not to serve him if he came in. Some of them asked Sal to stay away, but most of them told Carew to fuck off. And Sal, hell, he wasn't going to be told by anybody where he could go and couldn't go. He'd ride into town, bold as hell, and Carew's men would vag him and throw him in jail. That really pissed Sal off. He carried more money in his pockets than Carew made in two months and he was being busted like some bum. One night, he got thrown in the can four times. As soon as he'd make the bail, he'd go right downtown to the same club and there would be the cops waiting for him."

"Sounds like he'd have had grounds for harassment."

"Sure," she said, "but where were we going to take them? Hell, everybody was against us then. We had a different place then than we do now. It was about four miles down the road. Carew went to the Evans County D.A.—a guy named Anderson—and convinced him it'd help out his career if he joined in the fight. The two of them got a judge to declare our joint a public nuisance, and he issued an abatement order. When Sal didn't comply with it, Carew and Anderson led a posse of sheriffs out to the place with gasoline cans and they burned the joint down. There wasn't anything but ashes when they finished with it.

"That was the last straw for Sal. That was when he got his brainy idea to send the little sister of one of our girls over to seduce Carew. The girl was only seventeen, but she looked twenty-four if she looked a day, and gorgeous. Sal fixed it so she'd accidentally meet Carew in a bar he always went to and give him a story about how she was in Reno for a divorce. Anyway, Carew wound up balling her and Sal went up to see him the next day and told him that the girl was only a minor and that her mother knew about the whole affair and was raising holy hell. Sal told him he could cool her down and the whole thing would be forgotten if only Carew would ease up on us. He didn't know Carew was taping the conversation."

"And that was the extortion charge?"

She nodded.

"What about the girl?"

"She was going to testify, but Carew got to her and scared the holy shit out of her. He told her he'd send her up for ten years for perjury if she ever took the stand and hinted around that it might be a good idea if she just sort of left town for awhile. Without her, Sal was up shit's creek without a paddle." Her eyes drifted to the window and stayed there for a moment. "Those were tough times, let me tell you. All the time Sal was out on appeal, we had to keep operating, even though we didn't have a place. The goddamn legal bills kept coming in and we had to get the money to pay them somehow. We got a bunch of trailers and hitched them up to cars in a caravan and moved at night from one county to another. We'd set up in dry washes, any goddamn place. It's amazing how those customers found us, but they always did."

There was a faint smile on her lips and a faraway glaze over her eyes, as if she were right back there in those trailers, reliving the war, and enjoying the battle. Susan Mezzano must have been one hell of a woman in her day, I decided.

"What was Merritt in for?"

That brought her back. Her eyes snapped back over to me. "Burglary. That was what he was doing time for when he met Sal. Before that, he was up for assault."

I drew invisible circles on the table with a forefinger and asked: "Just what do you think your husband is trying to accomplish with these phone calls?"

"Who the hell knows? He's so goddamn unpredictable. I don't

23

even know how the hell he finds out where we're staying. All I know is I want this bullshit stopped. It's driving me out of my mind."

I tugged on the skin of my neck that lately had been working on the idea of becoming a double-chin. Looking at her neck, I suddenly felt self-conscious. I decided I would start doing neck exercises with Jack LaLanne in the morning. "As I see it, Mrs. Mezzano—"

"Susan," she reminded me.

"—Susan. You can go two ways with this thing. You can hire somebody to set up a voice-actuated tape machine that will trip on automatically when a call comes in. That could be expensive, especially if you're going to be moving around a lot, because you'd have to have the whole apparatus set up again when you got settled somewhere else. How long are you going to be in San Diego?"

"A few weeks maybe. I don't really know. It depends on what Jack lines up."

"See, it would really be a pain to keep setting that up. And the few people who have that kind of sophisticated equipment charge up the ass for it."

"You mentioned two ways to go."

I nodded. "You have a Stenorette?"

Her brow furrowed. "What's that?"

"A dictaphone."

"I've got a dictaphone," Schwartz piped up.

"Good. All you need then is an impedence microphone that will plug into your Stenorette. I've got one I can loan you. The mike has a suction cup on it that sticks it right on to the receiver. When a call comes in, all you've got to do is hit the record button on the machine and you'll pick up whoever's on the other end of the line. After you get the guy's voice, you call up Merritt on some phony pretext and tape his voice. There's a professor in the speech lab at UCLA who specializes in doing voice-prints. I think he charges $500 to make a comparison of the tapes. If the voices match up, he'll give you a sworn deposition saying they do. He'll even testify in court for the five hundred if you need him to. Once the cops have that deposition in their hands, they'll jump all over your husband's back with cleats on."

She gave me a puzzled look. "That's what I thought we were calling you for, to set all that up."

"Wiretapping laws in this state are very strict, Susan. If I got caught tapping your phone, the Bureau of Consumer Affairs would ream me. One investigator I know just got his license pulled for just *listening in* on one of his client's phone conversations. Besides, even if I did it, how do you know when the next phone call is going to come in? It could be a week, it could be a month, it could be never. And all that time, you'd be paying me a hundred and fifty a day just to do nothing but sit around and rob you of your privacy."

Her expression turned skeptical, but she didn't say anything.

"There are some operatives around I know of who would do the work, if that's what you really want," I said. "I can give you some names. But I think you'd be making a mistake."

She glanced over at Schwartz. "What do you think, Jack?"

He stared at her, then at me. "You called him for his professional advice. That's what you're getting."

She squinted at me suspiciously from beneath her false eyelashes. "How much do we owe you for this 'advice'?"

"Fifty bucks should cover it."

"And the microphone?"

"Like I said, I'll loan it to you. Just return it when you've finished with it."

She shook her head and her eyes narrowed suspiciously. "I don't get it. You must have known you weren't going to take this job when Jack called you yesterday. You could have told him what you just told me over the phone."

"I probably could have, if he'd told me exactly what it was all about, but he didn't. Besides, I was looking forward to meeting Carlos. I saw him fight Ellison three years ago at the Forum. That was one of the best heavyweight fights I've ever seen." I looked over at him. "You were really great that night."

The lumpy face broke into a wide grin. "Thanks. You nice guy." He pointed at me and said to Susan Mezzano: "He good guy. We do what he say, huh?"

I stood up. It was dark now and the hills beyond the balcony were full of lights. "I've got the microphone down in the car. I'll go get it."

Realango waved a meaty hand at me. "You no run off now. Plenty of time to get that. You stay and have drink with Carlos."

"No booze," Schwartz said forcefully.

"He's right," Susan Mezzano said. "You want Foster, no booze."

"Okay," Carlos relented with a sheepish grin. "No booze."

Carlos wound up drinking orange juice, but it didn't seem to matter. He must have gotten a contact-high from us, because the more we drank, the friendlier he became. He joked and laughed and threw his arms around Schwartz, who after a few Scotch-and-waters, began to shed his serious demeanor and became infected with Carlos' playful spirit.

Later on, we went out to a seafood restaurant on the water. All through dinner, Carlos would lean over and whisper something in Susan Mezzano's ear and she would guffaw and push him away and call him the "Bullshitter of the Pampas." If they were an incongruous-looking couple, they did seem to share a fondness for each other that was warm and real and after being with them awhile, I had to admit they somehow fit well together.

After dinner, we went back to the hotel and had a few more drinks and I finally pulled out of San Diego at midnight, minus one impedence microphone and suffused with a warm glow from the Wild Turkey and Carlos' exuberant declarations that he "loved me like a brother." It was nice to finally have a brother who could kick the ass of any big brother on the block.

3

It was ten days before I heard from any of them again.

I was in Pomona, looking for a bartender named Jim Tracy who had been a witness to a traffic accident a year ago in Inglewood. The attorney for one of the claimants smelled big settlement and was willing to part with a few bucks to have Mr. Tracy found. The only trouble was that Mr. Tracy had charged a few things during the past year on his Master Charge card he couldn't pay for and had been bouncing around quite a bit during the past year to keep ahead of the collection agency and finding him was turning out to be a pain in the ass. I did manage to track down his last known address—the apartment of one Ilona Wheaton, a cocktail waitress with whom Tracy had been shacked up with until a month ago—but I had not been able to elicit much from her except a few pithy epigrams describing the man's bedroom and bathroom habits and a vague reference he had made before leaving about Hawaii.

It was from downstairs in Ilona Wheaton's apartment building that I phoned my answering service and found out that both Susan Mezzano and Jack Schwartz had called. Susan Mezzano had left no call-back number, but had left the message for me to get in touch with Schwartz, that it was urgent. There was no number for Schwartz, either. He had told the girl that he would be moving around a lot that afternoon, but that he would be at the Main Street Gym at three-thirty and that I was to meet him there if I could.

It was two-twenty, and although I would have loved to have gone straight to L.A. International and gotten on a 747 to Honolulu to look for Mr. Tracy, I doubted that the attorney

27

would be willing to cover it on my expense sheet, so I went to the Main Street Gym instead.

The Main Street Gym was at 318½ Main, in the heart of L.A.'s Skid Row and its urban backdrop of ancient brick flop-houses and greasy cafes and dark and dingy bars haunted by alcohol-seamed faces, was somehow a perfect setting for it. It was a place where dreams came to die.

Through its decaying portals passed a constant parade of young comers and on-the-way-downers, most with black and brown ghetto-faces, all flat-nosed and flat-waisted, carrying nylon flight bags filled with sweat clothes and hand wraps and leather protective gear to make sure they didn't get their balls ruptured or their brains scrambled before they got paid for it. A lot fewer of them got their brains scrambled now than in the old days, but few of them got paid much for it, either. Most would stop bothering to come with their nylon bags well before they hit thirty and ninety-five percent of those would have little to show for all the sweat and blood and pain but a lot of scar tissue and a pocketful of yellowed clippings about the night they fought Buzzsaw Jenkins or Gorilla Murphy or Bazooka Ortiz and had their man "out on his feet" until he came up with a lucky punch and put the lights out. Right now, though, that was in a dim and unrecognizable future and they sure came in with a swagger and a cold hard light in their eyes that said they were the Next in Line, the baddest dude in the whole middle-heavyweight world.

Stepping off the street, I found myself in a grimy entryway filled with cardboard boxes full of trash and the acrid smells of stale bodies and Ben-Gay. A narrow flight of cement stairs, il-luminated only by a dirty skylight that turned the daytime gray, ran up to a flaking door on which a handpainted sign read: EN-TRANCE 50¢. I trudged up to it, feeling suddenly old and tired, as if the decay of the place had invaded my body and was settling in my bones.

Above the door, an ancient cardboard cutout of Jack Dempsey stared down at me, his fists raised in a challenge. To the right of

28

it was an office about the size of a broomcloset. Its door was open. I poked my head in.

Two men sat wedged into the space. Both were sixtyish and had thin, gray faces. One was leaning back in his chair with his feet on the desk and his thumbs hooked on his belt buckle. His lips were brown from the juice of the cigar stub jammed into the corner of his mouth. He was listening to the other man, who punctuated his sentences with assertive hand gestures.

"So Jerry is in a bind, see? One of the guys hurts his hand and he needs a heavy to fill in the card, otherwise he's in trouble. So he calls up Sammy Goldsmith and says, 'Sammy, I need a heavy for tomorrow night. Who have you got?' Sammy thinks for a second and says, 'Well, I got a white kid. Eye-talian. A real banger. Twelve straight knockouts. But I don't know if I should risk him. What's your boy like?' Jerry's coming in his pants. A white heavy who can whack, he's going nuts. He says, 'Don't worry. He's a tomato can. No chin. Your boy will put his lights out. How much?' Sammy says, 'Five hundred plus expenses,' and Jerry says fine. Comes fight time, the white kid comes in slugging and gets tagged and goes down like a fucking stone. They can't wake him up for two minutes. The next morning, Jerry calls Sammy up, real apologetic-like, and says, 'Sammy, I don't know how to tell you this, but your boy got KO'd last night,' and Sammy says: 'That makes *thirteen* straight knockouts,' and hangs up."

The other man laughed raucously, then shook his head and said: "That's Sammy, all right. Goddamn, that guy has balls." He looked up sharply as if I were some form of unwelcome bacteria and said: "Can I help you with something?"

"Jack Schwartz?"

"Inside."

I pointed to the admission sign. "Do I pay you?"

"Inside."

I left them and went through the door. An old, slump-shoul-dered black man in a coat about four sizes too large and an old fedora hat mashed down around his cauliflower ears sat on a set of wooden bleachers inside the door. I paid him my four bits and he thanked me through his toothless mouth and stood up and shuffled off.

It was cold in the room. The place was deep, with a high ceiling and dirty walls painted green and white and decorated with more cutouts of past heavyweight champions. On one of the walls, a large sign said:

DO NOT SPIT OR THROW GUM ON THE FLOOR

It smelled more like somebody had been pissing than spitting on it. It was almost overwhelming. The rank odors of sweat and cigar smoke and old leather had seeped into every corner of the place. The lighting was provided by overhead fluorescents and a row of dirt-streaked windows along one wall. In front of the windows were empty hooks where the speed bags were hung when in use, and down the middle of the room, suspended by chains attached to the ceiling, was a row of heavy bags. A Mexican kid was working out listlessly on one of the bags, his taped fists thudding dully as they pounded the leather. Besides him, the only fighters working out were two kids sparring in one of the two elevated rings at the end of the room.

I walked across the warped wood floor to the small congregation of men who stood below the ring apron watching the two fighters spar. One was a short Mexican, the other was a tall blond Anglo. Neither was working too hard.

Schwartz was standing slightly apart from the group, talking to a fat man in baggy slacks and a loud sports shirt with red and yellow flowers all over it.

Schwartz saw me approaching and acknowledged my presence with a nod. His eyes told me to wait, so I stopped a couple of feet away and watched the sparring session.

A cigarette dangled from the dark lips of the fat man. It bounced up and down while he talked. "To tell you the truth, Jack, I had Lujan in mind for Bobby's next fight."

"*Lujan?*" Schwartz said disbelievingly. "Lujan is a spoiler. You

30

know what kind of trouble Bobby's always had with southpaws. Jesus Christ, Chu Chu Lara had him out on his feet—"

The man took the cigarette out of his mouth and spat on the floor. "Bobby fought Lara when he had to starve himself to make 126. He had to spend two days in the fucking steamroom to make the weight."

"Come on, Solly, you know Bobby's always looked bad against southpaws. I'm telling you, he don't look sharp this time out and it'll blow the whole deal—"

"What deal? There ain't no deal."

Schwartz smiled. "I talked to Escobedo's people this morning. They know what an Escobedo-Torres match could be in L.A. They know what Bobby grossed against Lopez. The spics would drive in busloads to see it."

The fat man didn't say anything.

"Listen," Schwartz went on, "Bobby hasn't looked so hot his last two, but that's okay. He's got an excuse. He couldn't make the weight anymore and it was taking too much out of him. So okay, so everybody's waiting to see what he's going to do now that he's moving up a division. If he looks like dogshit again, you can write him off. He ain't gonna draw flies. Moreno is the man, I'm telling you. He'll stand up for six, seven rounds and put up a hell of a show. He'll make Bobby look like a million dollars. He walks through Moreno, I can guarantee I'll get Escobedo signed."

Schwartz put his hand on the fat man's shoulder and led him out of hearing range.

The men standing by the ring apron watching the sparring session were muttering in Spanish to one another. One of them, holding a stopwatch, shouted: "Ten seconds!" and the tempo in the ring picked up as both fighters practiced getting in their last-minute flurries.

The man with the stopwatch yelled, "Time!" and the fighters touched gloves and came over to the ropes where their trainer was waiting with two plastic bottles filled with water. Each took a swig from one of the bottles and rinsed out his mouth, then leaned over the ropes and spit the water into the bucket outside the ring.

31

The fat man dropped his cigarette on the wood floor and mashed it out with his heel, then turned and walked back toward the shower room behind the bleachers. Schwartz came over to me. "I see you got the message."

I nodded. "What's up?"

His face turned grim. "Looks like we've got some trouble."

"What kind of trouble?"

He took me by the arm and led me away from the crowd of men by the ring. "Susan called me this morning," he said in a subdued tone. "Apparently she got a phone call about three-thirty. It was the same shit, I guess, but it's the first time anybody has threatened her personally and she's shook up about it. She thinks Sal has finally gone flippo. She took a plane up to Reno this morning to try to reason with him. She wants to see if she can calm him down before he does something drastic."

"That's what she tried to call me about?"

He nodded. "Carlos went up there with her. She's afraid that if he and Sal get together, there could be fireworks. She wants you to fly up to Reno."

"If she wants a bodyguard—"

He shook his head. "She wants you to try to keep Carlos out of harm's way until she can get all this shit with Sal straightened out. Hell, I'd go myself, but I can't. I'm working on a package that could be big. Real big. If I leave it, it could all come apart."

"If she thinks there might be trouble, why didn't she leave him down here? Why did she take him at all?"

He held out his hands, palm up. "She tried. He wouldn't stay. And when Carlos gets an idea in his head, you can't reason with him. Suddenly you got a big language barrier, and he doesn't understand a word you're saying. No habla Inglès."

He made a face and put a hand on his stomach. He fished a package of Rolaids from his coat pocket, snipped one neatly from the pack with a thumbnail and popped it into his mouth. "None of this shit is helping my indigestion, I can tell you," he said.

"That's all I need is him to go up and get his Argentinian ass shot off."

"If she can't handle him, how am I supposed to be able to?"

"I guess she figures it's worth a try. Carlos took to you that night. She figures you might be able to keep him occupied at least until she can talk to Sal."

I was not enchanted by the thought of traipsing around Reno trying to keep a hot-headed heavyweight fighter who spoke broken English out of the way of a Looney Tunes Sicilian pimp. It smelled like trouble. But then you didn't run across too many jobs in this business that did not smell like trouble. "Is it snowing up there?"

"It was last week."

"I'd rather go to Hawaii."

"That's nice," he said in a hard voice. "But they're not in Hawaii."

"Jim Tracy is."

"Who the hell is Jim Tracy?"

"A bartender. I hear he makes a great martini. Stirs, never shakes." He looked at me as if he thought I was the one who'd gone flippo, not Sal Mezzano. "Skip it," I said. "What about expenses?"

"I'm supposed to give you the money to cover the flight up. The rest you can take up with her when you get up there."

The timekeeper yelled, "Time!" and the two young fighters came together in the ring and began trading combinations.

"I'll have to find out what time there's a flight leaving."

"There's one at six-ten. United. I already checked, they got space."

I nodded and watched as the Mexican kid head-feinted, then came over with a good right cross that set the blond kid back on his heels.

"What am I supposed to do when I get there?"

"She's got you booked into the Ponderosa," he said. "It's a big

33

hotel on Virginia Street. Anybody will be able to tell you where it is. Carlos is staying there, too."

"Where is she staying?"

"At her house."

"What about her husband?"

"He's moved out to Moonfire."

Both fighters grunted loudly as they threw and took punches, their labored breathing through their mouthpieces sounding like that of two overworked horses.

Schwartz gestured with his cigarette and said: "This little spic isn't bad. He's one of Solly's new boys. Not bad at all."

"How do I get in touch with her?"

"I've got her number here," he said. He put the cigarette in his mouth and squinted against the smoke as he dug through his coat pocket. He brought out a slip of scratch paper and handed it to me. It had a phone number on it and that was all. He reached into his pants pocket and brought out a wad of bills, unhinged the gold clip, and peeled off a fifty. "That's for the plane."

I put the fifty in my wallet along with the phone number.

"If there's any trouble," he said in a concerned voice, "you call me right away, huh?"

"Fifteen seconds!"

The blond kid stepped back and brought over a chopping right hand that made a loud slapping noise against the Mexican's headgear, then came up with an uppercut that caught him flush on the chin. The Mexican fell back against the ropes and the blond kid was rocking him with more punches when the keeper called time.

Schwartz made a face. Solly's new boy suddenly looked like dogshit. He grabbed my sleeve and stared at me intently. "I really mean it," he said softly. "If something happens, they need me up there, call me."

"Sure," I said and left him sucking on his Rolaid.

The old black man with the mashed-down fedora had resumed his station on the bleachers. I gave him a centurion's salute and went through the door. On the stairs, I passed two tiny Filipinos

34

who looked no more than sixteen, but who had their tote bags full of gear. They pointed at me as they went past and jabbered something to one another in their native language, then shook their heads and disappeared through the door.

Maybe I looked over-the-hill enough to have been a great one at one time.

4

I stopped tossing underwear and socks into the suitcase open on my bed long enough to dial Liz's number.

"Hello?"

It was Derek, Liz's fourteen-year-old.

"Derek, this is Jake. Is your mother home?"

If it had been any of the other men his mother dated, Derek would have said either, "No," and hung up immediately or put the phone down without saying anything at all and maybe or maybe not, depending on his inclination, informed his mother somebody was on the phone. Instead, he said: "She should be right back. She just went next door for a minute."

Derek did not like—maybe I should say did not approve—of the men his mother dated, maybe because there were so many of them or maybe because they were usually a lot younger than she was or maybe—if he wanted to get psychoanalytical about it—because of the rejection he felt because of his father. His usual method of expressing this disapproval was pretending the date of the evening did not exist, except in his imagination. Any attempt of the man du jour to engage him in conversation nine times out of ten would be answered with a: "I've got homework to do. I'm going to my room," and the sight of Derek's "Star Trek" T-shirt disappearing down the hallway.

Derek talked to me for two reasons: 1) Although I never wore a trenchcoat, I was still a "private eye" straight out of the pulp magazines, and pulp magazines and old comic books were Derek's main passion in life; and 2) My own childhood had been spent letting my imagination run wild through those same pulp magazines and comic books and I could converse knowledgeably about

Spider Man and Fu Manchu and the Fantastic Four and debate which was the best movie ever made, "War of the Worlds" or "Forbidden Planet." That enabled me to get a classification of "Intelligent" and be admitted into the Inner Circle that got to talk to Derek.

"If she comes in in the next half hour, have her call me. Otherwise, tell her I've got to break our date tonight. I have to—"

"Wait," he said. "I think she's coming in now. Hold on."

He put the phone down and I heard him say: "Jake's on the phone," and then Liz said: "Hello?"

"Liz?"

"Yezzz?"

"I'm glad I got you. I've got to break our date tonight. Something came up and I have to fly to Reno on business."

"Oh that's just great. You mean after I went to the doctor and everything, you're breaking our date?"

"What doctor?"

Her voice grew suddenly serious: "Derek didn't tell you?"

"Tell me what?"

"My nose fell off this morning. It's a rare form of leprosy. Very contagious. One minute I was looking down at my Rice Krispies and the next, there was my nose floating there in the milk. I took it to my doctor and told him I had an important date tonight and I couldn't go out looking like this, so he made me one out of Silly Putty until they can graft my own back on."

"How does it look?"

"Actually, I think it's an improvement. I can't smell with it, but the other one couldn't bounce or make impressions of comic strips."

"As long as I'm not embarrassed when you drive me to the airport in about twenty minutes."

A vexed sigh came through the earpiece. "So that's how things are. I'm beginning to feel used and abused."

"It would be doing me a tremendous favor," I said. "I won't have to leave my car at the airport and have an horrendous parking bill waiting for me when I get back. Isn't that clever?"

"Not clever, just cheap," she said. "What time is your flight?"

"Six-ten."

"Traffic is going to be a bitch," she mused. "I'd better leave now."

I hung up and thought about the first time I'd met Liz. She'd been standing in a dark corner of Freddie's, a Westwood disco filled with fishtanks and tacky panels óf stained glass and desperate faces frozen three-deep at the bar, with a Minolta in her hands. She had recently been divorced after twenty years of marriage to an orthopedic surgeon with a bad back, which, since the divorce, had kept him from working. And which coincidentally kept him from making alimony and child support payments. The pain in the good doctor's back was intermittent, however, and didn't keep him from working emergency rooms where the payments were strictly in cash, nor did it keep him from going out occasionally and doing the boog-a-loo, which was why Liz was lurking stealthily in the shadows of Freddie's with a Minolta in her hands. I doubted she would ever make it as a professional lurker. She was not what you would call your basic unobtrusive type.

She was a tall, mercifully freckle-free redhead with sharp triangular features and large green eyes that always seemed to have a faintly startled look in them. She also had humungus boobs that must have measured in around 40 Triple D somewhere, and she wore nothing but tight-fitting jeans and stretch tops that should have gotten time and a half for hazard pay. Since she had married so young and never really had a chance to experience men, she had run wild since her divorce, finding out what she had missed. And all the men had one thing in common: they were all young. She considered any man over thirty-five "old", despite the fact that she had a headstart on her forties. Since I was thirty-five, I figured I was approaching the top of the hill, but she never mentioned it. She was thoughtful that way.

But then I was thoughtful, too, by not mentioning certain things, for instance the fact that although she was still an incredibly sexy lady, that she was beginning to show signs of wear—especially around the eyes and the backs of the hands and that I could see a nervous day rapidly approaching when despite how far she threw that chest out, the men would stop looking and the roof would cave in. But even when that happened, she still had a ways to go, because she had a mind like a steel trap and an outrageous sense of humor that could take up a hell of a lot of slack. And some men—me, for one—found that a hell of a lot more attractive than a set of 40 Triple D's.

When I had been introduced to her in Freddie's, she had very demurely taken my hand and said with a perfectly deadpan expression: "Hello, there. I'm Liz. I come from Open Crotch, Montana. I have a big spread up there."

Since that night a year or so ago, Liz and I had worked into a casual, but at the same time, very close, relationship. Casual, because we both still dated a lot of other people, and close because there was a firm bedrock of friendship and understanding and respect underlying the whole affair that was more important than the heady excitement that comes with a strictly sexual attraction. If it had not been for a ten-year age differential and the fact that she had just come off a disastrous marriage and me a disastrous love affair, it might have developed into something a little less casual. As it was, I still gave it some thought every now and then.

"How long will you be gone?" she asked as we crept along the freeway through rush-hour traffic in her bronze XKE.

I shrugged. "I don't know. Maybe a couple of days, maybe a week. It's hard to say. I don't know that much about the situation."

"What's it about?"

"Just another example of connubial bliss," I said. "Husband is banging the brains out of a lot of broads, so wife gets herself a boyfriend, which husband gets angry about. Husband threatens to have wife and boyfriend encased in cement. Typical stuff."

"You're breaking a date with me for *that?* How dull."

"I know, but what can I do? *One* of us has to work. I doubt

39

you could support me and Derek on your unemployment checks in the style to which I am accustomed. By the way, how'd things go with the lawyer today?"

"Great. The asshole said I can't keep Bill from taking Derek on the weekends even though Derek doesn't want to go. He says it was part of the settlement."

"Paying you alimony was also part of the settlement."

"That's what I told him," she said. "He just shrugged. For that shrug and two letters his secretary wrote to Bill's attorney, he gave me a bill for three thousand dollars. I'm thinking of taking him to the State Bar for charging unethical rates."

She signaled for the Century Boulevard offramp and nosed the Jaguar up the ramp.

"You could, you know," I said. "But you won't."

"Why not?"

"Because you're a marshmallow. Your resistance to people pushing on your life is very weak. If you'd been born in China, you would have made a hell of a Taoist."

She bared her front teeth, put her hands together and gave a Mandarin bow to the windshield. "Ah-so."

"That's right. You big Ah-so."

The air was filled with the high-pitched whine of jets and the smell of jet fuel. A yellow Air West plane dipped over the freeway and shook the car as it passed over us on its approach pattern. I checked my watch. "The 5:15 from Phoenix."

She glanced over at me. "How do you know?"

"Because I used to live a few blocks from here, across the freeway. After a year, you get to know the schedules."

She looked at me disbelievingly. "How could you stand the noise?"

"The rent was cheap."

"It had to be awfully cheap."

"It was."

Traffic was thick heading into the airport. It seemed as if all of L.A. had finally gotten sick of the smog and was getting out. I just hoped they weren't all going to Reno. "Don't bother to park," I said. "Just pull over at the United terminal and I'll get the bag out."

She threaded the Jag through the tangled flow of cars and pulled over at the curb. A redcap started to scurry over, but I signaled him I'd get it myself and he frowned and pushed his dolly off in another direction. The car shuddered violently as it idled.

"What's wrong with the Great Beast now?"

She waved a hand in the air. "I don't know. I've got to take it in tomorrow and find out."

"Why don't you just dump it? It's nothing but a royal pain in the ass."

She sucked in a breath, seemingly shocked at the suggestion. "I *love* this car. I could never sell it."

"The only reason you love it is because it's a phallic symbol."

Her eyes widened and she blinked, confused. "What do you mean, 'symbol?' You mean that salesman lied? He said it was a vibrator."

I laughed and got out of the car and hoisted my bag out of the back. I went around to her side and gave her a peck on the mouth. "I'll call you in a day or so."

"Just be careful. Don't get encased in cement with any of those people."

"But just think: I'd be a living monument to my memory."

"I'm serious. Be careful."

"I think you've been reading too many of the detective stories your son collects," I said. "Four bodies on every page."

"Just as long as you're not on one of the pages."

"I'm not even in the story, lady."

She put the car in gear and said: "Let me know when you're going to be coming back and I'll pick you up. I should have my own nose back on by then."

"I don't know," I said, shaking my head. "Maybe you should leave this one. I think you're right. I think it's an improvement."

"Fuck you, too, Charley," she said, laughing, and took off, the Jag sputtering and coughing as it merged into traffic.

41

5

Aside from the dirty snow banked along both sides of the wet streets, the outskirts of Reno did not look much different than the outskirts of any Southern California town that had grown up in a hurry. The profile of the city was low and flat, the wide streets lined with motels and car dealerships and huge shopping center complexes and the omnipresent smattering of McDonald's and Sambo's and Pizza Huts. The Los Angelization of America.

It had probably been going on for some time, but in the past few years, whenever I had travelled, the trend had been striking. It was as if Los Angeles was one gigantic roll of concrete-and-glass-and-fluorescent-tube carpeting that was being laid by a secret group of city planners who had a Vision, to turn the country into one 3,000-mile-long shopping center. My only solace was that when it finally happened, which it inevitably would, at least I would be able to go anywhere and never feel homesick.

Schwartz had been right; the Ponderosa was easy to find. It was right on Virginia Street, Reno's main drag, and the three-story green neon pine tree out front made it hard to miss. I parked my rented Vega near the lobby entrance and went through the casino to the front desk.

The clerk was a prissy little man with a face like a dried apricot. He told me Mrs. Mezzano had made a reservation for me—Room 508—and had left word for me to call her as soon as I checked in.

The room was not what I would call plush, but it was roomy and comfortable. I tipped the bellboy a buck, then threw my bag on the double bed and unpacked. After I'd finished hanging and folding, I dialed Mrs. Mezzano's number.

She sounded relieved to hear from me. She asked if I had seen Carlos and when I said I hadn't, she told me he was staying in 505, just down the hall. That was as close to my room as she could get, she said. She gave me instructions how to get out to her house and asked if I could drop by about eight-thirty. I told her I'd see her then.

After a hot shower and a shave, I slipped into a black wool turtleneck and tan corduroy pants and jacket and locked the room. There was no answer to my knock at 505. The clerk told me Mr. Realango had left the hotel some time ago and had not been back. I checked out the casino and the coffee shop, just to make sure, then came back and left a note in his room slot for him to call me when he came in.

Susan Mezzano's house was in the foothills just south of the main part of town, in a development of houses that looked fairly new. The mailbox sat at the end of an inclined gravel driveway flanked by naked elms. The gravel crackled beneath the car's snow tires as I drove up the driveway to the floodlit house.

It was a modern, split-level with a brown shingle roof. It was made of red brick and wood and plenty of glass. The front yard was enclosed by a low brick wall topped by an ornamental wrought-iron fence.

As I pulled up and killed my engine, a huge white Alsatian dog came barking and snarling from somewhere around back. It planted itself behind the front gate, gave me a good look at all of its three hundred teeth, and kept on barking. I stood there like a dumb ass, wondering what to do when the front door of the house opened and Susan Mezzano stepped onto the porch. She had gotten one foot out the door when a twin of the dog at the gate plowed past her and roared down the brick walkway, putting its two cents into the frenetic din.

She shouted angrily: "Sonny! Cher! Get in here!"

At the sound of her voice, the dogs stopped barking and trotted back to her side, where they sat down and watched me. She pointed at the door. "Go inside now. Go on."

The pair eyed me suspiciously, but reluctantly obeyed.

43

"You can come in now," she called. "They won't bother you. Just lift the latch on the gate. It's on the right there."

I found the latch and opened the gate and went slowly up the walk, keeping an eye on the door behind her. She wore a loose-fitting gold silk housedress that went all the way to the ground.

"Have you seen Carlos?" she asked.

"The clerk at the hotel said he left a couple of hours ago. I left a note—"

She pursed her lips angrily. "That pig-headed—I told him to *stay* at the hotel, not to go out. Jesus, as if I didn't have enough to worry about as it is without him traipsing around Reno making a target out of himself."

"Is it that bad?"

She looked at me. "That's what I'm trying to find out."

She stepped out of the doorway and I went in. The stifling heat of the house rushed at me as I came through the door. The temperature inside must have been eighty-five degrees.

She closed the door and led me into a spacious living room with a high beamed ceiling. The carpet was about the color of a healthy lawn and about as thick and the furniture—mostly bright greens and yellows—was thick and expensive, displaying a taste for crushed velvet and gold leaf. Full-length cream-colored drapes ran the length of the far wall, which I assumed was glass, and the others were covered by marbled copper paper.

A fire crackled in the white brick fireplace and above it was a large oil portrait of Susan Mezzano dressed in a low-cut, long-sleeved evening gown. She was at least fifteen years younger in the painting, but the youth there was not merely in the absence of lines in the face of the skin or the fact that she was at least ten pounds thinner. The artist had captured a laughing lustiness that I had only gotten brief glimpses of ten days before.

She waved a hand toward a bright green patent leather bar at the other end of the room. "How about a drink?"

"Thanks."

"I could use one myself," she said.

We went over to the bar and I took one of the stools, while

44

she went behind it and started searching the glass shelves. "Bourbon, right?"

"That would be fine."

"I remember. You were hitting the Wild Turkey pretty good in San Diego."

"I don't think any of us did poorly."

"No, I guess we didn't," she said.

The two Alsatians did not waste any time getting my smells filed away in their doggie-brains. She told them to go lie down, which they did, side by side in front of the fire.

"Beautiful dogs."

She nodded and looked at them affectionately. "I sleep a hell of a lot better when they're around, let me tell you. Especially now."

While she mixed the drinks, I scanned the room. The knickknacks that littered the shelves and coffee tables were a mixture of Western and Oriental—cut crystal, carved ivory elephants, small bits of modern metal sculpture—and although individually there were some nice pieces, together they only managed to look tasteless.

She handed me my drink. "Let's go over and sit on the couch. It's more comfortable."

We went over to a huge U-shaped couch in front of the fireplace and sat down. "For Christ's sake, honey, take your coat off. I know it's hotter than hell in here. The only reason I got the heat on so high is that this cold weather plays hell with my back. I should really probably be living in Palm Springs instead of Reno."

I put my drink down on a coaster on the glass and gold coffee table that sat in the center of the U, and peeled my coat off. "So why don't you?"

"And do what? Retire? I may look it, but I'm not *that* old, honey."

I shrugged. "I'm sure the town could use a good whorehouse."

She smiled wryly. "Somehow, I don't think the local gendarmes would be as understanding as our local law."

"Is this the only county in Nevada where prostitution is legal?"

She shook her head and took a sip of her drink. "There are three others: Storey, Lyon, and Churchill. *We* were the first, though. We were the ones who took it to the Supreme Court. But you watch. Within ten years, it'll be legal in every county in the state."

"You really think so?"

"Damn straight I do," she said forcefully. She seemed to have temporarily forgotten about Carlos and why I was here. "It's got to. It's a service industry, just like any other. Look, you can drive along Interstate 80 and find a house in any town you stop in. As long as they don't get any complaints that somebody got rolled or the clap, the local authorities just look the other way and pretend they don't exist. But they're starting to look over here and see all that good tax money that's going down the drain and they're finding it harder and harder to turn their backs on it. You used to hear a lot of politicians around this state saying, 'We don't need whore money,' but you don't hear it much anymore. What else has this state got, except booze, broads and gambling? A lot of sagebrush and sand."

I nodded and took a swallow of my drink. It was strong. "What time did you get in?"

"Noon."

"Has anything happened since you got back?"

"No. Not unless you mean the electricity and water and gas to the house being shut off as something. He had the phone disconnected, too. I had to pull some strings to have everything hooked up again by this afternoon. He's also reported all my credit cards stolen, just to make sure I can't buy anything. He's trying to wear me down." She frowned darkly. "I'm worried, Jake. And I'm not the worrying type. I'm so worried I called the Reno P.D. from San Diego to make sure they could give me a police escort home from the airport, that's how worried I am. Sal has always gone through his Little Caesar moods, but lately, I think he's starting to think he's the Godfather. Ever since we built the new place. When I saw the architect's plans with the gun towers—"

"Gun towers?"

She nodded. "Two of them. Just like a damn prison yard. He's got all sorts of ex-cons walking around the place with badges and guns, playing the big role. He's gotten strange the past year. He never goes anywhere anymore without Merritt or Battaglia with him. Now I hear he's been seen riding around town with that new spic heavyweight of his—Alfredo whatsisname. Sal brought him up here originally to use as a sparring partner for Carlos; but then he bought his contract. He's from Colombia or one of those damn countries and he's mean as they come."

"What do you think it all means?"

"I wish to hell I knew," she said. "When I got that damned call—"

"Did you get it on tape?"

"No. The machine was in Carlos' room. I never figured he'd call me. As a matter of fact, I thought everything had quieted down. We hadn't heard anything more since we talked to you."

"Did you recognize the voice?"

She took a pull of her drink. "No. It was hoarse, like a whisper. Like he was trying to disguise his voice."

"What exactly did he say?"

Her face reddened angrily. "The jerk-off," she snarled, as if that were the most deprecatory term she could think of to describe someone. When I thought about it, it probably was. "First of all, he said something like, 'I hear the weather is nice and warm down there.' You got to realize it was three-thirty in the goddamn morning and I didn't know what the hell was going on. It woke me out of a sound sleep, and I didn't know what the hell was going on. I asked who it was and he said, 'Don't come back up north. You might get all crippled up from the cold,' and hung up.

"At first, I got really pissed off, that this jerk-off has the nerve to wake me up spouting off that crap, but then I started to get worried. I sat up until dawn, trying to decide what to do. I finally decided I'd better try to get back up here and calm Sal down before he really flips out and does something that can't be taken back."

"And you told Carlos about the call," I said.

She nodded. "That was a mistake. But if I'd tried to give him a line of bullshit, he would have just gotten suspicious and found out the truth anyway. I kept telling him I wanted to go alone, but he just kept saying, 'I go with you. I no let you go up to that nuthouse alone.' I gave up trying to argue with him. When he gets his mind made up about something, you might as well try to move a bridge. That's when I called Jack and then you."

"You think Sal might try to get rough with you?"

"I doubt it," she said, not too convincingly. "But if Carlos finds out I'm going out to Moonfire, he's going to insist on going with me, just to make sure."

She made little explanatory circles in the air with her hands. "Carlos, he—this is hard for him to understand. He's like a big kid in a lot of ways. He's never had the chance to grow up, really. His life has been organized for him since the time he was eighteen. He gets up and runs four miles, eats, goes back to sleep, works out in the gym, takes a shower, eats again, and goes back to bed. The only trouble is, that kind of a life doesn't prepare you for the shit that's out there. Life isn't that predictable. It's as messy and unpredictable as you can get. I've tried to explain to him what's going on here, how Sal is, but he just can't get it through that thick skull of his that this is one problem he can't solve with a left hook. He keeps talking about going out to Moonfire and talking to Sal."

"Have you talked to anybody out at Moonfire since you've been back?"

"I just talked for a couple of seconds to Gwen—the girl working the switchboard. She was scared to death to talk to me. She was afraid somebody would catch her talking to me and tell Sal. He's declared me off limits and issued orders that anybody who gets caught talking to me gets the axe." The thought seemed to upset her. She waved her drink in the air and some of the liquor sloshed over its rim and spilled on the carpet. She didn't notice, or if she did, she didn't seem to care. "That sonofabitch can't declare me off limits. That joint is as much mine as it is his. More. My name is on all the licenses. I was the one who kept the place

alive while he was in the pen doing laundry, for chrissakes. *I'm*
the one who's run things while he's gone off for weeks at a time
with some trashy little piece of tail. I've forgotten more about this
business than he'll ever know." She paused and her eyes narrowed. She waved the drink at me. I was out of sloshing range.
"You know what Sal's done since I've been away? I found out
today. He's set up a goddamn time-system for the girls. He's got
a time clock and everything. Now if a guy comes in and wants a
straight lay, he gets fifteen minutes, no more. A dollar a minute.
He's turning the joint into a Fur Burger King. I mean, a whorehouse isn't the most romantic place in the world, a broad checking you out for V.D., and then telling you to cough up bread up
front, but this, it's, it's *too* damn cold."

She finished, then flushed, a little self-consciously. We sat
looking at each other for a few seconds, not saying anything.
"What do you want me to do?" I asked softly.

"Do your best to keep Carlos out of the way for the next couple
of days. He likes you. He enjoyed himself that night. Take him
out drinking or gambling. Find a couple of broads, anything. Just
keep him away from Moonfire."

"Does he like to gamble?"

"He's not a heavy gambler, but he likes to play at it. Especially
blackjack."

"You think that's where he might be now?"

She frowned and shook her head. "I don't know. Could be. You
could check around. You might start at the King's Inn. He likes
the blackjack dealers there."

"Any others?"

"Harrah's. Maybe the Bonanza."

I nodded. "When do you figure to try to go out to Moonfire?"

"Tomorrow," she said. She brushed back a wisp of cotton-
candy hair and let her hand rest on the back of her neck. "All this
should come to a head in the next twenty-four hours, one way or
another."

I took a deep breath and raised my eyebrows. "I'll see what I
can do, Mrs.—Susan. I don't know how much that will be. If

49

Carlos is as stubborn as you and Schwartz say he is, I doubt that he's going to heed any of my sage advice."

Her face softened. "I'm not asking for miracles. I don't believe in them anyway. Just do what you can. Right now, I didn't know where to turn."

She put her empty glass down on the table and her face turned hard again. "Now. Money. I've instructed the Ponderosa to send your hotel bill to me, so don't worry about that. Jack gave you money for the flight up?"

"Yes."

"You'll want something up front, I take it."

"I'll take two days' salary. That's three hundred dollars. If you get everything straightened out by tomorrow, I'll keep one-fifty and deduct my expenses from the second one-fifty and return you the balance. Fair enough?"

Her mouth formed itself into a thin, lopsided grin. "Listen, honey, anything's fair at this point. You could charge me double and I'd pay it. Like I said, right now you're the best shot I've got."

She grimaced painfully as she hoisted herself off the couch. *Damn* this cold weather. The other day I heard some guy come up with a solution to the energy problem. He said all we had to do was eliminate the months of December through February, take all those days and put them in June and July. That way, we wouldn't have any winter. I think he had a right good idea. You wait right here. I'll get you a check."

She limped out of the room. Sonny and Cher lifted their heads off the carpet as she left and watched me. I didn't try to move. She returned a few minutes later and slipped a folded check into my hand. I put the check in my pocket, finished my drink and stood up. Sonny and Cher stood up with me.

"Don't worry," she said. "It's good. That's my personal checking account. Sal can't get to that, at least."

"I hadn't even thought about it," I lied.

She smiled slyly. "I would've."

I smiled back. "Of that I have no doubts," I said.

6

Beautiful downtown Reno was five square blocks of old, dirty gray stone buildings covered with a gaudy veneer of neon. Flashing and swirling and blinking lights spelled out names like Harold's Club and Harrah's and the usual hackneyed assortment of casino usuals like Nugget and Gold Dust and Bonanza. But one block off Virginia Street in any direction and the veneer chipped off like cheap silver plate. There one could find the illegitimate offspring of these neon promises of easy money, the pawn shops and second-hand jewelry stores and the seedy bars that offered cheap shots of courage or solace, depending on the need of the customer.

It was the off-season and the casino crowds were sparse. There was the usual smattering of housewives on three-day passes from their household chores, standing in front of the armies of slot machines and picking nickels out of their Dixie cups and pulling handles like those fixated chickens at the carnival that peck at the toy piano and wait for a kernel of corn. There were their husbands, who knew the slots did not get the name "one-armed-bandits" for nothing and who went for the "smarter" games and lost more. There were the old ladies in the polka-dot dresses who sat patiently blacking in their Keno sheets while the white-shirted man droned off numbers. There were conventioneers from the Fork Lift Manufacturers of America or the Tool-and-Die Workers Union, with their red faces and maroon-and-pink-and-green checked sports jackets, all snot-flinging drunk. And there were even a few tuxedoed, diamond-pinkied high rollers, chips stacked like miniature skyscrapers on the felt in front of them and a creamy blonde guarding each flank. About the only group not represented was Argentine heavyweights. And I would have settled for just one.

By two-thirty, I had hit every main casino downtown, and I could barely keep my eyes open. I had even tried a couple of topless bars by the railroad tracks that ran through the center of town. I decided to pack it in.

My message was undisturbed in Realango's room slot when I got back to the hotel. A quick check with the clerk confirmed he had not returned.

In my room, I undressed and, exhausted, fell into bed and fell asleep almost immediately. It seemed like two minutes later I was slammed up through ten layers of sleep by the ringing of the phone. My hand fumbled around in the dark while my heart beat wildly in my chest and I finally managed to locate the instrument on the bedside table. "What?"

"Jake, this is Susan," an urgent voice said.

My mind was still in a fog. "What?"

"Carlos just called me. Listen, are you awake?"

"Sure, sure," I lied. "What is it?"

"He told me Sal just called him at the hotel and wants to talk to him. To pow-wow. It's bullshit, a trick, I'm sure of it. I told him not to go, but he said he's going to get it over with. He said he's going to get everything all straightened out. He sounded like he's been drinking."

Her words were racing, stumbling over each other to get out of her mouth.

"When is he going out there?"

"Now. That's what I'm trying to tell you."

My mind was beginning to function now. I reached up and turned on the light. My watch was on the table. It said five-fifteen.

"It's kind of a strange time to hold a conference," I said. "Who does your husband think he is, Howard Hughes?"

"I don't like any of it," she said. "It stinks. You've got to see if you can stop him."

I told her to hold on a second and threw on a pair of pants and went across the hall. There was no answer to my knock. I knocked again, then went back into my room. "He's not in his room," I said. "How do you get out to Moonfire?"

"Go north on Virginia Street until you hit Interstate 90. Get on 90 going east and go about twelve miles until you see the Turner Road exit. You'll see signs after that."

"I'll get back to you as soon as I find out what's happening," I told her and hung up.

The clothes I had shed earlier were lying on top of the other bed and I threw them on hurriedly and went downstairs. The clerk said Realango had come in about an hour ago and gone to his room. About half an hour ago, he had received a phone call and had gone out again about fifteen minutes ago.

The streets of Reno were deserted, but the neon signs still blinked and swirled ludicrously, like an actor doing a monologue for an empty theater. I kept the Vega fifteen miles over the speed limit and my eyes on my rearview mirror for cops all the way out of town. The sky over the mountains was just starting to turn an insipid gray when I slowed down for the Turner exit.

The ramp dipped under a concrete bridge and my lights hit a sign that said: Moonfire Ranch—1 MI. An arrow pointed to a narrow concrete road that meandered like a drunken snake through a meadow of tall grass. I took it.

I had to drive slowly because of patches of ice on the road. Every once in a while, a boulder poked out of the dark grass with the words FUN AHEAD spray-painted on it in Day-Glo red, just to let me know I was still on the Road to Bliss. My tires clattered over the boards of an old trellised bridge that forded a small rocky stream and I found myself driving through a dense clump of birch trees. After a bit, the trees thinned and then the dawn turned bright red and I felt as if I had swallowed a cold stone.

The red dawn wasn't dawn at all, but the running lights of the half-dozen sheriff's cars that were parked at odd angles over a wide asphalt lot. Beyond the cars, on the far side of the lot, loomed the main building of Moonfire Ranch.

The building was huge and pinkish-purple and had a terra-cotta tile roof. From its central hub, which was hexagonal in shape and one story taller than the rest of it, wings ran out in all directions, like the spokes of a wheel. Hovering behind two of the wings, silent and menacing, in the quivering dawn, were two glass and wood gun towers and surrounding the whole architectural abortion was a ten-foot wrought-iron fence.

I parked next to one of the squad cars about fifty yards from the gates and stepped out of the car. A line of tousle-haired girls stood shivering behind the fence, their coats clutched to their throats, the revolving lights of the squad cars pulsating in their faces like bloody heartbeats. Their eyes were glued on a group of men—some uniformed, some not—who were gathered around a yellow Mustang II parked in front of the gates. The door on the driver's side of the Mustang was open and the men were standing by it, looking down at something. Before I could get close enough to see what the something was, I was intercepted by a lean-jawed deputy wearing a Smokey the Bear hat. He broke away from the group and strode up to me aggressively. "Just where in the hell do you think you're going?"

I pointed to the road behind me and assumed a bewildered expression. "The sign back there said the fun was right up this way."

"There ain't any fun here, mister, why don't you just get back in your car and head on back the way you came?"

I looked over his shoulder. "What's going on?"

He waved his nine-cell flashlight at me. "Nothing that concerns you."

"Has there been an accident or something?"

"That's right," he snapped testily. "An accident. Now move."

A tall hatless man in a fur-collared leather jacket stepped out of the cluster of men holding a .38 caliber revolver in a gloved hand. As he did that, the crowd parted and I got a glimpse of the crumpled form of Carlos Realango. He was curled into a fetal position by the door of the Mustang. His blood had stained the snow around him scarlet.

The hatless man with the gun walked over to a short, jowly man standing a few feet away. The short man had a bulbous nose and a wide, thick-lipped mouth that was working over an unlit cigar. There were a few strands of black hair on his head, but they looked terminal. He didn't look cold, despite the fact that he was only wearing a flimsy shortsleeved sports shirt, a pair of slacks, and loafers with no socks. The hatless man held out the gun to him and said: "You ever see this gun before, Sal?"

The man frowned. "It looks like my wife's gun. Where'd you find it?"

"In his boot."

The short man took the cigar out of his mouth and beamed triumphantly. "I *told* you, goddamn it. I told you he came out here to kill me."

The deputy had been distracted by the discovery of the gun, but suddenly he remembered me. He tapped me on the sternum with his flashlight and said: "I'm going to tell you one last time, buddy, get the hell out of here."

The tall man heard him and looked over. He handed the pistol to another deputy beside him, told him to put it in an evidence bag and made the ten feet to where we were standing in three strides.

"Who's he?" he asked the deputy, poking a thumb at me.

"Just a rubberneck, Sheriff."

The sheriff looked me over. He had a long, lineless face, with prominent temples and cheekbones, and premature gray hair that was cropped close to his head. His eyes were gray, too, but they did not give out much: they were cold and heavy. "Do your sightseeing somewhere else, mister," he said.

"Yes, sir," I said. "I was just leaving."

My mind was totally disorganized. I felt like a drunk coming home late at night and finding his wife had moved all the furniture. But there didn't seem to be anything else I could do but leave. I turned and started back to the car.

At the car, I paused and looked back. The deputy had gone back to the group around the body. I started to get in, but stopped when I heard the sirens whoop-whooping in the distance. All the faces snapped up and the short man shot a hard, questioning look at the sheriff, who merely shrugged. The group stood frozen in silence, their eyes focused on the road behind me like wild animals tensely sniffing the air for danger.

The sirens grew louder and finally, around the bend of trees, four blue-and-white cop cars peeled into the lot and slammed to a stop, their sirens dying with a throaty moan.

Mezzano grabbed the sheriff by the sleeve. "What the fuck are they doing out here? Did you call them?"

The sheriff gestured helplessly. "I didn't know what to expect out here, Sal. Whoever it was that called said somebody'd been shot, that's all. I didn't know if I'd need a backup or what so I called Washoe County—"

"You fucking idiot!" Mezzano said angrily. "Don't you think I would've *told* you if you needed a fucking backup? Jesus Christ!"

The doors of the squad cars were flung open and from them piled men dressed in khaki overalls and the black billed hats that identified them as SWAT. With military precision, one man quickly unlocked the trunk of each car and began handing out 12-gauges and .223 semi-automatic rifles.

That was enough for Mezzano. He started toward them waving his hands like a wild man. "Okay, you pigs, get the fuck off my property! Move it! Now!"

One of the men, a granite-faced man with sergeant's stripes on his sleeve, left the others and met Mezzano's charge with a cold stare, "Who the hell are you?"

"Sal Mezzano, that's who. You in charge of these guys?"

"That's right," the sergeant said stiffly.

"Then tell them to put their shit back in the cars and get out of here."

"Where's Sheriff Dierdorf? We got a call for assistance—"

"I don't give a shit who you got a call from," Mezzano yelled. "We don't need no assistance."

By that time, the rest of the men had assembled into an imposing shoulder-to-shoulder line, their guns at their sides. One of them, a sandy-haired man built like a cube, trotted up to the sergeant and said: "They're ready for their assignments, Sergeant. What's the situation?"

Mezzano stabbed a finger at him. His face was red now, and I didn't think it was just because of the running lights. "The situation is that we got a dead man here, so big fucking deal. Any of you guys think you can bring him back to life, you let me know. Otherwise get your asses off my property."

The sergeant's jaw tightened, but before he could say anything, Dierdorf came pushing his way past Mezzano, a conciliatory smile plastered across his face.

"I'm Sheriff Dierdorf, Sergeant. We've got everything under control. We've already got the suspect in custody. I'm sorry they got you out of bed for nothing, but I didn't know exactly what we had out here when I called for a backup."

The sergeant's eyes left Mezzano. "Where's the suspect?"

"What the hell difference does it make to you?" Mezzano said, pushing his face out. "You got no jurisdiction here. This ain't Washoe County. Now get your dogs back in their cars and off my property before I start waking people up in Carson City."

The sergeant pointed toward the building. "I was told there's a man with a rifle holed up in that whorehouse—"

His words were cut off by a shout from the direction of the gates. "They're coming out!"

All eyes snapped toward the gates. There was a nervous twittering from the girls as two uniformed cops, both holding 12-gauge pumps, stepped through the front doors of Moonfire, flanking a large, wild-haired man. The man had his hands cuffed behind him and his head was bowed so it was impossible to see what he looked like. He had on a pair of jeans and a long-sleeved blue work shirt that was unbuttoned down the front and shoes, but no socks. They opened the front gate and put him in the back seat of one of the squad cars.

"*There's* your suspect," Mezzano said, pointing. "So now you can beat it."

The SWAT sergeant nodded silently, his mouth a grim line.

He smiled at Mezzano like a maitre d' with gastritis, then turned to Dierdorf. "As long as you've got everything under control, Sheriff." He turned to his men. "Let's go home, boys. The pimp wants us off his property."

"Pimp?" Mezzano spat angrily and took a step forward. "You fucking pigs—"

The sergeant wheeled around, shifted his weight to his back foot, and dropped his hand toward his back pocket. Dierdorf stepped in between the two men quickly and put a hand on Mezzano's chest. "Easy, Sal."

The tenseness left the sergeant's body suddenly and he smiled, then turned briskly and marched back to his car.

Mezzano's eyes were fastened on his back like teeth as the sergeant walked by them without turning his head and said: "Pack it up, boys. We're going back to bed."

They mumbled and began to disperse.

While they were putting their rifles back into the trunks of their cars, a maroon Camaro pulled into the parking lot and made a wide arc around them.

"Now what the fuck?" Mezzano muttered as the Camaro parked on the other side of Realango's Mustang and a thin, dark-haired young man in a down ski jacket stepped out carrying a camera. Mezzano's face turned beet-red as the young man walked around the hood of the car and snapped off two pictures of Realango's blood-soaked body, and he broke into a trot, shaking his hands in the air like an ecstatic at a Baptist prayer meeting. "Get him out of here! No fucking pictures! Joe!"

The SWAT cops looked up with new interest as a thick man with curly black hair and a dark mustache left the group by the body and started for the photographer. The photographer's eye left the camera's viewer and worry clouded his face as he saw the mustachioed man bearing down on him. He quickly turned and ran back to his car and got in. He tried to close the door, but the man with the mustache had grabbed the handle and jerked it open.

The man with the mustache leaned in the car and said something and held out his hand. The photographer shook his head, but the man said something else, and the kid meekly handed over his camera. The man opened up the back of it, pulled out the film, handed it back to its owner, and jabbed a thumb toward the road down which he had come.

As the Camaro backed up, Mezzano walked back, mumbling. The Washoe County SWAT boys, anticipating possible trouble, were still standing around, watching the scene. Mezzano pointed. "You guys still here? I thought I told you to be missing."

Then, as if for the first time, he seemed to see me. He looked at Dierdorf. "Who's he? Another fucking reporter? Goddamn newshounds are like vultures. Take off, buddy—"

"I'm not a reporter," I said. "I was just out here for a little fun, that's all."

His round face softened and he patted me on the arm. "Sorry about that, buddy, but you can see we got our hands full right now. Look, come back later, why don't you, and I can guarantee you some fun. Okay? This is just a temporary inconvenience."

"It looks like it was a permanent inconvenience for him," I said, pointing at Realango's body.

Confusion registered on his features and his dark eyes widened. They had a feverish glow in them. "Huh? Oh yeah. Listen, this is nothing, see? It'll all be cleaned up in no time. Come back later."

Mezzano and Dierdorf walked back to the body. Mezzano waved his hands in a shooting motion toward the girls at the gate, who began to reluctantly peel off and go back into the building. Dierdorf began talking to the deputy who had brought out the suspect and then that man and the deputy who had tried to give me the bum's rush got into the car that held the prisoner and started up the engine. They turned on their running lights and drove out of the lot, their siren blaring.

The law from Washoe County watched in tight-lipped silence as the patrol car disappeared through the trees, then got into their own cars and began pulling out. I took up the rear, lost in thought and feeling slightly nauseous.

It was five minutes to six and the sun was just rising and was staining the mountains on the other side of the highway pinkish-purple. They stretched across the sky jagged and uneven, and whoever the artist was, I did not like his choice of colors: they were whorehouse colors.

7

The dogs were barking furiously inside the house as I drove up. A curtain stirred in the front window and then the front door opened and Susan Mezzano stepped out onto the porch dressed in a yellow bathrobe and slippers. The dogs brushed by her and ran into the front yard, still barking, but she shouted for them to shut up and they quieted down. She had no makeup on and her face looked drawn and haggard.

My stomach was churning as I opened the gate and went up the walk. As I neared her, she reached out a hand, as if to touch me. "What happened? Did you find him?"

"I found him."

"Where was he?"

"At Moonfire," I said. "Can we go inside?"

She pulled the door open without saying anything more and I slipped past her. The dogs tried to follow, but she told them to stay outside and shut the door.

I went directly into the living room and she followed. There was a fire burning in the fireplace. I went over and stood in front of it and pretended to warm my hands, trying to think of how to tell her. She stood by the couch, staring at me, her eyes questioning. "Why don't you sit down, Mrs. Mezzano—"

"What the hell is this?" she snapped angrily. "I don't need to sit down. Something happened to Carlos, didn't it?"

"He's dead."

"Dead." She repeated the word, as if trying to remember its meaning.

"Somebody shot him," I said. "The sheriff was already out there when I got there."

She was holding onto the back of the couch and I could see her nails dig into the fabric. "Who did it?" The words were so faint I could barely hear them. Her eyes stared at me vacantly.

"Some big guy with curly brown hair. At least that's who the sheriff had in custody."

"Merritt," she said. "Which sheriff was out there? Dierdorf or Washoe County?"

"Dierdorf," I said. "The Washoe County boys showed up, but your husband ran them off."

She shook her head in disbelief, walked slowly around the end of the couch and sat down. She bowed her head and ran a hand through her white hair, then began rubbing her neck with her right hand. "He just couldn't let it alone. He just couldn't let it alone."

I didn't say anything.

When she looked up at me, her eyes were watery. She took a deep breath and said: "You know what it's been like for the past ten years? Jesus Christ, look at me. I know I'm old and I'm ugly, but I deserve *something*, goddamn it, don't I? Don't I?"

I didn't know what to say.

She shook her head and kneaded her bathrobe with her fingers. "I've lived with Sal for nineteen years and never once have I tried to change him. I've always known he's the type of man you've just got to take like he is and that's that. So why the hell couldn't he take me like I am? How the hell was it going to hurt?"

She picked a piece of crumpled Kleenex out of the pocket of her robe and used it to wipe the tears out of her eyes. Her hands were trembling violently. She sniffled, then said: "Carlos made me feel young again. So what's wrong with that? Even if he was lying, he made me feel young again, like I was a woman and not just a goddamn adding machine that counts up the day's take, and hires and fires whores. It might not have lasted, but the sonofabitch could have let me have it for a little while. The bastard, I don't know what gets into that Dago brain of his . . ."

Her voice dropped suddenly and she buried her face in her

hands. Her shoulders were being wracked with sobs, but no sound was coming out. I stood staring awkwardly, then stepped up to her and put a hand on her back. "Can I get you something? A drink might do you some good."

She nodded without looking up.

I went to the bar and picked out a bottle of Ballantine's from the assortment of booze on the glass tray and poured her a double. When I came back over and handed her the drink, she seemed to have regained at least partial control of herself. She was sitting rigidly on the couch, self-consciously dabbing her eyes with the Kleenex. She thanked me for the drink and took a deep swallow. She kept the glass in her lap.

I sat down on the couch and watched her composure slowly return. After a few seconds, I asked: "Did Carlos have a gun with him?"

She shook her head. "A gun? No, why?"

"The sheriff found a .38 stuck down his boot."

"Somebody planted the goddamn thing. Carlos didn't have any gun." She searched my face with her eyes. "Who found it, did you say?"

"Dierdorf."

"That explains it right there."

"Falsifying evidence in a murder case is a felony, Mrs. Mezzano. You really think Dierdorf would stick his neck out that far?"

The lower part of her face smiled. "You don't seem to have gotten it through your head yet. Frank Dierdorf does what my husband tells him to do. Prostitution in Evans County is supposed to be regulated by the Prostitution Licensing Control Board. The sheriff is on the Board, so is the D.A., and the county commissioners. They're supposed to make sure all the ordinances are enforced, like making sure all the girls are checked out by a doctor once a week, assessing fees, making sure there aren't any houses operating within so many miles of any incorporated town, stuff like that. They also make damn sure nobody else gets a license to open a house in Evans County. Sal tells them what to do, every

63

last one of them. They all owe him their jobs and they know he could have them dumped out with the morning trash if they gave him any trouble."

She took another swallow of her drink. Her gaze shifted to a point somewhere over my right shoulder and she seemed to be talking to herself more than to me. "I know what Sal's doing. I know the way he thinks after nineteen years. He had the gun planted to make it look like Carlos was going out there to kill him. Between him and Frank and Wahrnke, the D.A., they'll try to work it so Merritt gets off on a justifiable homicide charge." She pursed her lips. "But the sonofabitch isn't going to get away with it. Not this time. This time he took away too much. Too goddamn much."

Tears welled up in her eyes again. Confronting her grief and faced with my inability to ease it, I was nagged by feelings of guilt. "I'm sorry I couldn't do anything to stop it—"

She shook her head and daubed at her eyes. "It wasn't your fault. It was mine. We shouldn't have come back here. I had a feeling something like this was going to happen, and I came back anyway."

"I'll be taking the afternoon plane back to L.A.," I said. "Is there anything I can do for you before I leave?"

She looked at me sharply. "Leave?"

"There's no sense in me sticking around."

"I gave you a retainer."

"I wasn't intending to keep all of it," I said, not being able to keep the irritation out of my voice.

"I want you to keep it," she said. "I want you to earn it."

That took me by surprise.

"I want you to prove Sal had Carlos killed," she said. "I want the bastard's hide nailed to the wall."

"That might be a little tough to do. Dierdorf is in charge of the investigation. With him in your husband's back pocket, things could get a little sticky—"

"I'll give you two hundred a day plus expenses."

I shook my head. "I'm not trying to put the squeeze on you,"

I said. "I'm just trying to tell you you should give this a lot of thought. You're worked up right now, and that's understandable. But what you're talking about getting into is, well, it can get pretty ugly and you should make damn sure it's really what you want to do—"

"I know what I want to do," she said, her voice a deadly monotone. The grief was gone from her features now and her face was a cold, hard mask. I felt myself recoiling from the sudden personality change.

"I'm sure there are a lot of local people who would know their way around the area much better than I would."

"I don't trust them," she said. "They can be gotten to."

"How do you know I can't?"

"It's just a feeling I have. And I'm not wrong about people too often."

"We'll talk about it later," I said. "Right now, I'm going to go back to the hotel and try to grab a couple of hours sleep. If you need me for anything, just call."

She nodded, but didn't say anything.

"You going to be all right here by yourself?"

"I'll be fine."

I went outside. The dogs didn't even bark this time. They sauntered up, their tails wagging, and I scratched them behind their ears.

I always did have a way with animals. At least the four-legged variety.

8

This time it was the sound of knuckles rapping on my door that woke me up. I rolled over and plucked my watch off the table. It said it was almost noon. Actually, all it said was twenty to twelve. I hoped it was twenty to noon and not twenty to midnight, although the way I felt I wasn't ruling out that possibility. I went to the door in my Jockey shorts and opened it a crack.

There were two men in the hallway. One was tall and built like an athlete. He had a square, smooth face and wide shoulders and a tapered waist and long, slim legs. The other was probably ten years older, a foot shorter, and about the same weight. He looked as if someone had set a steam iron down on his face and gone to answer the phone. They did not have badges pinned to their coat lapels, but they might as well have. The shorter one blinked and said: "You Jacob Asch?"

I scratched my head and stifled a yawn. "Well, if I'm not, I'm having a hell of a lot of fun with some of the women he knows."

He was a flasher. Some of them take their time with it, they open it up with both hands and hold it up to your nose so that you can take in all the details, the engraving and all. But he did it all one-handed, in one fluid motion. He dipped in to his inside pocket, flipped open his wallet so that I caught a brief glimpse of a badge, and it was gone again, safely back in his pocket. "Washoe County District Attorney's office," he said. "My name's Wallace, this is Zwerdling. Would you like to get dressed and come with us, please? District Attorney Carew would like to talk to you."

"Not until Soviet Jewry is freed," I said, stiffening.

Zwerdling the athlete looked puzzled, but Wallace simply looked annoyed. Since I could not see any percentages in having

66

him remain that way, I stepped back and opened the door: "Come on in. I'll be with you in a couple of minutes."

They came in. Zwerdling sat in the chair at the end of the bureau while Wallace perched himself tentatively on the end of the bed. He had his car keys in his hands and they made jangly noises as he fiddled with them. He looked like the impatient type.

I went into the bathroom, splashed some water in my face, then stuck my head out and held up an electric razor. "Mind if I shave?"

"Just hurry it up," Wallace snapped. Definitely the impatient type.

I ran the razor over my stubble, put on some deodorant, and made a feeble attempt to mat down my sleep-tousled hair with a wet brush. I came out and slipped back into the black turtleneck and corduroy suit and said: "Okay. Let's go."

We drove downtown in silence. They parked the unmarked Dodge in front of the county offices—in a red zone, of course, and we went up the front stairs and into a marble-walled lobby and took the elevator up to the third floor.

Carew's office was a thickly carpeted, wood-paneled affair with plenty of bookshelves filled with law books and volumes of the Nevada Penal Code. Mini-blinds covered the large picture window behind the walnut desk and through them, the weak afternoon sun suffused the room with a soft glow. The one wall that was not bookshelves or window was covered with various framed awards and plaques from groups like the YMCA and the DAR and the Veterans of Foreign Wars for meritorious service to the community.

Carew sat at the desk. He was a neat-looking sort, with carefully brushed gray hair and a face that was still handsome, although it was beginning to go puffy in places. He had a small, puckered mouth, a long, thin nose and small brown eyes that glittered with self-importance. He wore a conservative, three-piece, navy pin-striped suit, a pale blue shirt and a dark blue tie.

Susan Mezzano sat in one of the chairs in front of the desk. She gave me an unsmiling hello as I came in. She had on a dark green dress with a high neck and a matching turban from beneath which poked some wisps of platinum hair. She looked tired: there were deep lines around her nose and mouth, her shoulders were slumped forward, and she seemed to be making a monumental effort to hold herself erect.

"Sit down, Mr. Asch," Carew said, waving a manicured hand at the chair next to Susan Mezzano's. Wallace and Zwerdling took chairs against the wall behind us.

"I want to thank you for coming down," Carew said.

"I didn't know I had any choice."

He did not respond to that. On the desk in front of him was a cassette tape recorder. His eyes dropped to the recorder, then shot back up to me. "I understand you are a licensed private investigator."

"That's right."

"May I see your license?"

I brought out my wallet, opened it to my photostat and handed it to him. He merely glanced at it, nodded, and handed it back.

"If you want references from L.A. law enforcement—" I began.

"I already called some people in Los Angeles. Your reputation seems to be fairly good down there. At least nobody had anything particularly derogatory to say about you."

His tone was condescending and I didn't like it. "You sound surprised."

He smiled. There was faint amusement in it, but not much else. "Let's just say my experiences with private investigators haven't left me with an indelible impression of the integrity of the profession."

"Now, now. Didn't you know, Mr. Carew, that stereotypes are the basis of all bigotry?"

"They usually have some basis in fact, nevertheless." He kept the same faint smile and fingered the cord on the recorder. He took a sharp breath, as if he were going to say something, then paused. I was sure he did that for effect. All of his motions had a posturing, self-conscious flavor to them. He waited for the effect

—whatever he thought it was—to build, then said: "Mrs. Mezzano has told me why you're in Reno."

I waited for more. He was in no hurry to give it to me. He steepled his index fingers and pressed them against his lips. I guessed that was supposed to convey great thought. "She also told me you were out at Moonfire Ranch this morning when Realango was shot."

"After," I corrected him. "He was dead when I got there."

He nodded as if I had just made an immaterial distinction, then picked up the microphone from the desk and handed it to me. "I'd like a statement of what you saw there, as detailed as you can remember it."

I hesitated and looked over at Mrs. Mezzano. She nodded. I took the microphone from him and recited the events of the morning as accurately as I could remember them. When I had finished, Carew punched the "off" button and laid the microphone back on the desk.

"I'm very interested in that gun Sheriff Dierdorf found on Realango," he said. "Did you actually see Dierdorf pull it out of Realango's boot?"

"No. All I saw was him stand up with the gun in his hand."

He nodded, but didn't say anything. He picked up a pen from the desk and held the end of it in his teeth. "You'd never seen the gun before, then?"

"How would I have seen it?"

The lids of his eyes dropped slightly. "The gun was registered to Mrs. Mezzano. I thought perhaps you saw it in their room when you met them in Southern California."

"I told you," Mrs. Mezzano said, an edge in her voice, "I left that gun at Moonfire. We didn't take it with us when we left. Besides, why would Carlos take a gun out there anyway? He knew he couldn't get through the gate, even if he shot somebody. The gate's controlled from inside the house."

He shrugged. "You forget, he told you he'd gotten a call to come out there. He *did* get a call at the hotel around four-forty-five. The switchboard operator remembered it. Maybe he thought

69

he could use a little protection, in case it was just a ploy to get him out there. After all, the place is like an armed camp. Unless you're a total idiot, you don't go marching into an armed camp totally defenseless."

"Carlos wasn't defenseless," she said coldly. "He was the number five heavyweight contender in the world."

"Fists don't stop bullets, Mrs. Mezzano." He put the pen down on the desk and moistened his lips with the end of his tongue. "What do you know about a girl named Valerie Barrington? I believe she went by the name of Candy while she was working for you?"

She shifted uneasily in her chair. "Why?"

"I got through talking to Sheriff Dierdorf on the phone a little while ago," he said. "He's ready to release a statement to the press that Candy was part of a romantic triangle with Realango and Merritt. He says there was bad blood between the two men because of it."

"Frank Dierdorf is a liar."

Carew raised an eyebrow. "Isn't it a fact that she and Merritt lived together for awhile?"

"If you call sleeping in her room on her nights off 'living together.' I don't. Merritt did that periodically with a lot of girls at Moonfire. There was never any big—"

"Isn't it also a fact," he said, the question rising accusingly in his throat, "that this Candy and Realango were married at one time?"

I glanced sharply at Susan Mezzano, but her eyes were locked in combat with Carew. "Look, Carew, you want cooperation from me, don't try to play prosecutor. I'm not on any witness stand, so don't interrupt me while I'm talking."

"I'm sorry," he said with a small, tight smile on his lips. "Go ahead."

"Candy and Carlos were married for a total of two weeks. And it was only on paper. There was never any romance in it. It was strictly a business arrangement."

"What kind of a business arrangement?"

"Carlos wanted to become a U.S. citizen, but the State Department wouldn't let him. I thought if he married an American girl, they'd grant his application, so I asked Candy to do me the favor."

"I take it the arrangement wasn't very successful."

She shrugged. "Candy decided she wanted out of the business. She came to me and said she'd had enough of the life and wanted to leave Moonfire. So we got the thing annulled and she left. That was all there was to it."

Carew had picked up a pen and begun doodling on a piece of paper in front of him while she talked. He watched his own scribblings and asked: "And you don't think there was any animosity between Realango and Merritt because of the girl?"

"No," she said definitely. "Merritt hung around Candy for a couple of weeks, that was all. He didn't care about her. In fact, when I left Moonfire, he'd moved in with another girl, a new girl who'd just started to work a few weeks before. He was talking about cutting out and settling down with the broad and everything."

"Did he say where he was planning to cut out to?"

She shook her white head. "No."

"When he was arrested, Merritt gave his residence address as a saloon in Duncan. Do you know anything about that?"

She blinked and made a face. "I know he's been pestering Sal for the past year to loan him the money to buy some old saloon out there. He had some crazy scheme to restore the place and turn it into a tourist attraction. Sal wouldn't give him the money, though."

"Why not?"

"He said the place would need too much work and that Duncan didn't get enough highway tourist traffic. He said it'd be a bad risk."

"And Merritt was still living at Moonfire when you left?"

She nodded.

"What date did you leave?"

"December 12."

He looked up from his doodling. "What was the other girl's

name, the one Merritt was talking about settling down with?"

"Pebbles."

"I take it that's her whorehouse name." He lingered on the word 'whorehouse,' trying to use it as a barb.

She didn't seem to feel it. "That's right."

"What's her real name?"

"Evelyn something," she said, covering her eyes with her hand for a moment. "Bestar. Yeah, I'm sure that's it."

He had her spell it out and jotted it down. "Where was she from?"

"Some farming town in the San Joaquin Valley. Fresno or Salinas. I don't remember exactly."

He put the pen down. "You said she was new. When did she start working?"

"Maybe two weeks before I left."

He nodded silently and I took the opportunity to butt in. "One thing *I* don't understand. Realango's murder took place in Evans County, not Washoe. Why are you investigating it?"

He crossed his legs, smoothed down a wrinkle in his pants, then picked a piece of lint deftly off one knee and let it fall to the floor. "Reno gets its fair share of bad publicity, Mr. Asch, without this sort of thing going on next door. We have a nice, clean town here, filled with respectable, God-fearing people, but if Gallup or Harris took a straw poll around the United States, the consensus would probably be that law enforcement and local government here is controlled by a bunch of hoods from Chicago and Newark. People have the idea that just because there is gambling around that everybody is crooked or paid off. This kind of murder, involving an international celebrity like Realango, is going to get a lot of attention in the media. It would be more than unfortunate if somehow the incident managed to get whitewashed and confirm that erroneous image in the public mind."

"You think that's a possibility?"

"Anything is possible," he said.

"You still have no jurisdiction over the case."

"Jurisdictional lines are becoming blurred now. It looks like the

Nevada Crime Commission might step in."

Susan Mezzano's brow furrowed. "Why?"

"Because your husband has invited them to," Carew said. "Apparently he thinks that might help to quiet down all the allegations of collusion he knows will come up. A few people have already started to bring up the Hilltop Room thing."

"What's the Hilltop Room?" I asked.

"A restaurant outside Silverville Sal owns," Susan Mezzano said. "He had a manager there who was stealing the place blind. He fired the jerk, but by that time the place was in real trouble. That was last year. The court put the place into receivership and appointed Frank Dierdorf to take over as manager temporarily until things got straightened out. Frank straightened things out so good that after everybody got paid off, Sal asked Frank if he wanted to stay on as manager permanently. He did for about three months, but when the F.B.I. stepped in and said they didn't think that would be such a hot idea, Frank quit."

"What could the F.B.I. do about it?" I asked.

"They threatened to cut him off the national crime reporting teletype if he stayed on," Carew said.

He lowered his eyelids and gave me a hooded look. "Their local agent says no, but I'd frankly be surprised if he said anything else. The F.B.I. is notorious for keeping local law enforcement in the dark as to what they're doing. I know they've been curious in the past about some of the company Sal Mezzano keeps. On the basis of that, they might decide to do some poking around. It's hard to say." He put the pen down and said: "Their lab is going to be doing the ballistics comparisons. Evans County doesn't have the technical facilities or expertise to do that kind of work, so Dierdorf asked the Bureau to handle it."

"What about the autopsy? Who's doing that?"

"We are,"

"When?"

"Tomorrow morning. I've arranged for a pathologist from the Los Angeles Medical Examiner's office to fly in to assist on it, just to make sure there are no mistakes. He's supposed to be very

73

competent. Hitachi is his name. Ever heard of him?"

"No."

"Since you're from there, I thought you might have."

"No," I said. "Have you had a lot of mistakes in the past?"

"We have a competent coroner," he said without enthusiasm. "But this is no ordinary case and I want to make doubly sure everything is handled right."

We stared at each other for a little while, after which he smiled rather formally and said: "How long do you intend to stay in Reno, Mr. Asch?"

"That depends."

"On what?"

"A lot of things."

"Such as?"

I didn't answer him.

"Mrs. Mezzano and I had a brief conversation before you arrived. She told me you might be staying on in our fair city for awhile. I can't stop her from hiring you, but if I wanted to, I could make your stay here rather unpleasant."

"I don't doubt you could."

"She also assured me of your complete cooperation if you do decide to stay. That means keeping me up-to-date on what you find out, if you find out anything at all."

I waited.

"I just want you to know how things are."

"If I didn't before, I do now."

"I hope so," he said. "You'll be staying at the Ponderosa as long as you're in town?"

"If I decide to move, I'll let you know."

"Do that," he said. "If you want to reach me at any time and I'm not in, you can talk to Wallace here. He's my chief investigator. You've got the office number?"

I said I didn't. He reached into his desk drawer and pulled out a card and handed it to me, then stood up.

"That's all?"

"For now," he said. "Zwerdling, drive Mr. Asch back to his hotel—"

"That's all right," Mrs. Mezzano said, heaving herself out of her chair with a concerted effort. "I'll drive him. I'm going that way anyway."

Carew shrugged and offered her his hand. "Thank you for coming in, Mrs. Mezzano."

She took the hand stiffly. Zwerdling stood up and opened the door for us and we went through the outer office to the elevator. She didn't say anything until we were out of the front doors of the building into the chill of the afternoon. The sun was out, but it had no strength to it. The cold air had the bite of a knife on my cheek.

As we went down the steps she said: "So are you going to stay or go back to L.A. or what?"

"That's going to depend on the answers to a few questions," I said. "First of all, I want to know whether what he said about you assuring him I'd be keeping him informed is on the level."

"Yes."

"The reason I'm asking is I figure some pretty hard lines are going to be drawn around here in the next couple of days. If I can cooperate with Carew—and I mean *really* cooperate, not bullshit him, because he'll find out about that soon enough—at least I'll have some support somewhere from local law enforcement, even if it's tacit support. It's going to be bad enough going up against Dierdorf's people. If Carew lines up on the other side, you might as well forget it."

"Carew is an ambitious little prick, but he's the only one I would trust around here. He wants Sal just as bad as I do. Why do you think he didn't have you run out of town on a rail?"

"I was wondering that myself," I said.

"His jurisdiction ends at the Washoe County line, but you don't have any jurisdictions. You can go turning over rocks anywhere in the state and nobody can really do anything about it."

"Except try to stuff me under one." We walked a few more

steps and I said: "Then you're saying I can feed him what I get?"

"Yes."

Her powder-blue Mark IV was parked at a meter half a block down. Her limp was more pronounced and we had to walk slowly. "Why does Carew want Sal so badly?"

"Carew still has wet dreams about being governor and he knows he'll never do it as long as Sal's around."

"Why not?"

We got into the car and she started it up and pulled into traffic. "Because Sal pulls too much weight in this state now. A lot more than Carew pulls. See, Carew was still D.A. when Sal got out of the slammer, but things had changed. People were lining up to see movies like 'Deep Throat' and nobody gave a good goddamn about the evils of prostitution. We weren't an issue anymore, so Carew had to sort of leave us alone. Sal stepped out of the slammer to find out business had tripled while he'd been in, the money was coming in hand over fist. Anyway, Sal gets out of the can and sees all this going on and decides to put the icing on the cake.

"Anderson, the old Evans City D.A., was out and prostitution was still illegal then in Evans County. The county commissioners were all getting their grease, so nobody was saying anything, but it was still illegal to run whores, at least on the books. So Sal approached the county commissioner and D.A. about putting through an ordinance making it legal. At first everybody got nervous. None of them wanted to go in the record books as being the first ones to legalize whores in the United States. But they also knew Sal had built up a pretty good political machine that could dump them on their asses if they weren't careful." Her eyes narrowed and she said: "You know, one of the first things he did when he got out of the joint was to buy up land in a canyon a little north of Silverville. He moved a bunch of trailers in there and put in septic tanks and made the rents nice and low. And he made damn sure the people living there were aware they were lower than they could get anywhere else. All those people were just waiting around for Sal to tack up a poster to tell them how

76

to vote and those commissioners knew it. Some of them were still sort of nervous about it, but they calmed down when Sal told them he thought that $25,000 a year in license fees might be a nice round figure. The ordinance went sailing on through without a ripple and Carew couldn't bitch any more in the papers about the failure of Evans County to enforce its own laws.

"It also made Sal a celebrity overnight. Hell, he started getting asked by the Lions Club and the Rotarians to give speeches for their lunch meetings. Charities started asking him to give fund-raising speeches about what it's like to run a whorehouse and they packed 'em in. And he charmed the socks off them." She stopped and smiled faintly at the windshield. "That's one thing about Sal, he does have something—charm, charisma, whatever you want to call it—that people respond to. Anyway, people started finding it harder and harder to ignore him. He started buying up property and businesses around the area. Everything he touched seemed to turn to gold. And a lot of the money he made went for campaign contributions you'll never see on any declaration sheets. That's how he killed Carew's nomination for the state assembly."

"Carew tried for the assembly?"

She nodded. "That was two years after Sal got out. Carew decided to make his big bid for the Republican nomination. When Sal heard that, he right away started calling everybody he knew in Carson City. He poured money into Schlesinger's—that was Carew's opposition—campaign. By the time he got through, Carew might as well have been a leper as far as the Republicans were concerned. He ran for D.A. again and made it by the skin of his teeth, but he knows as long as Sal is around, he'll never get anywhere in state politics."

"And if he can pin Realango's shooting on Sal, not only will he be slaying the giant, but he'll be using his body as a stepladder."

"Now you're starting to get the picture."

She turned left onto Virginia Street. The neon signs were flashing, even in the daylight. There were quite a few people on the street, but my eyes were caught by an old wino who was trudging up the sidewalk, his thin shoulders weighed down by the sandwich board he wore like a sweater against the cold.

INSTANT CREDIT
OUT OF TOWN CHECKS CASHED
AMERICAN OR CANADIAN
24 HOURS

The sign didn't bother to mention the fact that the benevolent firm that was willing to cash your check instantly also instantly took out twenty-five percent of the amount as a fee. But hell, that was all part of the game, and if the game was crooked, well, it was the only game in town.

"That answers one question," I said.

"You mean there are more?"

"Two more. References to organized crime make me nervous. Is your husband hooked up to anything?"

"No."

"You're sure?"

"I'm sure. He knows people, but hell, *I* know people. Those people are like shit in Nevada—they're everywhere. You couldn't live in this state any length of time, especially running the kind of business we run, and not know people."

"He's not particularly friendly with anybody in the Mafia, then?"

"He has friends," she said. "Sal is infatuated with power. He likes to be around people who wield a lot of it. But he doesn't take orders from anybody." She paused and glanced over at me. *"Anybody."*

"I'm only asking because I've come up against those boys a few times and I'm not all that anxious to do it again."

"Don't worry about it," she said.

"What's the third question?"

"Did you mean what you said this morning about paying me two hundred a day?"

78

"Honey, I don't say anything I don't mean."

I nodded at that. "What's the story on this Candy chick that married Realango? All that went down just like you told it to Carew?"

"Yep. This story Dierdorf is coming up with is pure bullshit, just to take heat off Sal."

"Where was she from?"

"She went to high school right here in Sparks," she said. "She'd just graduated, in fact, when she came to me wanting to learn the trade. I don't usually hire local girls—nine times out of ten their parents turn out to be a pain in the ass—but I made an exception in Candy's case. Her mother came out and raised some hell about it when she found out her daughter was a whore, but I calmed her down and kept Candy on. I knew I was right about her. She turned out to be one of my most popular girls. I knew right away she'd be popular. She had that cute-cheerleader look a lot of men really get off on. Come to think of it, I think she was a cheerleader in high school."

"What happened to her? Is she still around?"

"I don't know," she said. "She may be. You get types like Candy every once in a while. They drift in and out of the business. A lot of whores—most probably—take up the profession out of necessity. They come from lousy homes and lousy neighborhoods and they use their bodies to eat. Some are just plain lazy and see it as an easy way to make good money, lying on their asses all day. But once in awhile, you get one like Candy who's bright and comes from a nice family and apparently has everything going for her, but for some reason sees the life of a whore as being exciting and glamorous. It doesn't usually take more than a year for them to find out there isn't much glamorous in having some fat, sweaty, greaseball lying on top of you grunting and panting like some animal. Then they get out of it and get married and move into their houses in the suburbs and have kids and don't ever tell their trusting little hubbies they once worked in a whorehouse."

There was a slightly sarcastic edge in her voice, but I could not

79

tell whether it was being directed at those trusting little hubbies or the girls who opted for the houses in the suburbs or the ones who stayed on at places like Moonfire.

"May I ask you a personal question, Susan?"

"What?"

"Were you ever a whore yourself?"

She smiled weakly. "Never was. I started out in the business as a madam when I was seventeen. I started out with the idea of being a whore, but the woman who taught me the trade thought I'd be more use to her working the front. I always had a business head on me and she needed somebody to help her handle the girls. After that, I had a few small joints of my own up and down Interstate 80. Nothing big, just five- and six-girl joints. That was where I met Sal. He came into one of my places. We talked and decided we could do a hell of a lot better by teaming up."

We drove for awhile and I asked, "What about this saloon Carew was talking about?"

She shook her head. "I don't know."

"Merritt bought it?"

"I don't know. All I know is what you heard me tell Carew."

"Where is Duncan?"

"On Highway 46, about 25 miles southeast of Reno," she said, then glanced over at me. "Are you gonna be sticking around or what? You never really said."

"I'll poke around for awhile, if you really want me to," I said. "But not at double my rate. The normal, 'steep' hundred and fifty will suffice. And if a time comes when I feel I'm not doing you any good, I'm going to get on the next plane to L.A. All right?"

Her smile was a little stronger now. "That sounds fair enough to me, honey."

"Now what about this Pebbles? What does she look like?"

"Big broad. Pale complexion, black hair. Wears it all piled on top of her head like one of those female Country-Western singers. I think that's what she is—a frustrated singer. Merritt used to sit around writing Country-Western songs on the guitar and she'd sing them. They did a couple of numbers for me one time. Jesus, were they bad."

"You say she's a big broad. How big?"

"Big enough to eat hay and shit in the street. She must be six-feet or so. She has shoulders like a wrestler and a big set of knockers."

"You know if she's still at Moonfire?"

"She was when I left."

The green neon pine tree of the Ponderosa appeared up ahead on the right and she slowed down to make the turn. She pulled into the driveway and parked under the canopy by the lobby entrance. "You want some more money?"

"Later," I said. "A couple of things I would like now, though—"

"Name them."

I took out a small notebook and a pen. "Where does your husband bank?"

"We have a joint account at the Bank of Nevada on Murray Avenue. He has a personal account at the Bank of America on Kietzker Lane. He probably has a couple of accounts I don't know about too."

She recited to me the number of the Moonfire account at the same branch of the Bank of Nevada, and her husband's social security number, which would come in handy as a cross-reference when the digging started. I put the pen and notebook away and asked: "What about the funeral? You need help making the arrangements?"

"Thanks for asking, but Jack's flying up tonight to take care of it. He called this morning. He couldn't believe it when I told him. He was . . ."

Her voice quivered and broke off. The terrible, unyielding reality of the morning was back with her and her eyes filled with tears.

I patted her sympathetically on the hand and told her I would talk to her tonight and quickly got out of the car.

She sat for a minute, composing herself, then took off, and I watched her, thinking about what Balzac had once said about the tears of the old being as horrible as those of children are normal. I kept watching the street a long time after she had gone.

9

A small flock of cars sat in the middle of the snow-patched parking lot, huddled together as if trying to keep warm. Not wanting to break up the effect, I pulled in and parked next to the end one.

Sunlight glinted off the glass of the gun towers. I kept my eyes glued to them apprehensively as I walked to the gates, almost as if I expected a nameless gunman to shout out a warning for me to stop and open fire.

They had done an efficient job cleaning up. They had shoveled up the blood-stained snow where Realango had fallen and scrubbed the asphalt beneath. But I still saw his body there, the knees drawn up convulsively, the life leaking out of him in a bright red pool.

A sign on the big iron gate said: RING BELL AND PUSH. I pressed the button and a buzzer sounded and I opened the gate. As I came through the front door, a middle-aged black woman wearing a stiff blond wig and a frilly pink maid's uniform flashed me a big grin, said, "Afternoon, sah," then turned and shouted: "Company, girls!"

The room was large and round with a high skylighted ceiling. The walls were covered with flocked red wallpaper and ornately framed oil portraits of glamorous nudes. A bar ran across the middle of the room and above it was a glass partition well stocked with liquor. A lavish assortment of girls was sprawled languorously across brocaded couches and love seats, filing their nails and chatting with each other. At the sound of the call, they dropped their conversation and their emery boards and immediately formed a line in the middle of the room.

There were tall ones, short ones, stacked ones, flat ones, white, black, and Oriental, about fifteen in all. They were dressed in bikinis and scanty black negligees with black garter belts and net stockings for those who like the more wanton look, and silk floor-length evening gowns complete with long white gloves and corsage, for those who had always wanted the Queen of the Junior-Senior Prom, but had never gotten within thirty feet. The only thing that was the same about all of them was The Smile. It promised a good time and it went about as deep as a USDA stamp.

There were two tall girls in the line, but one had the wrong color hair and the other was too thin. The smiles were turning a bit icy now and toes were beginning to tap impatiently. I felt intimidated by the stares coming from that wall of flesh, so I said to the black woman, loud enough for them all to hear, "I'm going to the bar first."

The smiles faded as fast as they had appeared and the platoon broke up and went muttering back to the couches and bar stools and once again began filing and talking. I went to the bar and ordered a Wild Turkey and water from the bartender, a middle-aged woman with a mannish haircut.

The bar was empty except for two telephone repairmen nursing a couple of beers and three girls from the lineup working diligently on a crossword puzzle. They occupied the last three stools on the end and from snatches I could get of their conversation, they were stuck on a seven-letter word meaning "to ease." Behind me at the bar, four archways marked the entrances to the hallways that led to the rooms. Every once in a while, a girl would come out of one of them and take her place on one of the couches. None of them answered Pebbles' description.

I was about halfway through my drink, wondering which girl to approach, when a black girl with a bushy Afro wig slipped casually onto the stool next to mine and smiled. Her teeth were very white and very straight. Her eyes were large and black and her false eyelashes could not have been more than a yard long. I thought I felt a slight breeze when she blinked, but that could have been my overactive imagination playing tricks on me. Her lips were thick, but her nose was upturned, not flat, with delicately flared nostrils. She wore a low-cut red pants suit that revealed a nice cleavage.

"Hi. I'm Dodie."

"Glad to meet you, Dodie. I'm Jake."

"You from around here, Jake?"

"L.A.," I said. "How about you?"

"San Francisco." She pulled the glass dish of salted peanuts on the bar over to her, grabbed a handful and began popping them into her mouth, two at a time. "What are you doing up this way?"

"Salesman," I said. "Auto parts. I'm on a selling trip."

"Ever been in here before?"

"I stop in whenever I come through. I handle the whole Southwest for my company. I come through Reno about once every five, six months."

"Mmmmmm," she said, making a half-hearted attempt to sound interested.

I waved at the room. "Looks like things are kind of slow."

"Always is, this time of day. That's why they call it the dog-watch."

"You work this shift all the time?"

She shook her Afro and smiled. "All the girls gotta take a week of dogwatches a month. We had our choice, we'd all be working seven to three in the morning. There'd be nobody on this shift to take care of old Jake, and we couldn't have that, could we?"

She snickered and took another peanut.

"I don't suppose that shooting this morning is helping business out any, either," I said. "I heard about it on the radio. Did you see it?"

Her smile disappeared and she turned away uncomfortably.

"Hell," I said, trying to backtrack, "I was afraid the place might be closed down when I got out here. Sure glad it isn't. I've been looking forward this whole trip to some real fun."

Just then the buzzer rang: "Company, girls!"

Dodie slid off her stool. "Duty calls."

She walked around the end of the bar and took her place in the line.

The man who came through the front doors had the self-confident stride of someone who had been through the routine many times before and knew just what he wanted. With barely a hesitation, he pointed at one of the girls who had been working the crossword puzzle, a petite, dark-haired girl in a silk Chinese dress slit up the side to the hip. She smiled and linked her arm enthusiastically through his and they disappeared down one of the hallways.

The assembly broke up. The remaining two of the crossword puzzle trio came back to the bar and resumed their search for the elusive seven-letter word meaning "to ease." Dodie came back and claimed her stool. After a couple of more peanuts, she leaned over seductively and smiled. "Listen, sugar, you want to have a party?"

"In a few minutes," I said, smiling back. "I want to finish my drink first."

"You can drink in the room." She paused, seemingly lost in thought. "You want two girls? Two girls is a trip. You don't have to do nothing', just lay back and let us do all the work."

I pretended to think about it. "Sounds real interesting, Dodie, how much?"

"We ain't allowed to discuss that out here. We got to go to the room, then I can lay it all out for you."

I shook my head regretfully. "I'm afraid I'm just a one-on-one guy, Dodie. I don't think I could handle two girls. It'd probably fuse something in my brain."

She snickered again. "Nothing' wrong with one-on-one. Let's have a party. I'll show you a good time."

I looked her over admiringly. "I'll bet you would, Dodie. You're really out of sight. But, well, it's strange, but I had a girl about a month ago when I came through here and I've been looking forward to getting it on with her ever since. I didn't see her in the line, though. Her name was Pebbles."

86

Her eyes once more became uneasy. She turned back to the bowl of peanuts. "Pebbles ain't here no more."

"Really? Where'd she go?"

She stared at me for a long moment, as if trying to read my thoughts. I kept thinking: spark plugs, distributor caps, U-joints. "She's got an old man. She moved in with him."

"Where'd they go? Duncan?"

"Ye—" She cut herself off, but the realization was there in her eyes that she had blown it. She clenched her teeth together and said: "Who are you, man, a motherfucking pig?"

I was saved by the bell. The call went up and she slid off her stool, glaring hatefully at me.

A grotesquely fat man with a cherry-red face waddled through the front doors. He was bald except for a neat fringe of white hair that ran around his head just above the ears, making him look like a modern-day Friar Tuck. He smiled warmly and made a wave-of-dismissal motion with his hand before the line had completely formed and headed directly to the bar.

With great effort, he hoisted his bulk onto a stool about four down from mine and ordered a Scotch on the rocks. His breath came in short, labored wheezes and he was sweating profusely. When Dodie came back to the bar, she sat down next to the fat man and smiled. "Hi, Jim," she said. "How do you want it today?"

The fat man took a handkerchief out of his back pocket and mopped his florid face with it. "I'll tell you, honey, the thing about being my age is that by the time you get all the way out here, you're too damn tired to do anything about what you came out here for."

She laughed politely. She was ignoring me, which was just as well. I decided to pay for my drink and leave before she changed her mind. She never looked at me when I passed her.

As I made the end of the bar, the dark-haired girl in the Suzie Wong dress came flying out of the hallway with an urgent expression on her face and a $20 bill clutched in her hand. She made a bee-line straight for her fellow crossword puzzle workers.

"Assuage," she said triumphantly. "He knew it right away."

They all twittered as they fit the word in. It was the most excitement any of them had had all day.

10

Duncan was a sad collection of decaying wooden buildings that
spread out along the highway for about four blocks before turning
back into snow and chaparral. At least half the buildings were
empty, CLOSED signs prominently displayed behind broken-out
windows and boarded-up doors, and the roofs of several had caved
in from the weight of successive snows. Above the town, the
snowy piedmont of the mountains was littered with the shells of
old cars and mining equipment—drilling machines, ore carts,
water pumps—thick with rust, like the skeletons of dead dreams.

The only saloon in town was called Ma and Pa's and it fit right
in with the rest of the street. It was a two-story building with a
squared-off façade and a peeling pillared portico above the front
doors, one of which was boarded up. Across the top of the portico
ran an ornamental balustrade that had half its spindles missing.
About the only signs of any restoration efforts were the two new
planks in the boardwalk out front and the freshly-painted sign on
the front of the building that said "ESTABLISHED 1896."
Those touches did for the place what a bikini would do for an
85-year-old woman.

There was a CLOSED sign on the front window, but I rattled
the doors anyway. I cupped my hands around my eyes and peered
through the window, but the afternoon sunlight was fading and
it was dark inside and I couldn't make out much. Around back,
a rickety wooden staircase led up the side of the building to a
landing and a door. I went up and knocked. I kept knocking until
I was sure nobody was going to answer, then went back down to
the car.

The town's only gas station was on the other side of the street, a block back in the direction I had come. I drove back to it and pulled up.

A tall, lanky man with a face like a weather-beaten rock shuffled out of the office wiping his oil-blackened hands on a rag. "What can I do for you?"

"Fill it, please."

"Sure thing." He cranked the handle on the ancient pump and the machine clicked and wheezed asthmatically. While he went over the windshield with a dirty squeegee, I got out and gazed at the tired old town. Just to get him talking, I asked: "Where's a good place to eat in town?"

"Only one place open," he said. "Ed's Cafe down the street. Ain't nothing fancy, but it's good home cooking."

"I'll try it out, thanks," I said. "Looks like things are pretty quiet around here."

"Always quiet this time of year. In the summer we get tourists driving through, but now, there's not much of nobody."

I nodded. "You own this place?"

"Yep."

I thought about trying to feed him a line about who I was and what I wanted, but rejected the idea. Those things rarely work out, especially in a town this size. Sooner or later—usually sooner —people start matching up your stories and come up with a three-dollar bill. And once they don't trust you, you could be Efrem Zimbalist, Jr. and they wouldn't give you the time of day. I decided to take my best shot with the man and if he didn't pan out, try somebody else.

"You seen the girl from Ma and Pa's around today?"

He stopped wiping the windshield and looked up sharply. "You a cop?"

"Private detective," I said. "My name is Asch. Jake Asch."

He stared at my outstretched hand for a moment, then took it hesitantly. "Jerry Cole."

"Glad to meet you, Jerry."

"Reason I was asking if you was a cop is that the sheriff was

90

around a while ago, looking for the girl. You here about her boyfriend?"

"Yes."

He nodded and finished the windshield. "That was a hell of a thing. A *hell* of a thing. You know, that Merritt buys gas in here all the time. I could always tell he was a mean bastard, especially when he had a few belts in him. He'd stare at you with that funny eye of his and it was like he didn't even recognize you, like he'd stomp you into the ground for two cents. But I never figured him for the type to go and plug somebody like that."

I didn't say anything.

"The sheriff said that fighter had a gun. That true?"

"That's true."

He cocked his head to one side. "Well, hell, then, who knows? It could have been self-defense."

"It could have," I admitted.

He squinted at me. "Private detective, huh?"

"That's right."

"Only private detective I ever seen is on TV. You don't look like you fit the part."

"Sorry about that."

"Don't take no offense, now. I didn't mean nothin' by that. It's just you build up an idea about what people should look like, you know? It's probably our own fault. You know that stuff ain't real, but you watch so much of it, you start to believe it anyway. Where you from?"

"L.A."

"You're a long way from home."

"I sure am," I said. "Have you seen the girl around today?"

"Not since this morning. I saw her come in around nine, I guess it was. Then she took off again like a bat out of hell around ten o'clock. She ain't been back. And I'd know, cause I've been here all day."

"What kind of a car is she driving?"

"Silver Cougar with a black vinyl top."

He left me and dropped the squeegee into a bucket of gray water, then went around to the back of the car and squeezed the handle of the gas nozzle. I followed. "How long has Merritt owned Ma and Pa's?"

"I don't know how long he's owned it," he said. "He moved in about a month ago, I guess, or thereabouts. He's been coming around looking at it for the past year, though."

The gas pump clicked off and he pulled the nozzle out of the tank and hung it on the side of the pump. "That'll be six-fifty."

I took out a five and two ones and asked him for a receipt. He disappeared into the office and came out with my change.

"I'd really appreciate it if you could answer just a couple of more questions, Mr. Cole. Do you know who owned Ma and Pa's before Merritt?"

He scratched his head which looked like a patch of windblown straw and said: "Well, Gus Pataki had it for twenty years. But he died about two years back. The place has been vacant ever since. I think Gus left it to his sister, but I wouldn't swear to it. He didn't have no kids."

"You wouldn't know where she lives, would you?"

He shook his head. "Afraid not."

I nodded. "Well, thanks a lot, Mr. Cole. You've been a great help. You have a pay phone around here?"

"Only pay phone in town is at Ed's."

"Fine. Thanks again."

Ed's was a three-booth and five-table, fly-blown cafe the walls of which were done in faded green paper covered with cuckoo clocks. Two locals sat at one of the tables, talking amiably with a tall man in a stained waist apron. I took one of the cracked and patched naugahyde booths by the window.

The man in the waist apron turned out to be Ed. He came over to the booth with a menu that was a typed piece of paper inserted into a plastic casing and I ordered a hamburger and coffee from him and asked where the pay phone was. He pointed to the door that said REST ROOMS.

All government offices for Evans County were in Silverville and all of them had the same number. The switchboard operator who answered it put me through to a sweet-voiced thing in the County Assessor's office. After a quick snow-job about being a buyer who was interested in the property at Ma and Pa's address, she came back with the name Mrs. Selma Weaver, 22 Sunnyvale Road, Incline Village, Nevada, as being the legal owner. I thanked her profusely and hung up.

I called Incline Village information and got the listing for Mrs. Selma Weaver, and dialed it.

Mrs. Selma Weaver, sister of the late Gus Pataki, sounded elderly, which was probably fortunate for me. I've found that elderly people usually make the most cooperative interviewees. They are comparatively immobile and therefore tend to live vicariously, a lot of the time through what they can pick up by keeping their living room curtains parted. But *this*—this was almost too much. Being involved, even peripherally, with a *murder*—of a celebrity yet—and getting a call from a real, live private detective, just like in the movies, would give Mrs. Selma Weaver enough material to keep her friends' ears burning for a year. She kept my ears burning, too, for at least ten minutes.

The reason Mrs. Weaver was still listed on the tax rolls as the legal owner of Ma and Pa's was that the deal with Merritt was still in escrow. She had sold him the saloon and one and one-half acres of property behind it for $10,000—$5,000 down and the balance to be paid off over the next year. Merritt had been interested in the place for the past eight months, she told me, and had called her frequently to discuss terms, but had never been able to come up with the down payment. Three weeks ago, he'd called her and said he had just consummated a big business deal and had the money for Ma and Pa's. The next day, she had met him at her bank, the Incline Village branch of the Bank of Nevada, where papers were drawn up and Merritt opened the escrow with $5,000—in one hundred dollar bills. She asked me a hundred questions about the shooting and I told her what I could without telling her anything she wouldn't read in the afternoon papers and it took every ounce of diplomacy I had to disengage myself and get off the phone.

My hamburger was waiting on the table when I got back to the booth. Hamburger Helper wouldn't have done much for it. I tried a half bottle of ketchup and a jar of mustard but gave up after a few nibbles. The coffee was drinkable and I nursed three cups while I watched the highway.

The sky turned a sullen gray, and began to darken. I ordered a piece of apple pie, ate it, then ordered another to keep my seat. A few more locals straggled in and settled into booths and Ed scurried around the room taking orders.

At five-fifteen, a silver Cougar passed by the window going in the direction of Ma and Pa's. I gulped down the rest of the coffee in the cup, hurriedly went to the cash register and paid Ed for the check, and trotted out to the car.

The Cougar was parked behind Ma and Pa's. I parked beside it and stepped out. Its doors were unlocked. The Nevada registration clipped to the visor said the car was owned by Evelyn Bestar, 100 Moonfire Road, Moonfire Ranch. The glove compartment was locked. I got out and closed the door quietly.

A light glowed orange through the curtained window upstairs. I went up and knocked.

The dark-eyed girl who opened the door was something straight out of "Nashville." Tammy Why-Not. She looked six-six, but about two of those inches were in the stacked heels of her red patent leather pumps and four more in her hair, which was piled and swirled on top of her head in a mass of jet-black ringlets and waves. Most of the six-feet that were left looked solid. She was wide across the shoulders, big in the bust, narrow in the waist. Her wide hips tapered into long slim legs. She wore tight blue jeans and a maroon T-shirt with a Dom Perignon emblem emblazoned on it. She didn't strike me as the Dom Perignon type, somehow. More like Boone's Farm.

Anxiety wired her features with an electric vitality. The pupils of her eyes jiggled and bounced in tiny, rapid movements, her brows were bunched over her long nose, her teeth nervously raked over her thin lower lip.

"Who are you?" she asked.

"My name is Asch," I said. "I'm a detective. I'd like to talk to you for a few minutes if I could."

"Look," she whined. Her voice had a redneck twang to it. "I already told a million cops I didn't see nothing. I stayed in the room when Gene went out there. I didn't see what happened."

"You were out at Moonfire this morning?"

She flung her hands out from her body. "Yeah, but I didn't see nothing—"

"What were you doing out there?"

"Gene had to work last night and I had a doctor's appointment in town this morning, so we stayed there." Suspicion began to crowd out the fear in her eyes. "Hey, I already told the cops all that."

"I'm not a cop, Pebbles. I'm a private investigator."

That seemed to give her courage. She shifted her weight to one hip, her body trying to take on a casual insolence. "I don't have to talk to no private dicks, so why don't you just get outta here and leave me alone."

"You're technically right about not having to talk to me, Pebbles, but we're going to talk eventually, one way or another, so why don't we just get it all over with now and I won't bother you anymore. Look, you don't want to be looking over your shoulder every time you go out wondering if I'm going to be lurking around a corner ready to spring out at you, do you? There's no sense in stretching out this unpleasantness any longer than necessary. A couple of questions, and I'm out of your life."

She sighed and rolled her eyes toward the sky, as if appealing to a higher power. "Jesus Christ. All right."

The room was small and damp and smelled of mildew, despite the fact that the place was carpetless. My eyes located the source of the smell in several large brown water-stains on the ceiling, reminders of melting winter snows or spring rains. Despite the efforts of a portable electric heater in one corner, the room was still cold.

The furnishings were sparse and old. There was a scuffed pine bureau, two chairs, and a double bed with an ornate brass headboard that needed polishing—ten years ago. There were two doors on the other side of the bed. One was partially open and led into a bathroom. The other was closed. I assumed it was a closet.

The top of the bureau looked like a store display of perfume, all French, all expensive. The contrast between that little bit of lavish indulgence and the shabbiness of the rest of the room was almost humorous. She leaned back against the bureau and crossed her ankles, waiting.

I sat down in one of the chairs and watched her for awhile. After her fingers began drumming nervously on the bureau, I asked: "Where are you from, Pebbles?"

"Is that what you came all the way out here to ask?"

"It's a start."

"Fresno."

"You came to Moonfire directly from there?"

"I went to Vegas first," she said, her eyes avoiding mine. "For a few months."

"When did you move out here with Merritt?"

"Two weeks ago."

"Seems like it'd be kind of isolated."

"That's why we like it," she said in a surly tone. "Anyway, it won't be after we get the place fixed up and people start coming in."

"What kind of plans does Merritt have for the place?"

"We're gonna make it into a Country-Western bar. We're gonna have shows and everything. Gene's gonna get a band and I'm gonna sing. It'll be a real tourist attraction once we get it going. Listen, this place has got a lot of history behind it. The whole town does. There was a big silver strike here in the 1890's. Fix some of these buildings up, and it could be as big as Silverville.

Bigger." The surliness left her voice as she tried to communicate her vision to me. She seemed to be getting caught up in her fantasy.

"What if Gene doesn't get off?"

The enthusiasm died out and the surliness returned. "Whaddya mean?"

I shrugged. "Your old man is a two-time loser, dear. One more time and *he's* history, never mind the town."

She shook her hand at me. "It was justifiable homicide. Gene was only doing his job. Carlos was going for a gun—"

"I thought you didn't see it," I broke in.

"I didn't. But a lot of other people did. They told me."

"Was Merritt in the room with you?"

She nodded. "Dora woke us both up on the intercom. She said Carlos was out front. Gene threw on some clothes and ran out."

"And you didn't bother to go out and see what was going on?"

"I didn't want to see," she said quietly. "I thought, I just can't stand to see that kind of shit."

"What kind of shit?"

"Blood. Violence."

"For somebody who can't stand violence, you sure picked a nice old man."

Her hand came off the bureau. She held a palm out to me. "Everybody's got the wrong idea about Gene. Everybody thinks he's bad, but he's really a mellow dude. That's why he wants this place so bad, so he can kick back and do his thing without a lot of assholes hassling him. He's got himself into some heavy shit before, sure, but it's not him. It's other people. They push him into things."

"People like Realango?"

"Yeah," she said. "Creeps like Realango."

"Why do you call him a creep?"

"Because he was. Everybody knew what Carlos was. He was just balling Susan because he thought he could muscle in on Moonfire."

"Is that what Merritt told you?"

97

"He didn't have to. Everybody knew."

"Is that why Merritt hated him?"

"Yeah," she said, nodding. "It pissed Gene off to see Sal being made a fool of like that."

"Is that why he went into Realango's trailer and set fire to all his clothes?"

Her eyes darted away nervously. "I don't know nothing about that."

"You mean Merritt never talked to you about it at all?"

She ran her tongue around her lips and looked away. "No."

"I find that hard to believe, Pebbles."

Her face snapped around. "I don't give a flying fuck what you believe."

I inspected my fingernails. I needed a manicure, but there was not much there to manicure. The ends of the fingers were ragged and bitten. "Where did Merritt get the money to pay for this place?"

"Huh?"

She was stalling, trying to gather her thoughts, but I pressed on. "Where did Merritt get the money to pay for this place?" I repeated. "He's been scrounging around for the past eight months, trying to come up with the down payment, then suddenly, presto chango, he materializes five thousand bucks in cash out of thin air. He told the owner of this joint that he just closed some big business deal. Now tell me, dear, what kind of a business deal could a guy with Merritt's talents make that would net him a quick five grand?"

She stared at me dumbly. "T-shirts."

It was my turn to say: "Huh?"

She walked to the closet door and yanked it open, bent down and picked up something off the floor. She tossed it at me.

It was a white T-shirt with a cartoon profile of Sal Mezzano on it, a long candy-cane cigar protruding from his mouth. Underneath the caricature was the logo: SAL MEZZANO FOR PRESIDENT.

"Gene had two thousand of these made up," she said proudly.

"They cost him a buck-and-a-half apiece. He sold them for four."

"He sold all two thousand?"

"That's right," she said. "So there's your goddamn fucking mystery."

I held up the shirt again and looked at it. "Where'd he sell them?"

"At Moonfire. Around. I don't know."

I tossed the shirt on the bed casually. I was feeling anything but casual. Her materialization of the T-shirt had taken me by surprise. She'd gained a momentary advantage I felt compelled to correct. I pointed at the shirt and said: "Some people think the guy on that shirt is setting your old man up for a fall."

Her body stiffened. "Sal would never do that."

I shrugged. "Dierdorf is coming out with a statement today that there was bad blood between Merritt and Realango over a girl. Candy."

She wrinkled her nose and stared at me. "Candy? I don't know no Candy."

"Your old man does, though. Or did. He lived with her for a couple of months this summer. She was a whore at Moonfire. A little while after she and Merritt broke up, she married Realango. That was annulled after a couple of weeks. The girl was into lasting relationships. I guess the story Dierdorf is coming up with is that Merritt never got over the girl and hated Realango because of that."

She looked dizzy, confused. "Gene never mentioned no broad named Candy. You're making all this up."

"You can read it in the papers tomorrow," I said. "The only reason I'm bringing it up is that I thought you might be able to make some sense of it. You're an intelligent girl." I looked down at the end of my nose to see if it was starting to grow. "It just seems strange to me that if Merritt's defense is going to be justifiable homicide, that the sheriff would bring up something like that and put it in the papers. I mean, if Merritt killed Realango over a girl, it isn't justifiable homicide anymore. You're like talking about second-degree murder, Pebbles."

She began to blink rapidly.

I leaned forward in my chair and spoke very softly. "Let me ask you this, Pebbles. You think Dierdorf would come out with a statement like that without Sal Mezzano's okay?"

Her face twisted grotesquely and she flung her hands up in the air and wheeled around. Her voice was whiny again. "I don't know. I don't understand. I just don't know how Gene could get mixed up in something like this." She began to pace and chew on the ends of her fingers, as if she was working herself into a state of nervous frenzy. "Sal told me Gene would be out in a couple of days. If he isn't, I don't know what the fuck I'm gonna do. I can't take this waiting around. If he doesn't get out, I'm gonna pack up and split. There's too much shit goin' on around here. It's blowing my mind. I'm really beginning to feel paranoid—"

"Just because you're paranoid, Pebbles, it doesn't mean they're not out to get you."

That snapped her. She turned on me suddenly, wild-eyed, and her voice was like a guitar string wound up too tight. "Why do you want to say things like that to me? I didn't do anything to you. Get out and leave me alone. I answered your questions. Now get the fuck out and leave me alone."

There was something touchingly pathetic in her pleadings and I felt sorry for her. She was desperate and lonely and I doubted she knew much more than what she'd already told me, and if she did, I was sure she wasn't going to spill it. Since there was no use flogging a dead whore, I stood up and went to the door.

She was watching me from the bureau when I turned around. I let myself out without saying anything and went quietly down the stairs.

11

It had been a long time since I'd been totally away from city lights, and the crystalline beauty of the night made me feel slightly giddy. There was no moon and the stars spread across the sky in a filmy gossamer, almost like a fog, they were so thick.

I was about ten miles outside of Duncan, my mind replaying the scene with Pebbles, when red light flooded the inside of the car. I glanced at my speedometer before I took my foot off the gas. Fifty-seven. I pulled over and parked with two wheels on the snowy shoulder.

There was a heavy, sinking feeling in my gut as I watched the cop get out of the patrol car in my side mirror. It was the lean-faced deputy from Moonfire. He came up alongside the car carrying a ticket book in one hand, and his trusty nine-cell tucked underneath his arm. He bent down and peered in the window and grinned. "Well, well, well."

Even the grin didn't make a line in his face. The skin was pulled so tightly over his face, it looked like a nylon stocking. "You work a long shift," I said.

"I sure enough do," he said. "But I don't mind. I like my work." He held out the hand that didn't have the ticket book. "Driver's license and registration, please."

I took out my wallet and held it away from him while I extracted my driver's license to keep him from getting a glimpse at my photostat. I handed him the license and got the rental receipt out of the glove compartment. While he ran the flashlight over them, I said: "May I ask what you stopped me for?"

He didn't look up. "Excessive speed. Eighty-five in a fifty-five."

"I was only doing fifty-five," I said.

He cleared his throat, handed me back the rental receipt, and clipped my license onto his ticket book.

"You up here on business, Mr. Asch?"

"You might say that."

"What business you in?"

"Ladies' lingerie."

He frowned. "That what you were talking to Pebbles about? Trying to sell her some lingerie?"

"That was it."

"She buy any?"

"No."

"Seems like a long way to come, just to pitch one customer," he said. "Don't seem like there'd be much market out here for ladies' lingerie."

I decided to end the game. It was over anyway. "You'd be surprised. Probably half your friends wear silk panties and you don't even know it. I have some samples in the back if you'd like to try some on."

That got a rise out of him. He jerked open the car door and stepped back. "Step out, please."

I was sure the "please" had come automatically, by rote. Paragraph Eight from the Peace Officer's Training Manual: Courtesy and Roadside Manners. I also had the distinct feeling that that was the last lesson he was going to practice on me that was from any manual—any printed one, at least.

As I stepped out of the car, he put the ticket book down on the hood of the Vega and shone the flashlight in my eyes. "Close your eyes and touch the end of your nose."

"You've got to be kidding."

"Don't do it and find out if I'm kidding," he growled.

I closed my eyes and touched my nose.

"Okay. Now keep your eyes shut—no, keep them shut. All right, now put your head back and stand on one leg."

I knew he was going to keep putting me through contortions until he found one I couldn't do. I opened my eyes and stared at him. "No."

His voice roughened. "Turn around and put your hands behind you."

"First I want to know what I'm being arrested for."

"Drunk driving. Resisting arrest."

"Fine. Let's go to a hospital. I want a blood test."

The flashlight made a tight little circle in the air. "Just turn around and keep your mouth shut."

I wanted to get to where there were lights and people. I wanted witnesses to my physical condition, before and after whatever he had planned. "I know my rights," I said. "You're arresting me for drunk driving, you've got to give me either a breath, urine, or blood test and I get to choose which. I choose blood. So let's drive to a hospital and take some."

"You're going to be leaking a couple of pints out of your head, asshole, unless you turn around right now and give me your hands."

He leaned back and stuck his hand into his back pocket. I knew he had a sap back there. I also knew he would love for me to give him an excuse to use it. I'd been sapped before; it was a very unpleasant experience.

I turned around and he pulled my hands behind me and snapped on the cuffs, so tight that I let out a yell. "Hey—"

That was all I got out before the fist slammed into my right kidney. My knees buckled from the pain and I fell forward across the hood of the car, gasping for air. He hit me twice more in the kidneys, then grabbed the collar of my jacket and flipped me over and pulled my face close to his. His face was grotesquely twisted, demonic in the red spotlight. His breath was heavy and rancid, and in the cold night it came out from between his clenched teeth in trails of steam. "Recite me your rights now, motherfucker."

I opened my mouth, but nothing came out, except a faint squeak. He shook me by the collar. "Come on. Recite. Let's hear it."

He let me go and hit me in the stomach and I doubled over and fell onto the freezing pavement, my mouth working like a fish out of water, trying to capture some air. He walked away abruptly and started back to the squad car and a jagged fear ran through my mind: He was planning to leave me out here like this, to freeze to death. But then I saw him coming back with something in his hand.

The snow had already soaked through my jacket and pants and I was beginning to shiver. I tried to get to one knee, but he pushed me and I rolled back painfully on my hands and I closed my lips involuntarily as my head slammed against the side of the car.

When I opened them, he was standing above me, holding a half-pint of something in the red spotlight. I found out it was Scotch when he unscrewed the cap and poured some of it over the front of my coat. He stood up, examined the bottle in the light again, then bent down once more and pushed the bottle toward my face. "You can finish it."

"Thanks," I croaked. My voice was barely a whisper. "But I'm a bourbon drinker."

He smiled and brought his sap out of his back pocket. He hit me on the ankle with it, not hard enough to break the bone, but hard enough to make me scream. He was the type who would know every place on the human body that would make somebody scream and not leave an obvious mark. Like he'd said, he was a boy who liked his work. He waved the sap at me and said: "You'll drink, all right, asshole. You'll drink."

He grabbed me by my hair and wrenched my head back. I opened my mouth to yell in pain and he jammed the neck of the bottle into it. I closed my eyes and tried to squirm my face free, but his hand closed around my jaw like a vise and the liquid fire was pouring into my throat and the only thing I could do was swallow, so I swallowed. I swallowed until I couldn't swallow anymore and then I threw up.

That must have been one contingency he had not prepared for. He yelled, "Shit!" and dropped the bottle and tried to leap back, out of the line of fire, but didn't quite make it. He danced around on the highway, holding the knees of his pants daintily between two fingers, looking down at the mess I had made of his pants and shoes. "You fucking asshole," he bellowed and came at me.

104

I was going to tell him it was his fault, but I didn't think he was in the mood to listen. The kick he was aiming was not at a no-mark zone, it was directly for my face. I tried to take my head out of its way, but was too slow. The point of his toe caught me on the side of the chin and the stars were wiped out as the night burst into daylight for a split-second, then turned back into night, then faded into something darker and more empty than night.

12

The moon had risen. It hung outside the car window in black space, full and cold and white. My head was resting against the back door so that it was shining directly in my eyes. I lay there staring at it, waiting for my numbed senses to return.

They did, all at once, and I wished they hadn't. My throat felt as if it had been cauterized, my jaw felt dislocated, and kidneys ached. The only parts of my body that did not seem to hurt were my hands. The cuffs were still biting sharply into my wrists, but below them was nothing.

The fact that I was lying on them couldn't have been helping matters, so I tried to sit up. A new wave of pain sloshed around in my head as I did and I groaned involuntarily. My chauffeur glanced over the back of the front seat, but didn't say anything. I didn't say anything, either. There was no sense in reopening old wounds, especially if the wounds were mine.

The road in front of us made a winding descent through a steepsided canyon dotted with scrub-pine, but then the pines were dwarfed by billboards advertising the "Suicide Table" at Big Sam's Saloon and the spittoon collection at the Silver Bucket and the daily hourly tours of the Aztec Queen Mine and I knew we were coming into Silverville.

The snow-topped tombstones of an old graveyard glowed eerily in the blue moonlight and we swished noiselessly around a curve past the sharp wooden steeple of an old church and into town.

The architecture of the town was straight out of the West of the 1870's and backlighted by the moon, the skyline looked jagged and foreboding, an uneven series of wood and red brick rectangles and parabolas. The main street was all saloons and antique stores and souvenir shops, almost all of which were closed for the night, and probably the season. A few rectangles of light from the windows of those saloons that were sticking out the winter lay across the deserted boardwalks. An old Scott Joplin tune tinkled with sardonic ghostly humor from a player piano somewhere behind painted glass doors. Bathed in the washed-out moonlight the entire scene was unreal and I felt as if I were floating through some outlandish nightmare conjured up by Zane Gray.

A few blocks into town, the deputy turned right and we headed up a steep hill. The courthouse was at the top of the hill, an old two-story yellow brick building with ornate leafing above its windows and doors. He parked in front of the stone steps and pulled me roughly out of the car.

Above the front doors was a bronze statue of a blindfolded woman in flowing robes, holding a sword in one hand and the Scales of Justice in the other.

"I'll bet she peeks," I said as we went up the stairs. The deputy answered by putting a hand in the middle of my back and shoving me through the doors.

The sheriff's office was a small paneled affair at the end of the hall. A waist-high oak partition halved the room and behind it, at a desk, sat a burly, crew-cut sergeant whose face was permanently fixed with that same tedious, dead-eyed expression all cops seem to think they have to wear.

He listened to the deputy's version of my arrest, made a few witty comments about the way I smelled, then booked me for drunk driving and resisting arrest. I didn't bother to dispute any of the details as they were fancifully laid out; the way I smelled, I had a feeling my credibility would have been a little low. Actually, I was almost looking forward to being booked. To book me, they had to print me and to print me, they had to take off the cuffs. By that time I was beginning to feel a mild panic over irreversible blood loss. I sighed in relief as I felt the blood surge back into my dead fingers.

After emptying my pockets and taking my shoes and belt so I

wouldn't try to hang myself, the sergeant and the deputy (whose name turned out to be Harris) marched me out of the office and down the hall to a heavy metal door.

I thought about asking for my one phone call, but rejected the idea. There was nobody I could call except Susan Mezzano and that was out. All I would succeed in doing by that swift move would be making her a target.

On the other side of the door was a naked cement corridor and two cells, both of which were empty. I wondered what they'd done with Merritt, but I didn't verbalize the question. The sergeant unlocked the first cell and Harris pushed me inside, and they left me alone.

The cold dampness of the place soaked through my stockinged feet and gripped me with a sudden chill. I turned and looked at the cell.

It had a high ceiling and the walls were covered with a thin layer of foam rubber which had been torn off in spots. Along two walls, facing each other, ran two low benches both covered with the same foam rubber padding that served as beds. A dirty toilet squatted alone at the back of the room. Into the ceiling was fixed a naked 100-watt bulb and a closed circuit television camera. The jail may have been old, but it had all the modern conveniences. I gave the camera the finger.

My stomach began to jump around. I went to the bars and began pacing. The silence sang steadily in my ears. I lay down on one of the benches and tried to close my eyes over the dread I felt beginning to constrict my chest, but even with my eyes shut, I could still feel the walls pressing in on me. I got up and began reading the pithy sayings the previous tenants had scrawled on the exposed patches of concrete where the foam rubber had been torn off, but the desperation and ignorance I found there merely added depression to my anxiety, and I got up and resumed pacing.

A few years back, I'd done six months in a cell like this one for refusing to name a source on a story I'd written for the *Chronicle*. I'm sure there are lots of people in the world for whom spending a night or a week or even a month in jail would be nothing. I may

108

have even been one of them at one time. But after spending six months in a concrete box, drastic alterations tend to occur in one's psychological makeup, and tolerances become dangerously low. Which was why I could never get uptight with those American prisoners of war in Vietnam or Korea who had gotten up in front of television cameras and faithfully recited their lines denouncing U.S. war-mongering imperialism. Like them, I had had a cause, but now, five years later, it seemed like a shimmering mirage, pale and wavering compared to the intense psychological pain of those six months, and if I had to do it all over again, I honestly did not know if I could. They had permanently peeled back the skin and exposed a nerve and that knowledge had me walking these days with a lot less self-assurance.

I bit my nails. I paced some more. I fumed. The anxiety gnawed at my chest like a hungry rat and I sucked in huge lungfuls of air to try to chase it away. I longed to see a clock—one with a second-hand—just so that I could be sure that time really was passing. I told myself over and over that they had to let me out in the morning for arraignment, that they couldn't keep me here indefinitely, but then I realized that nobody knew I was here and those chipmunks in my stomach began to run around in faster, frenzied circles.

This is no good, I thought, no fucking good at all. I lay down on the bench and closed my eyes and began deep-breathing in an effort to stave off complete panic. I started to calm down, and soon all I was concentrating on was my diaphragm expanding and contracting, expanding and contracting, and after what must have been a couple of hours, even managed to drift off to sleep.

That didn't last long. A man screamed me awake.

"Pigs! Fucking pigs!"

Harris and the desk sergeant were struggling down the hall with a drunk. The drunk was tall and thin and had dishevelled carrot-colored hair. Harris had the man in a chokehold and a hammerlock and the man was dragging his feet, which was slowing their forward progress, a fact which neither of the two cops looked happy about.

"I want my phone call!" the man screamed as the sergeant fumbled for the keys. "What about my phone call?!"

"Shut up," Harris snarled and tightened his elbow around the man's trachea. The shouting trailed off into indecipherable gurgling.

The sergeant finally managed to get the key into the door of my cell and the two of them pitched the drunk in. He skidded along the floor on his chin, then scrambled to his feet and raced for the bars, but the door had already clanged shut by the time he reached it. "I want my fucking phone call!" the man screamed in their faces. His face was bright red and the tendons in his neck stood out like iron cables.

Harris and the sergeant looked at each other, broke up laughing and went down the hall.

The drunk kept shouting, "Fucking pigs!" at them long after they were gone. Finally, he must have decided it was a lost cause, and turned to stare at me with glazed eyes. He plopped down heavily on the bench opposite me. "Where'd they get you?"

"On the highway."

He brushed back a wisp of orange hair that had fallen down over his forehead during the struggle and resumed his heavy-lidded stare. His wrist looked as if he had spaghetti for tendons, but it was not the booze that was the cause of that. "Driving?"

"Yeah."

"Hmmmmmmph," he said disdainfully. "I was walking. *Walking.*" The thought seemed to outrage him. He looked up at the television camera in the ceiling and shook his fists. "Pigs! Fucking pigs!"

That seemed to have gotten it all out of his system. He slumped back against the foam rubber wall and closed his eyes. There was something new in them when he opened them again. "What's your name?"

"Jake."

"Mine's Phil," he said, smiling. "Where are you from, Jake?"

"L.A."

"Oh. The big town."

110

The door at the end of the hall opened then and a young, long-haired trusty came in and began shoving a mop listlessly around the floor of the corridor. I went to the bars and shouted to him: "Hey, what time is it?"

The kid looked up. "Huh?"

I tapped my wrist. "The time."

"Oh." He looked at his watch. "It's a quarter to three."

From behind me, a lilting voice filled the cell. "There's no one in the place, except you and me. . . ."

When I turned around, Phil was smiling at me coquettishly.

"Jesus fucking Christ," I said to myself. "This is all I need." I stayed awake the rest of the night.

13

A different turnkey wearing the same expression as the desk sergeant came down the hall and unlocked the door.

Phil was curled up in the corner, snoring like a broken muffler. The turnkey looked at us both, then pointed at me. "Okay. You. Let's go."

All my joints were rusted and I was half-punchy from lack of sleep. I got up and followed him back to the office where he gave me back my shoes and belt and spilled my personal belongings from a manila envelope all over the top of the desk. I made it a point to count my money in front of him. Slowly.

He watched me impatiently, then said: "Hurry it up. The Sheriff wants to talk to you."

He took me through a door behind the oak partition, into a high-ceilinged paneled office. Dierdorf was looking very relaxed. He was leaning sort of sideways in his swivel chair, one hand casually gripping a wooden arm of the chair, the other wrapped around the pipe in his mouth. He took the pipe out of his mouth and pointed the stem of it at a chair. "Sit down. You want some coffee?"

"Thanks."

He nodded and said to the deputy: "Harper, bring Mr. Asch a cup of coffee. Black?"

"Cream and sugar," I said.

The deputy grunted and went out. The room was filled with the sweet smell of Dierdorf's pipe tobacco and the scent had a tranquilizing effect on my already fatigue-dulled senses.

The gray eyes studied me carefully. "I hope your night wasn't too bad."

"Not at all," I said. "It was a great night. One of the best nights I've ever had. I got kicked in the face, had a bottle of whiskey shoved down my throat until I puked, I had a front tooth chipped that is going to cost me a pretty penny to have capped, I had "One for the Road" sung to me by a flaming faggot and I'll probably be pissing blood for a week from the job your lovely deputy did on my kidneys. It was a great night. I wish I could spend every night just like it."

That got to him. He sucked on his pipe, frowned, took it out of his mouth and peered at the dead ashes in the bowl. Then he tapped them into a ceramic ashtray on the desk and began repacking it from a pouch of tobacco he brought out of his desk drawer.

The deputy came in with a large Styrofoam cup of coffee, then went out again. I sipped it eagerly. Too eagerly. I took too much the first sip and burned the roof of my mouth.

Dierdorf picked up a sheet of paper from the desk in front of him and glanced at it. "I've been looking over your arrest report. Drunk driving is a bad thing to have on your record. It's a charge that tends to follow you around. Plays hell with your insurance—"

I made a face. "Come on, Sheriff. We both know why I'm here."

He leaned back and reached into his pocket and brought out a Zippo lighter. He held the flame over the bowl of his pipe and kept his eyes on it as he methodically drew in air. "Really?" he said between sucks. "Why is that?"

"For asking questions about the shooting of Carlos Realango."

He put the lighter back and took the pipe out of his mouth. He tapped the paper on the desk and said: "It says here you were stopped for going eighty-five in a fifty-five, that you were intoxicated, abusive to the arresting officer—"

"I was doing fifty-five and I wasn't drunk."

He raised an eyebrow. "The desk sergeant who booked you says otherwise."

"The desk sergeant can testify that I smelled like Scotch and puke. He can't testify how I got to smell that way. I got that way from having a bottle crammed down my throat. To prove in court

113

that I was drunk, you'd have to have a sample of my blood. No blood, urine, or breath test was taken last night. I asked for one but all I got for my request was my kidneys worked over. Who knows? Maybe your storm trooper thought he'd take the blood and urine together."

"It says here you refused a blood test and that you became violent when told by the arresting officer you had to submit to one."

"That's what it says, huh?"

"That's what it says."

"It'll never stick," I said.

He shrugged. "Maybe not. Then again, you never know. Justice is a very uncertain process. It's run by human beings and therefore is contaminated by human error. You could get a judge who might see things your way, then again, you might get one who didn't give a good goddamn about any blood test. He might just think the testimony of the arresting officer and the corroborating testimony of Sergeant Willis were more important than any little old blood test. Now, that could be wrong, but you'd be found guilty just the same. You could appeal, of course, but that would take time and a lot of money for lawyers and Lord knows how many trips all the way from California because of postponements—"

"Make your point."

He adjusted the pipe in his mouth and it made a clicking sound against his teeth. "The point is this. I say a man's entitled to a second chance. I'm willing to wipe this whole thing right off the books, drop the charges and forget it ever happened."

"That's conditional, I take it."

"Just one condition and it'll be very easy to meet. Just stay out of Evans County." He put on his best professorial face and said: "See, we're proud of our highway safety record here in Evans County. We like to keep our roads free of people who are prone to drink while driving."

I thought about it. I thought about last night, about the cell, about how it would go for me if I didn't do what he said. I thought about all the things I had told myself about exposed nerves and ephemeral causes. And I could feel myself starting to get mad. "When will I be arraigned?"

"I just told you," he said, smiling. "There won't be any arraignment. The charges will be dropped."

I took a sip of coffee and shook my head. "I think I'd like to go to trial on this, Sheriff. Win or lose, I think I can generate some nice publicity with it, and just between you and me, my business can use the boost. 'Private Detective Assaulted and Jailed for Asking Questions About Murder.' That'd make a nice headline, don't you think? From what I hear, there are some reporters over at the Reno *Gazette* who'd drool to get hold of a story like that, especially with all the accusations floating around now about collusion between you and Sal Mezzano. I'm sure Leland Carew would love to get his hooks into it, too—"

The mention of Carew's name sent a network of dark lines criss-crossing his face. "Carew has no jurisdiction in Evans County."

"No, but the Nevada Crime Commission does and he'll be working with them. Your boss asked them to step in, as you must know, just to quiet down all those nasty rumors about you two being too chummy. I wouldn't worry about it, though, Sheriff. I'm sure they won't find any skeletons in your closet, just in case they decide they would like to take a good, hard look at law enforcement in Evans County."

His tone grew hard and he said: "What was that crack about 'your boss' supposed to mean?"

"Come on, Sheriff. The door is closed. We're both politically astute. Your situation here isn't any different than that of any other sheriff in any other county. It just stands out because you've got one man you owe your job to instead of two dozen and because the county's too damn small to hide in. Now I'm not saying that you do a bad job as sheriff because of that, I wouldn't be one to say something like that. As a matter of fact, I'd go so far as to say that except for hiring baboons like Harris, you probably do a damn good job as sheriff. But to do a job at all, you have to make certain concessions. Just like me. And I'm willing to make one now."

He stared at me. His face was solemn. "Now it's your turn. Make your point."

"The point is this. I say a man's entitled to a second chance. I'm willing to forget this whole unfortunate incident ever happened. I'll forget about suing for false arrest and police brutality, I'll forget about the shitty night in jail, I'll forget about talking to Leland Carew and the Reno *Gazette* and the Nevada Crime Commission, and who knows? I might even succeed in forgetting your deputy's ugly face—providing I never see it again. And all you have to do is drop all the charges, wipe this whole thing right off the books. Period. Unconditionally. No strings attached. Because I might as well tell you right now, I'll be crossing the county line again and I don't want to see Christmas lights behind me when I do."

He didn't say anything, so I went on. "It was all unnecessary. More than that. It was stupid. The girls didn't tell me anything anyway. Your boy could have just let me go on my way back to Reno and nothing would have come of it. But no, he has to go and try to shake me down. I don't think he was acting under your orders, by the way. I just think he's a sadistic punk who starts sprouting hair in the palms of his hands when he puts on a uniform and a Sam Browne belt. That's why I'm willing to forget about it. I realize how hard it is to find good help nowadays."

He frowned and shook his head. "Forget it."

I leaned back and sighed. "I guess we sort of have a Mexican standoff, then."

It was all a bluff, of course. There was no standoff. I would have taken his deal, whether I meant it or not, rather than go back to that television-monitored box.

He put the pipe down in the ashtray. "Listen to me, Asch, and listen good. I know who you're working for. I didn't figure Susan would lay back and let us handle it. She's not the type. But I don't intend to let you wander around in this county, bothering its citizens and screwing up this investigation. We're a small force here, but we can handle our own problems—"

116

"I know. I've had a personal sample of how it handles its problems."

He leaned forward and pushed his jaw out at me. "You want another sample? They keep getting bigger and better."

He waited for me to say something, then leaned back once more. "You've been told. Get out of Evans County and stay out."

"Does that mean I'm free to go?"

"That's what it means."

"What about my bail?"

"There isn't any bail. The charges have been dropped. Now get the hell out of here."

I drained the coffee and put the cup down on the edge of the desk. "What about my car?"

"It's outside. I had it driven up this morning."

"That was very thoughtful," I said, and stood up. I looked down at him. "One question, Sheriff—"

"What?"

"Where's Merritt?"

"I had him taken over to Nevada State Prison."

"Why?"

He smiled thinly. "I thought it might help quiet down some of those nasty rumors you were talking about, you know, about collusion and special treatment, and all that sort of thing."

"That was a pretty good idea."

The smile faded. "I'm just chock-full of good ideas," he said softly. "Push me and you might find out just how good they can get."

"I'm sure they get pretty damn good," I said. "But ideas can play funny tricks on you. Sometimes they can seem pretty good when you first think of them and then, after a little reflection, they turn out to be not so good after all. Sometimes they even stink."

I waved and went to the door. "Thanks for the lovely evening, Sheriff. I'm sure we'll be in touch."

117

14

I stopped at a liquor store on the outskirts of Reno and picked up a morning edition of the *Gazette* and a half pint of Old Grand-Dad to match the way I felt. The thought of booze made me slightly nauseous, but I had no choice; I needed sleep badly and I knew I would not get it without help. Somewhere in the early morning hours, I had punched through the other side of fatigue and was now tapping that mysterious source of mechanical energy that turns on automatically after so many sleepless hours and I was going to need something to short-circuit the connection.

If the desk clerk at the Ponderosa was shocked at the way I looked or smelled, his expression did not betray it. He gave me my room key and a message Jack Schwartz had left for me last night. It said he was in Room 327 and to call him when I got in.

I went up to the room and got undressed. I put my soiled clothes outside the door to be picked up and took a shower as hot as I could stand it. I stood under the stream of hot water for a long time, letting the heat work the knots out of my neck and back, and after toweling off, I felt at least half-human again. A very easy shave around the black-and-blue egg on the left side of my jaw and a thorough tooth-brushing completed my physical rehabilitation, and I was ready to talk to people.

Jack Schwartz was shaving when I called. I suggested we have breakfast together and we agreed to meet in the coffee shop in twenty-five minutes. Next, I dug my little black book out of my suitcase and looked up Leon Rosen's number in L.A.

Leon Rosen was a 59-year-old ex-bank examiner who had retired after being struck by the revelation ("It came to me in a flash of light," he once told me, "a truly religious experience") that banking was a venal business run for the most part by venal people and that he could make more money expending a hell of a lot less effort by tapping some of that venal reservoir. Things had been slow at first, but never one to quit, Leon had hung in there, and now he was knocking down a good twenty-five G's a year by sitting in a cubbyhole of an office making tunes on his touch-dial telephone. The tunes he made were to the friends he had made in his twenty-odd years in banking and he made the twenty-five G's by selling the classified information they gave him —for a fee, of course—to private detectives and other shady types.

Leon didn't have a bank account. He kept all of his money in safe deposit boxes. He didn't trust banks.

He answered, and after going through the customary niceties, I gave him the information I had for both Merritt and Mezzano and asked him to get me a list of all transactions on any accounts he could find for both of them for the past two months. He said he would do what he could and that it probably wouldn't cost more than a hundred and fifty. When I got through screaming, he calmly explained that since the accounts were in Nevada, he would have to go through at least two people to get the information, which would mean double juice. That was the way things were in the world of banking. Seeing that further argument would be fruitless, I gave him my number and told him to get me the information as soon as he could and hung up.

As I sat there, staring at the phone, a vague depression settled like a damp fog in my chest. Maybe it was the events of the past two days catching up with me or a residue of last night's humiliation, but I felt as if I were sinking. Suddenly I remembered I had not called Liz and I felt the urgent need to hear her voice.

"I was wondering when you were going to call," the voice said.

"I probably should have called you last night. I could have used some cheering up."

"Why didn't you?"

"You're supposed to get one phone call, but I didn't want to aggravate the zookeepers by asking for it. I was in bad enough shape without getting my hand accidentally caught in a closing cell door. Anyway, I doubt the sheriff would have been willing to foot the bill for long distance."

The cheerfulness left her voice. "You were in jail?"

"Yep."

"What for?"

"It's a long story. I really don't want to go into it now. I'll tell you all about it when I get back."

"When will that be?"

"I don't know. Did you read the paper this morning?"

"Yes, why?"

"Was there anything in it about the fighter that was shot to death up here yesterday at Moonfire Ranch? Carlos Realango?"

She sucked in a little breath. "Was that who you were supposed to watch?"

"Yeah. Only it didn't quite work out the way everybody was hoping it would."

"What happened?"

"That's what I'm trying to find out. The wife doesn't trust the local law. She thinks they might be a little biased. After last night, I think she might be right."

"It sounds nasty."

"It is."

"Just be careful."

"Don't worry, if it gets much rougher than last night, I'm checking out and coming home."

"It was that bad, huh?"

"Yeah," I said. "It was that bad." Then, to change the subject, I asked: "How's Derek?"

"I've got to take him to the doctor today to get his hand X-rayed. He keeps falling off his skateboard and hurting it. It's really been bothering him lately, but he won't stop riding that damn skateboard."

"Take it away from him."

"Ever try cutting off a chicken's lips?"

I laughed. "You're not taking him to the good Doctor X, I trust."

"Hell, no. I have trouble enough keeping him away from Derek as it is. The bastard bounced another child support check off me yesterday. But I ran it through his Ready Reserve account and the bank made it good. You wouldn't think that after twenty years he'd still underestimate my resourcefulness, would you?"

"I've only known you one and I wouldn't think of it." I glanced at my watch and said: "I've got to run. If you need to reach me for anything, I'm at the Ponderosa Hotel, Room 508."

"Okay," she said.

"Hey," I said, "you know what? I miss you."

"I miss you, too."

I felt a sudden surge of feeling and I wanted to tell her more, a lot more, only I didn't know how much of what I was feeling for her was real and how much of it was just my battered body and emotions crying out for a nurse and a pair of healing hands. Our relationship had always been guarded; without saying it, we had both been haunted by the possibilities there, but we had always hung back, afraid of the logistical problems. I had taken myself right to the edge more than once, but had always taken a step back, telling myself I'd better hold off, that she deserved better than having me say things I would take back later or never bring up again. Maybe it was really the fact that I wouldn't want to take them back once I said them that made me step back.

"Maybe—"

"What?"

"Never mind."

"I hate it when you do that. What were you going to say?"

"Nothing," I said, making my voice sound as light as possible. "I'll call you in a couple of days."

I hung up feeling more depressed than before. I got dressed and went downstairs to meet Schwartz.

The coffee shop was three-quarters empty. I slid into a booth in the back and told the waitress I would wait for Schwartz before ordering, but that I would take coffee and a glass of milk whenever

121

she got around to it. Then I spread the paper out on the table and started reading.

The bad blood story was splashed all over page one, with a high school graduation picture of Valerie Barrington, a.k.a. Candy, suggestively positioned between pictures of Realango and Merritt.

Merritt's picture looked as if they had just cropped the numbers hung across his chest. He had a sullen, pock-marked face, surrounded by wild hair that stuck out in all directions. He had one wall-eye which somehow made the blank stare he was giving the camera convey terrible malice.

Candy, by contrast, did indeed have that well-scrubbed, pug-nosed cheerleader look, only according to the article, she had been a Pom Pom girl at William Simpson High in Sparks, not a cheerleader.

The article said she currently lived in Sparks with her mother, Mrs. Wanda Barrington, and that she was unavailable for comment, so the reporter proceeded to make up for that deficiency by providing a sketchy account of Candy's relationships with Merritt and her short-lived marriage to Realango and fattening it all up with quotes by Sheriff Dierdorf about the animosity the two men felt for one another over the girl. The article made no mention of Mrs. Mezzano's version of the marriage, that it had been arranged solely to obtain citizenship for Carlos, but it did mention the fact that Carlos had been a bigamist, that he had a wife of eleven years sitting back in Argentina.

The murder seemed to have succeeded in awakening some of the sleeping puritanism of the locals, because accompanying the article on the same page was an editorial labeling Moonfire as an institution "dedicated to the corruption of Reno's youth," and calling for the "eradication of the poison at our doorstep." It cited, of course, the case of Valerie Barrington, the "cream of Reno's youth," ex-Pom Pom girl, ex-Simpson High Homecoming Princess, now ex-prostitute and the pivotal part of a bloody love triangle. Could she have come to this state of degradation without outside influence? "Advocates for the legalization of prostitution and pornography call these 'victimless crimes,' " the outraged journalist wrote. "But in reality there is no such animal as a 'victimless crime'! All of our homes are victims."

I would like to have seen the statistics on how many star quarterbacks in high schools throughout the country had missed a game or two this past season because they had been slipped a dose of the clap by a representative of the "cream of the town's youth" who also liked to pull trains behind the stadium bleachers, but I doubted I ever would. The people who bought the *Gazette* were the mothers and fathers of those pug-nosed, Dial-soaped Pom Pom girls and they were not about to dish out fifteen cents to read crap like that about their daughters. It was a lot safer to tell them to go get a can of gasoline and a torch and burn down Moonfire Ranch.

My thoughts drifted from the paper and I looked up to see Jack Schwartz walking through the casino toward the coffee shop. He was wearing a long-sleeved beige sports shirt and dark brown slacks. He spotted me and waved and came over.

He slid into the booth and the waitress came over and she gave him coffee and a menu and went away. He scowled and pointed a chubby pink finger at my face. "What the hell happened to you? You look like you went ten rounds with Kenny Norton."

I shook my head. "One round with the steel toe of a cop's shoe."

I told him what had happened and when I finished, he sucked the inside of his cheek and said angrily: "The dirty bastards."

I nodded in agreement. "Dierdorf was very understanding about the whole thing, though. He realizes what kind of stress everyone has been under the past couple of days and he understands how a guy could go out under those circumstances and have a few too many. He even offered to drop the charges if I gave him my solemn assurances I wouldn't cross the county line again."

"He actually said that?"

"More or less. I don't know if those were his exact words, but it's the thought behind it that counts."

123

His eyes left me and searched the room impatiently for a waitress. When they lighted on one, he waved until he caught her attention and formed the word "Coffee" silently with his lips. Then he turned back to me. "Sorry, but I have to get some fucking coffee before I die."

"Rough night?"

"Not as rough as yours," he said. "I couldn't sleep, thinking about everything. So I stayed up until about four shooting craps."

"How'd you do?"

"I wound up about four hundred to the good."

"You're right. That wasn't as rough as mine."

"I was up about a grand," he said, disgustedly. "I should have quit then."

The waitress came over with coffee and while she poured it, Schwartz ordered a large tomato juice with tabasco, scrambled eggs, and white toast, and Sweet 'n Low for his coffee. I ordered bacon and three eggs over easy and whole wheat toast. After she departed with the order, I said: "Have you seen Susan?"

"Last night," he said. "She was pretty bad off. I guess I got over there around eight-thirty and she was already pretty well juiced. All she talked about was Carlos, Carlos, Carlos. She was talking about having her attorney draw up a new will naming Carlos' kids in Argentina as her heirs, all sorts of screwy crap like that."

"She seemed all right yesterday afternoon when I left her."

"She wasn't last night. She was a basket case. She started crying, I didn't think she was ever going to stop." He put his pink hands flat on the table and leaned forward. His expression was very somber. "I'm worried about her. She sleeps with his crucifix, you know that? The one Carlos wore around his neck."

I said I didn't.

He nodded. "She called somebody she knows in the Coroner's office, I guess, I don't know, she wasn't too coherent, and they gave it to her. It was still on the body when they brought it in."

He shook his head, then wrapped his fingers around his coffee cup as if to warm his hands, and stared down at the table. "You know, seeing her like that blew my mind. She's always been such

124

a tough old broad, it was really a shock. I've sat ringside through hundreds of fights and I've been splattered with blood from guys up there getting their faces pounded into hamburger, but I see one woman cry and I come unglued."

Schwartz watched his fingers play with his spoon, turning it around and around, and he said: "This whole thing seems unreal, you know? I just talked to Carlos a couple of days ago. It's hard to believe he's dead."

I remained silent and took a sip of coffee.

"What kind of a gun was it?" he asked. "The papers didn't say."

"I only saw it from a distance," I said. "It looked like a 30.06."

He shuddered and his eyes grew distant. "Jesus. A 30.06. When I was just a kid my father used to take me deer hunting with a 30.06. That bullet will really do a job. I hope to God he was hit clean."

"Right through the heart."

"At least it must have been painless, then," he said. He stared into his coffee cup for awhile, then said in an emotional voice: "I can't help thinking that it's my fault."

"Why?"

He looked up beseechingly. "If I hadn't introduced him to Sal, none of this would have happened," he said in a self-pitying tone. "He'd be alive right now."

"Maybe he would be," I conceded. "Maybe he would've gotten run over by a truck or been in a plane crash or fallen into an open sewer—"

"This wasn't any accident," he said, his head jerking up. "This was murder, goddamn it."

"That's right. And you can walk around gnashing your teeth and wearing a horsehair shirt and he'll be just as dead when you get through. If you'd had a crystal ball or could read tea leaves, you probably wouldn't have brought him to Mezzano. And if I had wheels, I'd be a trolley. You can't hold yourself responsible for all the ifs in life. There are too damn many of them."

That seemed to make him feel better. He thought for a moment and then said quietly: "It's funny, you talk about ESP and telling the future and all that; yesterday, just before I called Susan, I had the goddamndest feeling something was up. Nothing definite, just a creepy feeling that something bad was happening somewhere. It's enough to make you believe in that stuff."

I shrugged. "You knew there was the possibility of trouble, that's why you called me. You were probably just reacting to the situation. We all get those feelings of foreboding every once in awhile, only most of the time nothing bad happens and we forget about them. They only seem significant when something bad does happen and then we run, don't walk, to our local soothsayer to hear all about what the future has in store."

"I guess so," he said.

Breakfast arrived. Schwartz picked at his unenthusiastically while I dug into mine ravenously. If you didn't count the greasy hamburger at Ed's—which I didn't—the last decent meal I'd had had been nearly thirty-six hours before. Between mouthfuls I said: "You say Carlos has kids?"

"Three, I think."

"I read in the paper this morning that he had a wife in Argentina, but it didn't mention any kids. It was kind of a shock when I read it. Nobody told me he was married."

He shrugged. "I didn't think about it, and I guess Susan didn't think it was important. Is it?"

"I guess not."

"That was one reason the State Department still wouldn't give him residency papers, even when he married Candy. They knew about the wife." He took a little scrambled egg on the end of his fork, inspected it critically, made a face, and laid his fork on his plate. He made an attempt at a smile. "One good thing will come out of this maybe. I could lose some weight."

He folded his arms on the table and watched me eat for awhile, then said: "Are you going to try to talk to Merritt's girl friend again?"

"I don't know. I don't know what good it would do. She's not about to tell me anything voluntarily and I don't see much hope

126

in breaking her down. She's about as soft as a concrete sidewalk. The only time I got any rise out of her at all was when I suggested Sal Mezzano might be planning to let her boyfriend play the Lone Ranger. That upset her a little bit."

"Is that what you think Sal is going to do?"

"It'll be interesting to see. If he leaves Merritt holding the bag, it means he didn't order it."

He shook his head. "I don't get you."

"Merritt can't stand the fall. He's a two-time loser. In this state, third-time felons get life. Merritt wouldn't go up for life, no matter what kind of loyalties he feels for Mezzano. His only chance would be to make a deal with the D.A. He'd spill it all, and Mezzano couldn't allow that."

After a minute or so, Schwartz looked up from his eggs and said: "Maybe Sal figures no matter what he does, Merritt has only one way to go. Even if he was following orders, it's still murder, and that's still a felony. If he wants to take his neck out of the noose, the only way he can jump is justifiable homicide. Maybe Sal is just figuring, 'Fuck it, let him work it out.' "

"I don't think Mezzano is that sloppy a planner. I don't think he'd leave that much to chance. Besides, if there was the slightest chance he could be implicated, he'd be trying to take pressure off Merritt, not put it on. That story of Dierdorf's definitely hangs a couple of weights on Merritt's balls."

I wolfed down the last bit of egg on the plate, then sopped up the leftover yolk with a crust of toast and popped it into my mouth. I washed it down with coffee and leaned back. "How long are you going to be up here?"

"I don't know," he said. "I really came up to help Susan with the funeral, but now that there isn't going to be any funeral—"

"Hmm?"

He looked puzzled, but I was sure no more puzzled than I. "Don't you know? Carlos' brother is flying in from Buenos Aires tomorrow morning to claim the body. He's going to take it back to Argentina with him."

"When did all this take place?"

127

"We heard about it last night."

I nodded. "I was in jail."

"That's right."

"So you don't know when you're going back?"

"I should go back in the next couple of days. That Escobedo deal is heating up and I shouldn't leave it sitting on the back burner too long. Torres' manager has given me the nod if I can line up Escobedo for April. I may have to fly to Puerto Rico next week to close it." He made a face. "I hate to leave Susan, the way she's feeling, but I don't know what help I can be there anyway. It'd probably be worse for her if I stuck around. All she'd do is reminisce about Carlos and make herself feel rotten."

He turned away guiltily, as if afraid I was going to accuse him of copping out. The truth of the matter was that my thoughts were floating freely from exhaustion and I was having trouble keeping them focused on what he was saying. I picked the check off the table and stood up.

Schwartz stretched his hand out and said, not too convincingly: "Let me get that."

"Get the tip," I said. "Are you going to talk to Susan this morning?"

"I'm going over there in a little while."

"Tell her I'll call her later. I've got to try to get some sleep or I'm going to drop. I must have totaled six hours in the last two nights."

"Sure," he said. "How's your room, by the way?"

"All right, why?"

"I was just wondering. The cold water doesn't work in my shower. I turned it on this morning and nearly burned my pecker off."

"My shower is fine."

"Figures," he said, as if he was confronted by this conspiracy all the time. "I usually stay at Harrah's, but there's some scrap metal convention or some other bunch of fucking loonies booked in there and I couldn't get in."

"Did you tell the manager about your shower?"

"Yeah. He said he'd fix it this morning. I told him he's going to test it out. He can burn *his* pecker off; I need mine."

"Sometimes I think it'd be easier getting along without one."

He nodded seriously. "They can get you into a hell of a lot of trouble."

"That's what we're all doing up here, isn't it?"

He didn't answer me. I paid the cashier for the check and went up to the room, feeling more like Old Grand-Dad than ever.

15

Sparks was Reno's sister city, the older sister who could not afford a face lift, who had bad teeth and a touch of pleurisy and who was living on Social Security and welfare. Its residential drives were quiet streets lined with bare-branched elms and cracked sidewalks and run-down wood frame houses in front of which were parked 1964 Chevy Novas or battered VW vans with "Save the Whales" stickers on their bumpers and stained-glass decals covering the windows.

The address the telephone directory gave for Mrs. Wanda Barrington was 412. It was a chocolate brown two-story wood house with gabled front porch and a sharply peaked roof. A 1972 Ford Galaxie was parked in the driveway. I parked on the street and went up to the door.

The woman who opened it was a short and squat fifty. She had unkempt brown-gray hair and skin with the unhealthy blue-white pallor of skimmed milk. Her small, sharp eyes regarded me suspiciously. "Yes?"

"Mrs. Barrington?"

"What do you want?"

"My name is Asch," I said. "I'm a private investigator. Is Valerie at home?"

"No." Her eyes drew a narrow bead on me. "What do you want her for?"

"Are you expecting her home later today?"

My avoidance in answering her question broke her down. "Why don't you people leave us alone? My daughter's got a decent job now. She's trying to make a new start for herself and get back some of her self-respect and all you reporters and detectives have to come around, digging up the dirty past and trying to make people believe my daughter had something to do with that shooting, just to sell a few newspapers. It's disgusting. You shouldn't be allowed to print that garbage."

Her eyes were wild. She seemed confused, disoriented. "I'm not a reporter, Mrs. Barrington. I'm a private investigator. And I agree with you that the stories the *Gazette* has been printing have been misleading. That's why I want to talk to Valerie. I think her name should be separated from this mess. But in order to do that, I've got to talk to her, to get at the truth—"

"The truth?" she shouted. "The truth? The truth is that it's all the fault of that, that, woman, that Susan Mezzano. There's your truth. She's the reason my Valerie's mixed up in all this trash. I never should've listened to her in the first place. I should've had Valerie taken out of there by force. I knew all this would come to no good."

"How did you listen to Susan Mezzano?"

She tossed a hand in the air. "When I found out Valerie was out at that filthy place, I went right out there and told Susan Mezzano I was going to make plenty of trouble for her and her husband unless they fired her. Oh, she was real understanding, all right. She sat me down and gave me some tea and said although she'd never had any children of her own, she understood the way I felt as a mother. But she said there was nothing I could do about it. She said Valerie had come to them looking for a job, they hadn't gone to her, and since she was over eighteen and prostitution was legal in Evans County, there wasn't anything I could do legally to prevent her from working there. She said as long as Valerie was bound and determined to go into that line of work, wouldn't it be better for her to do it in a place that was clean and where she wouldn't be on dope or be getting arrested all the time or having some pimp beating her black-and-blue? She was real persuasive, all right. Then she called in Valerie and Valerie said she was going to stay and that was that, so I might as well go on home."

She stopped and shook her head. "Her father would have

turned over in his grave if he could have seen where she was, but I didn't see what I could do, so I left her there. I should've caused some trouble. Then maybe she would've been fired and none of this would've happened."

I nodded, trying to look as sympathetic as I could. "What time do you think Valerie will be home, Mrs. Barrington?"

Her eyes, which had been slightly out of focus, snapped up. She began waving her hands at me, in a shooing motion. "Just get out of here. We've got nothing to say to you. Leave us alone."

She was about to close the door in my face when a brown Mercury Capri pulled into the driveway and parked behind the Ford. Valerie Barrington stepped out and slammed the car door, then started across the snow-covered front yard.

There was a smattering of freckles across her nose and cheeks that had been touched out in the paper and her auburn hair was cut in a shoulder-length flip instead of being long and straight and her mouth was a tight angry line over those even white teeth, but other than that, she looked exactly like her high school photograph. Despite her stint at Moonfire, she still had that fresh, athletic—incredibly, almost naive—cheerleader look. She wore a thin white canvas overcoat, belted at the waist, and white work shoes.

Mrs. Barrington opened the door and stepped out. Her gaze was riveted on her daughter and she seemed to have forgotten I was there. "What are you doing home so early? You're not supposed to be home until five."

"The sonofabitch fired me," the girl said when she got to the bottom step of the porch. "He saw the story in the paper and he fired me."

"He can't do that," Mrs. Barrington cried.

"No? Well, he did. He said the publicity would hurt the store. He said I could finish the shift, but I told him to shove it up his ass and walked out." She looked at me sharply, then back at her mother, her eyes asking who I was.

Mrs. Barrington stepped between us as if to shield her daughter from assault, and said: "This man is a nosy detective, that's all.

132

You don't have to talk to him. Come in the house. You'll catch pneumonia out here."

Valerie ignored the last suggestion. She stepped up on the porch and said to me: "What kind of a detective?"

"Private." Feeling like a used-car salesman about to lose a prospective buyer, I rattled off my spiel. "It would really be a great help to me if you could spare a minute or two. I promise I won't take up much of your time."

Her green eyes burned with an inquisitive light. She tilted her head to one side. "Who are you working for?"

I thought about that. I didn't figure it would make much difference if I told her. Everybody else and his brother already knew. And I felt as if I had to make some kind of a first move, to establish trust. "Susan Mezzano."

Mrs. Barrington flushed and waved her hands at me. "I won't have it! I won't have you—"

Before she could finish the sentence Valerie wheeled on her and screamed: "Shut up, Mother!"

The older woman took a quick step backward and her hand flew to her throat as if trying to dislodge the unspoken words which had lodged there.

Valerie continued to glare at her, then said to me: "You want to talk, come inside."

I went in and Mrs. Barrington tarried behind us, her head bowed like a whipped dog.

The thought immediately struck me as we walked past the carpeted stairway into the small living room that if Valerie had been revolting against her upbringing by becoming a prostitute, or whether she had gotten into the profession for other, more obscure reasons, the gaudiness of Moonfire was as far away from this as she could get. The walls were natural wood, stained dark, the carpet a worn beige pile. The furniture was cheap Early American maple with a lot of spindly legs and covered in dull brown and gray fabrics. The backs of several of the chairs and the hump-backed couch in front of the stone fireplace were covered with shawls of white lace. The gray afternoon light seeping heavily

133

through the half-closed curtains over the front window helped lend the room the depressing aura of a spinster's tearoom.

I sat down in a lumpy gray easy chair in front of the unlit fireplace. Valerie took off her topcoat and laid it over the back of the couch and sat down. She had on a green nylon uniform from work and her plastic name badge was still pinned over her right breast. Her body looked lean and supple beneath her uniform, which was short and about a size too small. She had a tiny waist, narrow hips, and breasts that were not large, but firm and beautifully-formed. Her legs, which she was showing me a lot of, were muscular and perfectly proportioned, with well-rounded calves and neat, trim ankles. She caught me looking at them and crossed her legs.

Mrs. Barrington hovered over us like a nervous servant waiting for an order. Valerie glanced at her and asked me if I would like some coffee.

"That would be great," I said, picking up my cue perfectly.

"Mother, why don't you go out and make some coffee?"

"But—"

"Mother," Valerie said, her voice hard now.

Mrs. Barrington hesitated, then left the room reluctantly. Valerie watched her go and said: "She means well. She's just behind the times by about twenty years. She was out of touch before, but since my father died five years ago, she hasn't been out of the house hardly at all. Sometimes when she looks at me, I think she still sees me in bobby socks and penny loafers."

I would have liked to have seen her in bobby socks and penny loafers—and nothing else. I gave myself a serious mental flogging for my lascivious thoughts, with an imaginary strand of very limp spaghetti. She watched me silently for a moment, then held out her hand. "Let's see some ID."

I opened my wallet to my investigator's license and showed it to her. She looked it over, handed it back, then pointed at my coat and made a couple of quick swipes in the air with the backs of her hands. "Open the coat."

I stood up and unbuttoned the coat and turned around and lifted up the back. "I'm not wired."

"You never know around here."

I sat back down.

"You say you're working for Susan. Can you prove it?"

"Call her," I recited the number for her.

She must have believed me, because she made no move for the phone. She just said: "What are you supposed to be doing for her?"

"Trying to find out what happened at Moonfire yesterday morning."

She flipped a hand at me and said: "Why? What's it going to accomplish?"

"She wants to know. Wouldn't you, if you were her?"

"I don't know. Maybe. But I'd sure as hell think twice about whether it was worth it."

"What do you mean?"

She shrugged and gave me a small, sarcastic smile. "Look what a hassle it's causing me, and I wasn't even involved that bad."

Her purse was on the maple coffee table in front of her. She leaned forward and rummaged through it until she came up with a package of Shermans. She lit one with a match, then dropped the package and the book of matches back into her purse and leaned back. With the first drag from the cigarette, some of the tenseness seemed to dissipate from her body. "I'm going to tell you right now, the only reason I'm talking to you is because you're working for Susan. The cops have been out here to ask me questions and I wouldn't tell them shit. But I like Susan and I can sympathize with what she's going through, even if Carlos wasn't worth it. She treated me like I was family when I was working at Moonfire. That's why when she came to me and asked me to do her a favor, and marry Carlos, I said sure. If I'd have known it was going to rain shit two months later, I probably wouldn't have done it. But I don't blame her for anything. You can tell her that for me when you see her."

I nodded. "What about the story in the paper today?"

"Pure bullshit," she said, then raised a curious eyebrow. "Why, what does Susan say about it?"

"Pure bullshit. She says it was all strictly a business arrangement."

"That's what it was supposed to be. She said she'd make it worth my while. Only the whole thing wound up costing me nearly half a G."

"How come?"

"Carlos was a con artist, that's how come. He was a lovable con artist and he could be a hell of a sweet guy, but you shake hands with that dude and you'd better count your fingers afterwards."

"How'd he con you?"

She inhaled from her cigarette, turned her head away and blew out a mouthful of blue smoke. She didn't look good smoking, I decided; it chipped away at her façade. "He nickel-and-dimed me to death. He'd always be borrowing twenty bucks for this and ten bucks for that or using my car and giving it back to me with an empty tank. It got to be like I was supporting him. I went to Susan and told her about it, and she said not to worry, she'd take care of everything, but I don't know, something snapped in me then and I said fuck it, I just want out. Things were beginning to back up on me anyway and I knew I was going to get away from the life pretty soon, but that was kind of the straw that broke the camel's back. You get your body used all day and night and you don't expect to have your so-called friends use you, too. You know what I mean? So I just took off. Susan tried to pay me for what Carlos had spent, but I told her to forget it, just take care of the annulment and I split." She stopped, then said: "I kick myself in the ass for it now. I should've taken the money. But all I wanted to do then was get away from that whole scene as fast as I could. I was right on the edge of a nervous breakdown and I just wanted out."

She shifted her position on the couch so that she was facing me obliquely. Her nylon uniform made a crisp, rustling sound as she moved. I tried not to think about it.

"What about Merritt?"

"What about him?"

"What was your relationship with him like?"

"There wasn't one. Gene hung around for a couple of weeks, that was all. He hung around with a lot of the girls. He'd sort of pick a girl and move in with her for awhile. After me, he moved in with Zelda for a couple of weeks. Then it was Joni. You couldn't get into anything heavy with Gene. He was just too fucking dumb. A nice guy, but I think his I.Q. and his temperature hover around the same spot. It wasn't as bad for some of the girls, I guess, as it was for me, but I couldn't take that shit for any length of time. Gene's a nice guy, but Jesus, you can listen to somebody talk about Country-Western music or great barroom brawls he's been in or that old piece of shit saloon he's dreaming about buying, just so long and then you start to go nuts."

"He talked about the saloon a lot?"

She nodded and leaned forward. She took a last drag off her cigarette and mashed it out in the ashtray on the coffee table. "He even drove me out there one day to look at it. The way he talked about it, I expected the San Francisco Opera House or something. I couldn't even believe it when I saw that old claptrap bar. He said the owner only wanted ten grand for it. I wouldn't have given him ten bucks, never mind ten thousand, but I didn't say anything. Why should I rain on his parade? We're all entitled to a dream, even if it'll never come true."

"He made half of it come true."

Her eyebrows arched into question marks. "What half?"

"He bought the place."

"No shit?"

"You sound surprised."

"It's just I never thought Gene would ever put the bread together. I thought he was just talking. He was always talking about how he was going to do this and that and make a million dollars. Only Gene is the type of guy who'd talk about buying a pineapple plantation in Alaska because there was no competition up there."

"How did Merritt act around you after you married Realango?"

She shrugged. "The same. I told you, there was no big love story between Gene and me. He knew the thing with Carlos was just an arrangement anyway."

"How did he act toward Carlos?"

She tilted her head toward the light and her auburn hair reddened. "He hated Carlos. But it had nothing to do with me."

"Who did it have something to do with?"

"Gene thought Carlos was trying to get Susan to divorce Sal. He thought he was trying to cut Sal out of Moonfire."

"What do you think?"

She frowned. "Who the hell knows? Look, you see a young dude with an old broad like Susan and right away you think, Jesus Christ, the guy's either a real sicko with a mother complex or he's after her money. It's natural. But I saw those two together a lot and there was something there. I don't know if you could call it love—I'm not sure I know what love is myself—but Carlos really seemed to care for her. I guess it could've been an act, but it was a hell of a good one if it was."

I had to agree with her. I'd felt pass between them on that one evening in San Diego the same thing Valerie had. "Did you ever hear Merritt threaten Realango?"

"To his face?" she said scoffingly. "He wouldn't have dared. Gene was scared of Carlos."

"He told you that?"

"Gene would never admit to being afraid of anybody. But you could tell the way he acted around him. He'd never say anything around Carlos."

"What about behind his back?"

"He might have said a couple of times that he'd like to kick Carlos' ass, but nothing heavy like killing the dude or anything like that, if that's what you mean. But then I left before all the heavy stuff started coming down. As long as Sal let Carlos stay around, Gene couldn't really say much. He just sort of stayed out of Carlos' way."

"And when the wraps were taken off?"

She shrugged. "I wouldn't know. I wasn't around."

"You think Merritt hated Realango enough to have been carried away by the moment? You said he hated him and was afraid of him at the same time. Hate and fear can be a deadly combination."

She scratched her chin, then uncrossed and recrossed her legs. "Maybe. I saw Gene get worked up a couple of times. He could really flip out, especially if he'd had a couple. I remember one time this summer a couple of kids were outside in the parking lot, spinning doughnuts in a Corvette. Gene took a gun and went out there and stopped the car and made the two of them get out and lie down in the dirt and then he started kicking them, real hard, in the sides and legs. They were just *kids*, for chrissakes, they couldn't have been more than sixteen, but he was really kicking the shit out of them with those heavy cowboy boots of his until Joe Battaglia ran out of the place, screaming. Joe pointed at the kids and asked Gene what the hell he was doing. You know what Gene said? He just looked at Joe and said, 'This ain't no dirt track,' and walked back inside. The parents of the two kids sued, but Sal squared it with them somehow."

"He sounds like a real sweetheart."

"Strangely enough, he could be. He was never anything but gentle and kind around me. He was really thoughtful. He'd do a lot of little things, bring me flowers or perfume or wash my car for me."

"You think his feelings for you could have been less casual than your feelings for him?"

"No," she said firmly. "He was that way around all the girls."

"Why do you think Dierdorf put that bad blood story in the papers?"

"I don't know."

"Sal had to okay the story," I said.

She didn't say anything.

"It could mean that Merritt got excited and blew away Realango and Sal is preparing to throw him to the wolves."

Something moved warily behind her eyes, but her voice came

out cool and dry. "I don't know what it means. Guessing about it isn't going to help."

The light in the room got suddenly dimmer, as if the sun outside had gone behind a cloud. She turned toward the window and a small, wry smile spread across her lips.

"What are you thinking?" I asked.

"Nothing. Just how funny it is."

"What?"

"How we all screw things up. All Gene ever wanted was that saloon and finally he gets it and he goes and blows it for himself. Not only that, he blows it for all of us while he's at it—Carlos, Sal, Susan, me, everybody." She sighed. "My shit's minor compared to the rest of them. All I've lost is a lousy job. I can always pack up and split town. They can't."

"Carlos is packed up and ready to split town now."

She glanced over sharply. "Hmmmm?"

"His brother is coming in today to take the body back to Argentina. They're going to bury him there."

"Oh. Yeah, I read that."

"Is that what you're going to do?" I asked. "Leave town?"

"I don't know. Probably. I sure don't guess I'll be able to get another job around here too easily."

"Where will you go?"

She shrugged. "Who knows? Vegas maybe."

"Vegas?" a voice said behind us.

Mrs. Barrington was standing in the hallway, her hand still at her throat. "What would you do in Vegas? That town is no good. You'll only get into trouble there."

"I couldn't get into any deeper shit than I am right here," Valerie said.

"I wish you wouldn't talk that way," her mother said.

Valerie rolled her eyes. "Jesus Christ."

"I'd better be going," I said, and stood. "Thank you very much for talking to me. You've been a great help."

"Doesn't anybody want coffee?" Mrs. Barrington asked, making helpless gestures with her hands. "I made coffee."

"No, thank you," I said. "I'd better be going."

The woman's eyes bored hateful holes in me. When she transferred the look to her daughter, tears began to well up in her eyes. I went past her to the door and by the time I reached it, they were at each other again, the mother tearfully clutching, Valerie swearing and backing away.

I was struck by a sudden vision of where they would both be six months from now. I saw Valerie as Candy again, hooking in Vegas or waiting for a live one at a bar in some roadside house on Interstate 80, and Mrs. Barrington as a serious candidate for the Laughing Academy or on her knees five hours a day in some musty church, praying for her daughter's salvation and for forgiveness for her own failures as a mother. She had that kind of ascetic, self-immolating personality that could go that way.

I hoped the vision was wrong, but I doubted it was. I did great readings for other people, the only future I could never see into was my own. I opened the front door feeling I was probably better off.

16

I spent the next three days interviewing bartenders, cocktail wait-resses, blackjack dealers, and a hooker or two, trying to trace Realango's movements on the eve of the shooting.

The earliest I could place him anywhere was shortly after two A.M. at the King's Inn. He had had a couple of drinks there and joked with some people at the bar, then spent an hour or so participating in the "world's most liberal blackjack game," as the establishment advertised it. It must not have been liberal enough, because he had wound up losing about two hundred bucks before going over to the Bonanza where he'd dropped another hundred. He had left the Bonanza around four-something, which put him back at the Ponderosa in time for the fatal phone call.

Leon Rosen had called on Friday to tell me Gene Merritt had a checking account at the Security Pacific Bank on Macadamia Road in Reno. The balance in the account had fluctuated between $300 and $800 during the past month, but had never been more than that. He had managed to find two accounts at different banks for Sal Mezzano, but neither of them showed any withdrawals in the past thirty days to the tune of five big ones.

Jack Schwartz flew back to L.A. the day after Carlos' younger brother arrived in Reno to take possession of the body. The brother's one statement to the press during his short stay had been rather vituperative. "The U.S. capitalists cheated my brother of his money time and time again, now they have cheated him of his life."

According to AP and UPI, thirty thousand Argentinians were waiting at the airport and along the road into Buenos Aires to pay homage to their fallen hero. A hundred and fifty thousand more showed up at the local soccer stadium for the funeral service, which was open to the public. There had not been such a unified display of grief in the capital city, the papers said, since the death of Alberto Rosa, a tango dancer who had been shot to death by a jealous dance partner in 1930.

With Susan Mezzano's permission, I turned over what little I had to Leland Carew. He seemed very interested in Merritt's financing of Ma and Pa's and made notes while I talked. After I finished, he filled me in on what they had pieced together so far about the way the killing had gone down. He told it all like an initiation rite, as if it were all very hush-hush and that by telling me, he was allowing me into some privileged secret inner circle, and I went along even though I knew it would all be appearing in the papers in the next couple of days.

At five-thirty, Realango had arrived at the front gate of Moonfire, demanding to see Sal Mezzano. The girl working the security desk, one Dora Wells, knew Realango was persona non grata and woke up Joe Battaglia, who threw on some clothes and ran outside. While he was talking to Realango, Dora woke up Merritt, who was sleeping in one of the unoccupied rooms in back. Merritt ran to a back room where the guns were stored and grabbed a shotgun, but couldn't find any shells for it. Watching Merritt's frenzied search was a maintenance man at the ranch, Pete Schumacher, and wanting to be helpful, he ran and got the 30.06 from the front gun tower and handed it to Merritt. Merritt took the rifle and slipped out the kitchen door and Schumacher, not wanting to be hit by a stray bullet, scurried back into the main room. Consequently, he was not a witness to what happened after that.

While all that was going on, the conversation between Realango and Battaglia was growing heated. After exchanging bitter words, Realango turned and walked back to his car, opened the door and stepped behind it. Some witnesses claimed that Realango then bent down suddenly as if reaching for something, others said he was standing erect, glaring at Battaglia, when a voice yelled "Freeze!" and a shot rang out. None of that mattered to Realango. He was already dead by the time he hit the ground.

The bullet entered three and a half inches to the left of the midline of the chest, dead-center on the heart. It passed through the heart, nicked the lower lobe of the right lung, and exited through the back by the right tenth rib. The Sheriff's people admitted they had moved the body before the coroner's investigator had seen it, so it was impossible to tell exactly how Realango had been standing when he'd been shot, but according to the path of the bullet, he had to have been in a crouch to have been shot from the kitchen doorway.

Tests by the FBI lab had confirmed that the bullet had been a high velocity 30.06, but it was too fragmented to make any meaningful ballistics comparisons. And since Dierdorf had not bothered to run paraffin tests on Merritt's hands after taking him into custody, there was no way to positively identify the gun Merritt had been given as the murder weapon, or even prove that Merritt had fired a gun at all that morning.

Carew was worried about what Merritt's attorney would do with all that. Apparently the man had done more with a lot less.

That was how things stood on Monday when I drove over to Silverville to Merritt's bail hearing. I spent the entire drive in a state of adrenal rush, my eyes darting rapidly between the road ahead and the rearview mirror in a constant scan for cops. I didn't see any until I reached the courthouse, and then I saw quite a few.

A small crowd of newsmen stood at the base of the courthouse steps, cameras and notepads and cassettes ready, their white breath mingling in the cold air. Some were hopping up and down, some stamping their feet on the hard ground in an effort to warm them. Their entry into the building was being barred by two uniformed deputies, who stood on each side of the door with their thumbs hooked casually on their Sam Browne belts.

I walked to the edge of the crowd and tapped the shoulder of a man in a rabbit skin parka. When he turned around, I noticed the PRESS badge pinned to his furry chest. "They're not letting anybody in?"

"You kidding?" he asked gruffly. "Just whores and pimps

144

allowed. The press can freeze its collective ass off."

After a couple of minutes of standing around, the cold began to seep through the soles of my shoes and I began stamping my feet with the rest of them. Then a ripple went through the crowd as a tall, broad-shouldered man emerged from the courthouse and planted himself on one side of the door. His face was dark and there was something coldly primitive, even reptilian, in the way his slitted black eyes scanned the crowd. Those features that hadn't been flattened by punches were Latin and I guessed this was the Colombian sparring partner Susan Mezzano had told me about.

That guess got partial confirmation when Battaglia and Dierdorf came through the door, followed by a short, ashen-faced man wearing a navy blue camel overcoat and matching blue-fur Russian Cossack hat, and carrying a large leather briefcase.

When nobody else came out after ten seconds or so, murmurings began to spread through the crowd that we'd all been hoodwinked and Mezzano had gone out the back way, but then he stepped through the doorway and there was a surge toward the steps.

He looked like a stage act in Vegas. He had on a snow-white leather suit covered with silver studs and white cowboy boots. Wrap-around dark glasses covered his eyes and a black hairpiece covered his balding dome. He had two of the Moonfire Revue with him, one clinging to each arm, and each of them was as flamboyant as his suit.

Both were at least six inches taller than he was and both were spectacularly beautiful in their own way. One was a pale blonde with high cheekbones and clear, almost transluscent skin, the other a brunette who looked as if she might have had a touch of Asian blood somewhere in her ancestry—Filipino or Thai, maybe. Both wore identical miniscule white leather bikinis and even shorter tan suede jackets with fox collars. They stood smiling idiotically as reporters shouted questions at Mezzano.

Mezzano dropped the girls' arms and waved everyone quiet. After the cacophony thinned out, he grinned impishly and made

145

a supplicating gesture with his hands. "Why the hell should I talk to you boys? I wouldn't say you've been particularly nice to me lately."

There was another clamorous bout of shouting and Mezzano waved them quiet again, smiling broadly. He seemed totally at ease, almost enjoying himself. "The facts in this case are simple. You guys just don't want to hear them because they're not sensational enough, they don't make good copy. It was justifiable homicide plain and simple. The only reason it's gotten as far as it has is because the D.A. and the Sheriff here are running scared from all the hubbub whipped up by you boys. If they had any guts, they'd throw the charges against Merritt in the trash where they belong."

"Does that mean Merritt is admitting he shot Realango?" a voice called out from the crowd.

"It doesn't mean anything," the ashen-faced man in the Russian hat said. He looked annoyed. "I'm sorry, but the judge has imposed a gag rule in this case and we're—"

The reporters ignored him and kept shouting questions at Mezzano. "How much has the bail been set for?"

"Two hundred grand," Mezzano said.

"Are you going to put it up?"

Mezzano gestured to the man in the Russian hat. "My attorney, Mr. Jacobson, is going to see what he can do about getting it knocked down. We feel the bail is unjustified in the face of the facts. But if worse comes to worst, hell yes, I'm going to put it up. That nut came out to my place looking for me with a loaded .38 in his boot. Now I don't know what that judge in there thinks Realango might have had in mind to do with that gun, but me, I got a pretty good idea. If Merritt hadn't of done what he did, I wouldn't be standing up here talking to you now. I'd be dead."

That was enough for Jacobson. He stepped in front of Mezzano and shouted: "I'm sorry to cut this off, fellas, but the judge has requested silence from all parties in this case. We'd like to talk to you, but we're under orders from the court, so if you'll excuse us—"

146

He took Mezzano by the arm and started down the steps with him, pausing to let Dierdorf and Battaglia and the big man with the brooding face form a wedge in front of them. The reporters resisted the push and kept shouting questions.

Dierdorf was the first one through. He pushed out of the crowd about four feet from where I was standing and we locked stares. He strode over to me and said through clenched teeth, "I thought I told you to stay out of the county?" He looked angry, but he kept his voice down so that the reporters would not pick it up.

Mezzano broke through the crowd just then, flanked by the fighter and Battaglia, who were keeping away the photographers at arm's length. Mezzano gave me a puzzled look, then came over. "You were out at Moonfire the morning of the shooting. I never forget a face."

"This is the detective," Dierdorf said softly.

Mezzano looked at me curiously. "What's your name?"

"Asch."

He smiled easily and stuck out a small, plump hand covered with a coarse matting of black hair. "Glad to meetya, Asch. Sal Mezzano. But I guess you already know that."

I took the hand.

"You come on for a ride," he said, more as a command than a request. "There are some things we gotta talk over."

He spoke rapidly, in short, staccato bursts, and all his movements, from his hand gestures to the way he walked, gave the impression of dammed-up energy that was being barely held in check. He had been frenetically hyper when I'd seen him right after the shooting, too, and at the time, I'd put that down to the situation. Now I could see my conclusion had been false. His personality still crackled like a broken high-tension wire. "I've got my own car," I told him.

"I'll bring you back," he said, and turned quickly away, as if that settled it. I guess it did, because I followed.

The crush of reporters was still trying to get to him and a shoving match was beginning to flare up between the photographers and Mezzano's two bodyguards. The two girls and Jacobson

147

jostled through the crowd and came up behind us. "You two girls go with Joe and Lou," Mezzano told them. "Go get a drink somewhere. I'll meet you back here in twenty minutes. Take Alberto with you."

"Where are you going?" Jacobson said apprehensively.

"For a ride. This man and I got some things to talk about."

Jacobson gave me a hard look. "He's not a reporter—"

"Course he ain't a reporter," Mezzano said. "Relax, Lou. You're gonna harden a couple more arteries, you keep worrying like you do."

"Sure, relax," the lawyer snapped. "How the hell can I relax when you make statements like you did back there? Either you're going to take my advice—"

"Sure," Mezzano said, patting him on the shoulder. "That's what I'm paying you for, ain't it? We'll talk about it later. Right now, I gotta talk to this guy."

He left Jacobson fuming and started down the block. Alberto and Battaglia formed a guard in front of us and continued to hold the reporters at bay until we got to Mezzano's car. It was an Eldorado convertible, pure white inside and out, with chrome wire wheels. I watched out of the back window as the photographers moved into the wake we left as we pulled out, still grinding out footage.

I turned around in the seat and said: "Your lawyer seemed a little upset."

"Lou's a great attorney," he said smugly, "but he's from Frisco. He don't understand these small-town juries like I do. With these people, you *gotta* get your case in the papers. In a big town, it may hurt you, but here, it helps."

I didn't say anything.

"You from L.A., huh?"

"Yeah."

"L.A.'s a good town. I go there a lot on business. I'm from Frisco myself. Before that, New York. Before that, Sicily. I don't remember much about Sicily, though. I left there when I was only eleven."

148

When I didn't say anything to that, he materialized a cigar from his jacket that looked as if it might have been part of a wall of a log cabin at one time. He stripped off the cellophane wrapper and shoved the cigar into the corner of his mouth.

"I just chew on 'em," he said. "Sometimes I light 'em, but the smoke bothers a lot of people."

I said it wouldn't bother me, but he made no effort to light it. He hung a right at the bottom of the hill and started through town. When the buildings began to thin out, he stomped on the accelerator.

The road twisted sharply down the mountain in a series of hairpin turns and he took them all about fifteen miles an hour over the recommended limit. My right leg began to cramp from pressing down on the imaginary brake pedal, but I didn't think he was driving that fast to try to scare me. The squealing of the tires really seemed to relax him.

I've known a few men like that who actually relaxed under pressure and if it was not being supplied from the outside, they supplied it themselves in one form or another. On the surface, they could appear perfectly normal—even superior—due to the aggressiveness and cool self-confidence they displayed in stressful situations that would render us mere mortals helpless and blithering in self-pity. It was when the pressure was removed suddenly you had to watch out. Not having any way to siphon off all the internal energy they had built up, cracks would appear and steam would start coming out of their ears. All you'd have to do would be book Sal Mezzano on a two-week ocean cruise and stand back and wait for the explosion.

He smiled dreamily over his cigar and said: "Rides nice around the curves, don't she?"

"Nice."

"Know how much this baby cost me?"

"No."

"Twenty big ones," he said proudly. "You can't get Eldorado convertibles anymore, you know that? They stopped makin' 'em. The guy I bought it from wanted twenty-five, but I gave him twenty. All in cash." He chuckled. "He just about shit when he saw all those bills. Wanted to know if the money was all right. He thought I'd got it in a bank heist or something. Course it cost me another G-note to get it all fixed up the way I wanted it. Had to get special shocks and suspension. I don't like the way these big cars ride, all mushy, like you're in a fucking boat or something. I like to feel the road under me when I drive."

We sailed around another curve and the rear end started to fishtail, but he applied an adept flick of the wrist to the power steering and the car righted itself.

"So you're working for Susan?"

"Yeah."

"How is she?" His voice sounded genuinely concerned.

"Some days better than others," I said. "She'll make it. She's a strong woman."

He nodded, keeping his eyes on the road. After a pause, he said: "Is she really trying to nail me for this thing?"

"She's trying to find out what happened."

"And she thinks I had Realango blown away."

"Let's just say that she doesn't have a hell of a lot of faith in Dierdorf's objectivity."

"What about the Nevada Crime Commission? She thinks I tell them what to do?"

"All I can say is that she's paying me to stay on the job."

He grunted. We passed a sign that said SILVER CITY, and he took his foot off the gas. I took mine off the imaginary brake pedal and we coasted past a series of wooden shacks and curio stores plastered against the side of the mountain. "You can tell her for me I didn't have Realango offed. I told Merritt to keep the sonofabitch off my property, but I didn't tell him to shoot him."

I didn't say anything.

"You don't say a hell of a lot, do you?"

"Depends."

"On what?"

150

"On whether there's anything to say. And who I'm saying it to."

He smiled with his mouth. The dark glasses prevented me from seeing whether his eyes were smiling, too. I wondered if that was why he wore them. "That's okay. Listen, I like people who can keep their mouths shut. I don't trust guys with big mouths. I hear you even spent some time in the slammer because you wouldn't open your mouth."

"Where'd you hear that?"

"I told you. I go to L.A. a lot. I got friends there. I did some checking on you. The consensus down there is that you could cause me some trouble."

"People usually cause their own trouble."

"That could be. It could be." He stopped then went on. "You know, Asch, you may not believe it and Susan may not either, but I'm really sorry things have turned out like this. I really am. It's stupid. We've built up something over the years, Susan and me, and I hate to see it get all torn up this way. And I don't mean just Moonfire, although I'd be lying if I said that wasn't a part of it. But I mean us. Her and me. I've fucked thousands of broads in my time and I've been through the love bit, with the bells and the buzzers and the hot flashes and all that shit, but it don't mean anything compared to what we've got. I mean, you sit across a breakfast table from somebody for a whole lotta years and try to solve all the day-to-day crises that come up—everything from trying to keep the D.A. and the IRS off your ass to trying to calm down some whore who wants to take a meat cleaver to a guy because he tried to take a dump on her chest—and something happens to you. You become sort of one, you know what I mean? You start to think alike, to understand one another. Love don't last, but that understanding does."

It was not exactly the love speech from *Cyrano de Bergerac,* but he sounded in earnest. "So why did you want to talk to me? To tell me that?"

The buildings were gone now He began to accelerate again.

"Look, when I heard what Frank pulled on you, I jumped down his throat. I told him that rough stuff don't accomplish anything, but give you a bad impression of me. I thought we should get together and talk man-to-man, so we could get this thing hammered out. I thought maybe you'd want to ask me some questions. I figured it's better than you going around talking to a lot of people who don't know shit from Shinola and getting all the wrong ideas about me."

"You mean you're going to answer them?"

He rolled the cigar from one side of his mouth to the other. "Sure. Why not? I got nothing to hide."

I kept my eyes on him to keep from watching the road. "Okay. Why don't we start with who you used to make the calls to your wife and Realango in San Diego?"

"What calls?"

I sighed. "Let's just turn around and you can drive me back. This is just wasting both our time."

"No, I'm not kiddin'," he demanded. "What calls?"

"The death threats," I said. "The warnings at three in the morning not to come back to Reno unless they wanted to be planted there."

"I don't know anything about no calls," he said.

"Why do you think your wife came back up here?"

"I don't know. I haven't talked to her since she left."

"What about the call Realango got at the hotel the morning he was shot? You don't know anything about that either?"

"No."

"Realango called your wife at five that morning and said somebody from Moonfire had called and said you wanted to see him."

"That's a lie," he said sharply.

"The call came through the hotel switchboard."

"I don't care if it came through the White House switchboard. Nobody at Moonfire made that call."

"Then why did Realango go out there? He knew about the security and the guns. He knew he didn't have a chance in hell of getting in if you didn't want him to."

152

"Because he was crazy," Mezzano said. "Crazy like a fucking fox. He was coming out there to kill me, plain and simple, and he told Susan I called him because he thought it'd back up a claim to self-defense." He took the cigar out of his mouth, and made a gesture with the soggy end of it. "If Susan and I got divorced —which wasn't likely—and she married Realango, all he'd have gotten was half of half the joint. And he knew if I was around, sooner or later, I'd get the other half back. But with me dead, he would've had the whole fucking works in the palm of his hands. He always had that in his mind, from the first day he came sucking around."

"You know that for sure?"

He put the cigar back into his mouth and said: "Sure, I do. Toward the end there, before I booted his ass off my property, he was walking around acting like he owned the joint. The night before I had Merritt go in and clean out the trailer where he was staying, I threw a big bash for some of the local bigshots, politicians and the like. Realango was standing by the front door, smoking one of my fucking cigars, asking everybody: 'How you like my joint?' *My* joint, he says. That sound to you like he didn't have any ideas about taking over?"

"So you sent Merritt over to burn his clothes."

"Yeah, I—" He stopped and retreated rapidly, realizing he had made a tactical blunder. "Merritt went overboard with that. I only told him to clean the place out. I didn't tell him to set fire to anything. Merritt just sort of went crazy. He hated Realango's guts anyway."

"Why?"

"'Cause he knew what kind of a scumbag Realango was, that's why."

"You mean you're not going to try to sell me any stories of jealousy and unrequited love?"

His mouth tightened over the cigar. "That story never should have been given out. I chewed Frank's ass out for it when I saw it."

"You want me to believe Dierdorf did that on his own?"

153

"I'm telling you he did it on his own. I don't care whether you believe it or not. The only thing I care about is the fact that I'm talking to you about it. If it hadn't been for Merritt, I wouldn't be. Realango came out to Moonfire to kill me, I'm tellin' ya, only it didn't work out like he expected. He tried to get cute one time too many and it finally caught up with him. With all the crap he pulled, it's amazing he didn't get a bullet in his black heart before this. It's just a good goddamn thing they're burying him in Argentina, cause if he was being laid out over here, they'd have to get a couple of Doberman pinschers to dig the grave."

"What kind of crap did he pull?"

He glanced over at me, then turned his black fly-eyes back to the road. "You really want to know what kind of a prick Realango was?"

"Sure."

"You know I owned his contract for awhile—"

"Yes."

"Yeah, well, that was one of the biggest mistakes I ever made. After one fight, I found out how big. The bastard tried to screw me out of five grand."

"How?"

"You know about the fight Schwartz set up up here with Masters?"

"I heard about it."

He nodded. "It was at the Coliseum. We had a pretty good crowd there to see Realango knock out this stiff and I was watching the prelims, feeling pretty good, y'know, when ten minutes before fight time, I get word Realango wants to see me in his dressing room. I can't figure out what he'd want to see me about, so I go in there and the spic bastard is just sitting on the massage table, smiling, and he says: 'I want five thousand more or I no fight.' Well, I start to get hot and I tell him he's gonna fight or I'll guarantee he'll never fight again, but he don't budge. Five grand more, he says, right now, or he don't fight. What am I gonna do? I already had more than twenty grand tied up in the deal. I'd lose it all plus have a lot of people pissed off at me on

154

top of it, so I dish out the bread, right there, in cash, and he says okay and goes out. I was waiting in his dressing room when he came back in and I told him if his spic ass wasn't out of town by sunset, he'd be walking on his hands."

"Jack Schwartz never told me any of this."

"He wouldn't. Realango was Schwartz's boy. Schwartz was the one who sold me the bill of goods on Realango in the first place. He was also the one who paid me back the five grand."

"His own or the five grand Realango soaked you for?"

"I didn't ask," he said gravely. "I went to Schwartz after the fight and told him I wanted my money back and I didn't care how he got it. He found me a little while later and gave me the money and apologized all over the place. Then Carlos came to me, laughing, and said it had all been a big joke, ha-ha-ha. I didn't care for the joke, but I said what the hell, I've got my money back and let it slide. Then I started making some calls and found out it wasn't a joke. He'd pulled stuff like that on everybody."

"You mean extorting money from people?"

"Everything," he said, screwing up his face. His dark lips worked on the cigar. "He must have sold his contract to fifty people. He'd get an advance for a fight from the poor bastard who thought he owned him, then split town leaving the guy holding the bag. He nearly broke some doctor down in Miami doing that, and another guy in New York who owns a chain of $1.49 steak houses, I can't remember the guy's name now. Stein or something. Jewish guy. Anyway, that was his racket, and the bastard got away with it. One time, though, it nearly backfired on him real bad. He went down to Puerto Rico and sold his contract to a guy named Sartucci for thirty grand. The very next day, Realango gets a call from Madison Square Garden offering him eight grand to fight Ali in New York, so Realango, not wanting to have to dish out all that money in agent's fees, goes back to Sartucci and says he feels real bad about taking his thirty grand, that he's not worth that much money and that he'll buy the contract back. What he doesn't know is that Sartucci has got some heavy mob connections, and after he starts checking around, Sartucci calls up

Realango and tells him to be nice or he'll break his legs."

"What happened?"

"Realango went through with the Ali fight and Sartucci got his cut."

"How could he keep getting fights?" I asked. "The people in the business had to know about his reputation."

He shrugged. "Realango had a lot of things going for him. He could look great against mediocre opponents and put up a hell of a good fight against the great ones. And he was white. Finding a white heavy that can stand up and go the distance with the class niggers is like finding the crown jewels in that business. Greed gets the better of you. You look at the sonofabitch and say, 'Hell, I can handle him. He just had bad management.' Even Marcello Truzzi got taken in. I hear he has fits now, anybody even mentions Realango's name."

"Who's Marcello Truzzi?"

He took the cigar out of his mouth again and opened the dashboard ashtray with his free hand. He picked a couple of tiny bits of soggy tobacco off his lower lip and flicked them into the ashtray, then he inserted the cigar in his mouth. "The biggest fight promoter in Europe," he said. "Realango went over there a couple of years ago and somehow got hooked up with him. Like a jerk, Truzzi gave him a new Mercedes and a complete wardrobe and lined him up with a few fights where Realango could bring his own music. Then Truzzi's booking agent for non-Europeans got Realango a shot with Joe Frazier in Melbourne for seventy-five G's. Everything was signed, Frazier's people were all packed, then, three weeks before the fight, Realango disappeared. What happened was Realango got a call from Paddy McGuire, who's a hatchet man for Don Smith, the black promoter, offering him a ten grand advance to fight George Foreman in Mexico City."

"I don't remember Realango ever fighting Foreman."

Mezzano smiled. "That's because he didn't. He went to Mexico City, collected the ten grand and split to Vegas."

I shook my head, trying to take it all in. "How did you find out about all this?"

"I know people," he said smugly. "It wasn't hard."

"Does Susan know about it?"

He took a hand off the wheel and shook it. "Sure she knows. That's what I could never understand. Susan is really good at reading people. She can be at some hotsy-totsy dinner party and take one look at a guy all dressed up in a white tie and tails and looks like William Powell, and say, 'That asshole is a burglar,' and you check it out and I'll be a sonofabitch if she isn't right ninety percent of the time. When she came to me and said she wanted to handle Realango, I couldn't even believe it. I told her she was nuts, the guy's a flake, and I laid it all out for her, but she kept making me crazy about it, so I finally gave up trying to talk to her and said go ahead, but don't come to me crying when you get burned. I'd already told Carlos I didn't want anything to do with him, that he could wipe his ass with his contract. The next thing I know, the spic has turned on the charm and she's running around acting like a lovesick cow, buying him clothes and a car and giving him money." His mouth hardened and he didn't seem to be talking to me anymore, just himself. "The biggest mistake I made was not running his ass out of town in the beginning."

He was very good, there was no doubt about it. A master of illusion. Like a stage magician who distracts his audience from what his hands are doing by laying down a constant stream of patter, he had lulled me to sleep with his verbosity. It seemed as if he'd been talking for hours and my head was buzzing with facts, but when I sifted through them I couldn't latch onto one that seemed of any significance. He'd given me a damn good reason why he would have wanted Realango dead—which I already knew —and an alleged reason why Realango might have wanted him dead, which might have been born out of fiction, reality, or paranoia, but that was about all.

He pulled off the road onto a dirt shoulder and made a U-turn. He started back up the highway the way we'd come.

"A few weeks ago, Merritt put $5,000 in cash down on a saloon in Duncan. He'd been trying to raise the money for a year and couldn't. I hear he approached you on it."

The tires squealed in protest as we rounded a corner too fast. "So?"

"I hear you refused to bankroll him."

"I couldn't see sinking five grand into that shitbox. So what?"

"Got any idea where he got the money all of a sudden?"

He hesitated. "No."

"You didn't loan it to him?"

"No," he said, but his voice wavered.

"His girlfriend, Pebbles, says he got the money by selling SAL MEZZANO FOR PRESIDENT T-shirts. She said he had them made up and sold them, but she wasn't too clear on just where he got them or how they were sold, or who he sold them to. You wouldn't know anything about that, would you?"

He shook his head and rolled the cigar around on his lips. "No."

"He never put them on consignment out at Moonfire, then?"

"He may have mentioned something about some T-shirts at one time," he said. "I don't remember. We sell a lot of souvenirs out there. Ashtrays, lighters, crap like that. The tourists eat it up."

"But you'd remember if he'd put a thousand or so T-shirts on consignment, wouldn't you?"

"Yeah. I'd remember."

"And he didn't?"

His hairy hands clenched and unclenched around the steering wheel, but it seemed more out of a growing irritation rather than nervousness. "I think he talked about it. I told him it'd be all right if he wanted to do it, but he never came through."

We rounded a bend and once more passed the curio shops of Silver City.

"You know where he would have ordered the shirts from?"

"You'd have to ask him."

"I'd like to do that," I said. "You think it might be arranged?"

He grinned. "That might be kind of hard, I mean, with you back in L.A. and everything."

"What is that supposed to mean?"

He kept grinning. "Look, I've been cooperative, right? I've answered all your questions. I've told you what started all this crap, so there's no reason for you to stick around and keep poking around and stirring things up. Hell, since I'm a generous guy, I'll even throw in two thousand bucks as a bonus. You couldn't ask for anything fairer than that, could you?"

I watched him in silence, then said: "What am I supposed to tell your wife?"

"That you've looked into the whole thing and decided there's nothing to it, that Merritt acted on his own and that's all."

I nodded pensively. "Let me ask you one more question."

"Shoot."

"If you're Mr. Clean, like you say you are, why are you so anxious to get me out of town?"

He shrugged casually and said: "Like I told you, this vendetta Susan has going ain't doing anybody any good. It's no good for her, it's no good for me, it's no good for business. Whatever's done is done. Nobody can bring the dead back to life. I don't want it to get to the stage where the wounds will never heal."

"It may have already gone past that stage."

He stiffened against the suggestion. "You gonna go?"

"Sorry."

He didn't say anything for a few seconds. "Don't be a jerk. You're gonna lose. You'll be off the case anyway. Susan can't keep fighting me. She's got nothing to keep fighting with."

It was my turn not to say anything.

Then he made the first mistake driving I'd seen. He sailed around a blind horseshoe turn and went over the center line and nearly took off the left front bumper of a camper driven by a panic-stricken octogenarian and his wife. The camper's horn blared away from us, and Mezzano slowed as we drove past the first old buildings of Silverville.

My hands were trembling slightly from the near-collision, but it didn't seem to have affected Mezzano in the least. He took off the dark glasses and set them down on the dashboard and turned to look at me. His eyes glittered intensely like two black star sapphires. "Maybe Frank was right," he said in a voice that was strangely subdued.

159

"About what?"

"He said I wouldn't be able to reason with you, that you were too hard-headed. He said you'd have to learn the hard way. If you learned at all." His eyes watched the smattering of camera-laden tourists marching up and down the boardwalks of Silverville, window-shopping and pointing out representative examples of 19th-century Western architecture to their spouses, lovers, or children.

"You know what, Asch?"

"What?"

"For a simple guy who only made it through the sixth grade, I make a hell of a good teacher."

"You have special teaching techniques for slow learners?"

"I guess I could think some up," he said.

I nodded. "Well, maybe you'd better start thinking."

17

Action in the Ponderosa casino was lethargic as I passed through on my way out. A few men, obviously dressed for dinner, were playing at putting chips down on the felt while they waited for their wives or whatever to put on the finishing touches and meet them downstairs. I had no idea where I was going for dinner; I was just determined it was not going to be the Ponderosa coffee shop.

I was almost to the front doors when I heard my name being paged to the phone. I picked up a house phone and a voice said: "Asch? This is Leland Carew. What are you doing?"

"I was just leaving to get some dinner. Got any suggestions where I should go?"

"You want to take a ride?"

"Where?"

"The Wishone Lake Indian Reservation. It's about twenty miles northeast of here."

"At least I won't need to make a reservation there," I quipped. It may not have been good, but at least it was fast. "What's there?"

"Maybe Evelyn Bestar."

It took a second for the name to click. "Pebbles?"

"Yeah."

"What's she doing there?"

"If she's in her car, not much. They're trying to pull it out of the Truckee River right now."

"I'll be waiting outside," I said.

It took him four and a half minutes to get there. Zwerdling was driving the green Dodge Charger and Carew was sitting shotgun in the front. Zwerdling gave me a taciturn grunt when I said hello and climbed in back. He didn't seem to care much for my new position of favor. I reminded myself to lose some sleep over that tonight.

"So what's it all about?" I asked Carew as we pulled away.

"All I know is a car identified as Evelyn Bestar's is sitting in the Truckee River. It was spotted about forty minutes ago by a passing motorist. I don't know how long it's been there or how it got there."

I took that as a tacit request not to ask him any more questions about it, so I shut up and sat back to enjoy the ride.

Zwerdling and Mezzano had one thing in common: they drove the same. He cut a pattern through traffic like scissors through cloth, all the way to the freeway, missing cars' bumpers by inches, keeping his foot to the floor the whole time. A couple of minutes out of town, I looked over the seat at the speedometer. It said 85. There were undeniable advantages to being a cop.

Carew broke the silence by turning sideways and draping an arm across the back of the seat. "I hear you were at the bail hearing this morning."

"You have good spies."

"You left with Mezzano."

We stared at each other. "He had a few things he wanted to talk over with me."

"Such as?"

"He wanted to assure me of his innocence," I said. "Then he wanted to offer me a nice chunk of change to get out of town."

"Strange behavior for an innocent man," he mused.

"That's what I told him."

"Did you take him up on his offer?"

"I'm still in town."

He nodded casually. "You know he put up the bail."

I came forward in my seat. "When?"

"This afternoon. A few hours ago. He sent a bondsman named Abe Friedlander down to Silverville with a check for $200,000. He put his restaurant up as security for the bond."

Reno was just a thin layer of foamy light behind us now. The night had turned black and sullen, the moon an uncertain glow above the blanket of clouds that covered the sky.

"Bail or no bail," Carew said, "this time it looks like Mister Mezzano has bitten off more than he can chew. He's stirred up a lot of attention with this one. And none of his political friends will be able to help him bury it."

"What's up?"

He smiled slyly. "This afternoon, while Mezzano was sending Friedlander down to Silverville, his bodyguard, Joe Battaglia, was handed a subpoena at his home in Sparks to appear before the federal grand jury."

"What for?"

"Nobody knows. The Feds aren't saying. It could be the IRS. It could be about a possible violation of federal gun laws. Mezzano had some nice artillery out there, a couple of submachine guns and the whole bit. And half his so-called security force handling them was ex-cons. He fired most of them real quick after the shooting, but they might want to talk to Battaglia about it. One thing is for sure, though—it's coming out of the shooting. And it may be just the thing that'll send Mr. Mezzano up for a few years, no matter how Merritt's trial comes out."

"Income tax evasion?"

He nodded. "Those broads out there all drive their new sports cars and they have closets stuffed with expensive clothes and fifty-dollar bottles of perfume sitting on their dressers and most of them have a trail of bad paper behind them a blind man could follow in the dark. Bad checks and unpaid phone bills and leases they've skipped on made out to twenty phony names. You start rattling their chains about all that and talk about things like interstate flight and federal prison and their knees would get all shaky and they'd drop their loads in those perfumed silk panties. And once they lose control, let me tell you, some of those girls make the best witnesses on the stand a prosecutor could hope for. They seem to have a great memory for detail, like how much they took in on a certain day and how much Mezzano told the government

163

they took in for that same day. They round up a few of those good, fun-loving gals and Mezzano is as good as gone."

He paused and looked out the window at the black landscape. His face hung in the glass, pale and unsubstantial, reflected by the lights of the dashboard. "We've filled in Realango's missing hours the night he was killed."

"Where was he?"

"With a whore," he said, as if it was to have been expected. "Elena Montoya, a.k.a. Spanish Rose. She works at Moonfire, but she's been off for the last couple of weeks. She has an apartment on Sutter Street in Reno. She says Realango came over that night about five-thirty. They fucked and then went to watch the kids playing in the park for awhile. I guess Realango was a sucker for children. Then they went out to dinner at Emilio's downtown and had some drinks and he drove her home around two."

"Which puts him at the King's Inn."

He nodded.

"How'd you stumble onto her?"

"A waiter I know at Emilio's called me. He'd seen her before."

"Why didn't she come to you?"

He shrugged. "Said she didn't want to get involved. She saw what the papers did to Candy. She was afraid Sal would fire her."

"What kind of a mood did she say Realango was in when he left her?"

"Good. Very relaxed. She said he was joking and laughing the whole time."

"That tallies with what the people at the King's Inn told me."

"Yeah. And she'd be the one to know his moods if anybody would. She was around him a lot. She says when Realango and Susan Mezzano went out, a lot of times they took her along, to act as an interpreter." He added as an afterthought: "She's Puerto Rican."

We glided through the black landscape. At a small town called Wilson, we turned and headed north up a narrow two-lane highway that wound through a rugged mountain range. Scrub pine wheeled away from the sides of the car like bicycle spokes. On my side of the car, the dirt shoulder of the highway ran to a sharp edge and then dropped a hundred feet or so into a steep-sided ravine. The river was black except for occasional spots where it beat itself into a white froth. I put my hand against the window of the car. It felt like ice. The thought of anyone being down there in that water, alive or dead, made me shudder.

We came around a bend in the road and ahead were the flares strewn along the road. We slowed down and stopped behind a pickup truck that stood empty in our lane and a state highway patrolman came over to the car and bent down. His breath was pink vapor in the flare-light. "You'll be here a few minutes, gentlemen—"

Zwerdling cut his speech short by whipping out his badge. "Washoe County District Attorney."

The patrolman straightened up. "Oh. Sure."

We stepped out of the car. "Have they gotten the body out yet?"

"The doors are too jammed up," the patrolman said. "It took an awful pounding on the way down. We'll probably have to torch it out when we get the car up top."

Up the hill in front of the pickup was a line of cars, and twenty feet beyond the line was a collection of black and whites, several unmarked but obviously county cars, and an ambulance, clogging the highway at all angles. Backed up to the snowy shoulder of the road were two heavy tow trucks with EDDIE'S GARAGE painted on their sides. Their winches jutted over the embankment and white fingers of light from their zinc spotlights probed the river below.

As we trudged up the hill toward the tow trucks, we were met by a not-quite middle-aged man who had one of those clean-cut, characterless faces they seem to stamp out with cookie-cutters in military academies. He had on a long, pale trenchcoat that went to the knees and although I couldn't see what he was wearing beneath it, I would have been willing to bet he was dressed like

165

a salesman for Xerox. Plain gray suit, narrow lapels, starched white shirt, narrow tie, gray, carefully knotted. "Hello, Lee," he said.

"Hello, Jeff," Carew returned.

"Jeff Bick, Jake Asch. Asch is an investigator working on the Realango thing. Jeff is our local FBI agent." Bick and I shook hands.

"Since we're on a reservation," Carew went on, "I guess this makes it your baby."

"If it's anything more than an accident."

"Any reason to believe it is?"

The smooth planes of the FBI man's face were broken by a faint smile that conveyed nothing more than politeness. "Not yet."

Carew nodded, then said to me: "Asch, why don't you go take a look, see what's happening?"

I took the hint and trudged up the hill, while Carew took Bick's elbow confidentially and walked a few steps off. "What's going on with this federal grand jury . . ." I could hear him say before his words were drowned out by the squawk boxes of the police cars.

A bitter-cold wind blew down the canyon and I pulled my coat up around my throat. I walked up to the edge of the ravine and stood beside two long-haired Indians in flimsy windbreakers who were silently watching the salvage operation. They turned and gave me that discomfiting stare only Indians can give, the same intense, unreadable stare a cat gives you when you don't know whether it wants to be petted or whether it's about to take your ear off or it thinks you've just totally lost your mind. It had probably taken them two hundred years of dealing with the white man to perfect that stare and being a white man it made me feel damned uncomfortable. I was about to move off, but as if sensing this, they suddenly turned away from me and resumed watching the tow trucks work.

Forty feet below, the truck spotlights were focused on the silver body of the Cougar. The white water of the river boiled and

166

churned as it parted and flowed around the car, as if angered by this unexpected intrusion into its privacy. Two men in waders stumbled around the car, slipping on rocks and swearing, trying to adjust the hooks of the steel cables that ran up to the truck winches.

One of them straightened up and cupped his hands over his mouth. "Okay! Try her now!"

Two men in down jackets who were standing by the backs of the trucks, waved and got into the truck cabs. The steel cables groaned as the winches started up. The Cougar didn't budge and for a moment I thought the taut cables were going to snap, but then the nose of the car turned slowly upward, like an animal testing the air for danger, and the battered wreck began to inch its way up the boulder-strewn side of the ravine.

I noticed Carew and Bick were up by the trucks now, talking to a tall Highway Patrol sergeant. Since Zwerdling was there, too, I figured it would be all right to join them, so I left my Indian companions and went over.

"So what does it look like?" Bick was asking the sergeant as I came up.

The sergeant pointed to two parallel skid marks on the asphalt and a gaping hole in the snowbank where the car apparently went through. "She must have been coming around the turn and hit some ice. There's a patch of black ice back there. You can't hardly see that stuff in the daytime, never mind at night. From the way the car skidded, it looks like she hit her brakes, but brakes won't help you on that shit."

Bick nodded and a shout went up from the edge: "Here she comes!"

The front end of the Cougar poked up over the edge of the road and the two trucks gunned their motors and pulled forward. The car came over the top of the shallow snowbank and slammed down on the highway.

It looked as if it had rolled quite a few times on the way down. Both sides, the grille, and the front part of the roof were completely caved in. We all moved forward, crowding around the car.

Pebbles stared dully at us through the shattered front windshield. The steering wheel had crushed her chest and pinned her against the bucket seat. Her black hair hung down in limp, wet strands, forming a somehow appropriate funereal frame for her face, which was a bloodless blue-white color. Her forehead and cheeks were covered with lacerations but the freezing water had washed them all clean of blood and now they were just a network of open, black cuts. A garment bag lay across the back seat, and the contents of a broken cosmetic case were strewn about the floor and the front seats.

The two drivers from Eddie's Garage moved around the car, trying the doors. One of them shook his head and said to nobody: "We'll have to torch 'em."

The Highway Patrol sergeant told him to go ahead, then turned to one of the ambulance attendants who was peering intently through the side window. "What about it?"

The attendant shrugged. "You don't have to rush to get her out of there, if that's what you mean."

A short, graying man with a soft, pale face muscled his way past the attendant and said gruffly: "That body has been chilled. That means rigor will begin developing pretty goddamn fast which means you'd better get her out of there before it gets too far along, otherwise you'll have to cut half the car away to get her out at all."

The young attendant shrugged and slouched off under the man's dark scowl. "Hello, George," Carew said. "I see you finally made it."

George transferred his scowl to Carew. "Hell, I was right in the middle of dinner when they called me." He bent down and looked through the glass. He stayed that way for a good ten seconds, then straightened up, grimacing and holding his back. He shoved his hands deep into the pockets of his tweed overcoat and said: "They sure pick some places to die, don't they? It's colder than a well-digger's wallet out here."

"What do you think?" Bick asked, brushing aside the man's comment on the weather.

George made a clicking sound with his tongue and shook his head. "The river is going to make it awful tough. It's going to be a bitch trying to pin down a precise time of death, unless we can find out when she ate last. Her body temperature must have dropped like a rock in that water. When was the car spotted?"

"About an hour ago," the highway patrol sergeant offered.

George rubbed his chin. "That puts it before six-thirty."

"I can pin it down a little for you," Carew chimed in. "She was seen alive at two-oh-five. If she drove directly here from there—which she probably didn't—it would have taken her at least twenty minutes. That means the earliest she could have gone over is two-thirty."

George nodded silently.

"When do you think you'll be able to get me a preliminary report?"

The man shrugged. "Depends on who else is scheduled for the morning. I know there's at least one. A hit-and-run—"

"I want this one first," Carew said.

"What's the rush?"

"I just want this one first," Carew said, as if that closed the matter.

George gave him a hard look. "I don't set up the schedules, Lee. You want this stiff given priority, you pass it on to Nevens. I'm sure you've got a lot more influence than I do." With that, he moved around to the other side of the car where one of the truck drivers was setting up an acetylene torch. Carew muttered something inaudible under his breath as he watched the coroner's man walk away.

The other driver came over to us and asked: "Where do you want us to take it?"

"Justin Brothers in Reno," Carew said. Then turning quickly to Bick, he said in a falsely deferential voice: "Is that all right with you?"

Bick shrugged.

"That's twenty miles towing," the driver said. "It's gonna cost—"

Carew dismissed him with a wave of his hand. "The County

will pick up the tab, don't worry about it."

The other driver had his goggles on and was working on the door now with the torch. We watched the shower of orange sparks and molten metal rain down on the pavement and then they got the door open and lifted the body carefully out of the car and laid it down on the concrete. George bent down and felt here and there on the blue-white thing that had once been Pebbles.

He stood up and shook his head. "Looks like massive injuries. There's no way to tell anything here."

The Highway Patrol sergeant tried the trunk with the key from the ignition. There were two good-sized suitcases inside. The men lifted them out and the sergeant opened them while Carew watched eagerly. "Just clothes," the sergeant said, looking up. "Looks like she was going on a trip."

"She went on one," Carew mused. "The biggest one she could take."

After ten minutes more of standing around, hugging ourselves, Carew said: "Come on. There's no use freezing our asses off. There's nothing we can do here."

The two Indians had moved up next to Zwerdling and were looking at the corpse with the exact same expression they had looked at me. Carew signaled to Zwerdling and he followed us down to the car.

As we drove back down the highway, I asked: "Did Bick tell you what the federal grand jury business is all about?"

"He claims he doesn't know any more than I do," Carew said. "He's a liar."

After another half a minute, I said: "Where was Pebbles seen at two-oh-five?"

He thought about that one before answering. "Moonfire," he said slowly.

I felt a sudden surge of resentment toward him, as if he had been conning me. He had known that all along, but hadn't mentioned it. And if I hadn't asked him, he probably never would have mentioned it. When I thought about it, of course, I had no right to feel resentful at all. He was not obligated to tell me a damned thing, which set me to wondering why he did. It was certainly not because he had taken a sudden liking to me. He was playing some sort of a game here, but what his motives or the rules were, I had no idea. "What was she doing out there?"

"I'd love to know. All I know is that an hour after she left Moonfire, Sal Mezzano sent his bail bondsman out to Silverville with two hundred grand. It could be just a coincidence, but I don't believe much in coincidences. I have what you might call an organic view of the universe. I believe everything's connected in some way."

"If Mezzano paid Merritt for the hit, she could have known about it," I offered. "She could have gone out there to do a little arm-twisting to make sure her boyfriend got out of the slams."

"Maybe," he said, and turned to stare out the window. "I'd sure like to mention that little possibility to Merritt, and see what he'd say. It might get an interesting reaction."

I could feel the tenseness in his body as he gazed out the window at the night. After awhile, I said: "You really want his head, don't you?"

He turned slowly toward me. "Yeah," he said quietly. "I do."

"Why? Because you think he's guilty or because you want to hang it on your office wall with your plaques so you can pose in front of it for all the papers and maybe make the Senate?"

I don't really know why I said it. I was not trying to bait him. He smiled strangely. "You think my motives are really any of your business?"

"Probably not."

"Then why ask?"

"Just curious, I guess."

He nodded. "Well, since you're just curious, maybe there's a little of both mixed in with why I want Sal Mezzano. I'd be a fool to try to deny it. It's no secret I want to get into politics. It's also no secret that Sal Mezzano is in my way. But I wouldn't railroad him to get where I want to go." He paused and studied my face. He said with a mock sadness: "You don't approve."

171

"I don't judge people," I said. "I gave that up a long time ago."

"But you do, mister," he said in a cutting voice. "Your judgment was implicit in your question."

I shook my head. "I just think you have to be careful when you're dealing with ambitions like that, that's all. It's too easy to make yourself believe something when it's convenient."

"What about you, Asch?" he asked tartly. "What are you after from life if not pursuing the follies of fame and power and wealth like the rest of us mere mortals?"

"I don't know," I said, ignoring his sarcasm. "I wish I did. It changes on me from day to day. One day I think one thing is important, the next day, it fades out."

"There's got to be some constant in your life, some driving force."

"I guess I'm trying to absorb experience. Most people I know don't have the capacity to do even that. Life never touches them. It's like they're standing in the middle of a river in a rubber suit and the water's rushing by them but they never get wet. I don't know, I guess I'm just trying to get wet."

"Well, you see, my friend," he said, "everything is relative. If Pebbles was alive, she'd probably wished one of those people would have loaned her his rubber suit."

I could see he was not going to let the conversation go anywhere, so I picked up his thread. "I've been wondering about Pebbles. Her bags were packed and in the car, right? She was obviously going somewhere."

"Yeah?"

"So what's at the end of this road?"

"You saw those two Indians standing by Zwerdling?"

"Yeah? So?"

"About two hundred more just like them."

"That's it?"

"That's it."

"Then what the hell was she doing up here?"

He hesitated a beat. "There's only one reason I can think of."

172

"What's that?"

"The same reason this whole thing is going to be a pain in the ass," he said, turning to look at the passing night. "The river. The dirty whore-bitch of a river."

18

I could hear the music all the way up the street, the wavering hillbilly voice and the plaintive, whiny wail of a steel guitar. I looked at my watch. 10:15.

A brown Ford Bronco was parked in back of the saloon and I parked next to it and got out. I had started for the back door when I was stopped by the sweet smell of something burning. I turned away from the building, sniffing the air, trying to pin-point the source of the smell. I spotted it about thirty feet from the car, a large black mound against the white snow.

It was still smoking and I bent down and began to pick at the smoldering pile with a stick I found on the ground. The ashes separated into big chunks and my eye was caught by something white among the black mass. I hooked it with the stick and pulled it out.

It was a singed piece of cotton cloth, about two inches by four. Four of the letters had not been damaged by the flames.

ZAN
R

I put it in my pocket and went back to the door. The steel guitar was still wailing inside. I knocked. Nothing. I listened to the song. The man was accusing his girl friend of "frying her bacon in another man's pan." I pushed on the door. It gave with a loud creak and I was assaulted by the deafening volume of the music.

I stepped into what seemed to be a long, narrow kitchen. The moonlight fell in a pale blue shaft through the window and made a square patch on a greasy drainboard. There was no other light in the room.

"Merritt?!" I shouted. No answer came back.

I broke the patch of moonlight and felt my way along the wall to a door. The door led into the main barroom. It was dark in there, too. Several slot machines stood in a row against the back wall, staring at me with fluorescent lemon and cherry eyes. The only light in the room was the faint glow from the rainbow-front of the jukebox in the corner from where the music blared.

I stepped forward and stumbled against the back of a chair.

"Merritt?" I shouted again, as much to alleviate the case of nerves I was working up as to get a response. It was somehow comforting to hear my own voice. Assaulted by the music and the darkness, I felt insubstantial, like some wayward spirit trying to make contact with someone from the physical world.

After a few seconds, my eyes began to adjust and carve dim shapes out of the dark, a bar, tables, chairs. A bulky figure, outlined by the glow from the jukebox, occupied one of the chairs in the middle of the room. I went toward it.

Merritt was sprawled in the chair, perfectly still. His chin rested on his chest, and his hands dangled loosely by his sides. On the floor beside the right one was an empty bottle of something. I couldn't tell what in the dark.

The steel guitar died away and a silence almost as loud as the music flooded the room. I took the opportunity to make myself heard. "Merritt?"

The hulk stirred. The head rolled ponderously off the chest. His face was black, featureless, his disheveled hair backlit by the jukebox. "Get the fuck out of here," he said slowly, in a slurred Texas accent. His tone was flat and unemotional, but there was a rage behind it as real as a brick wall.

I took another step forward. "My name is Asch, Merritt, I'm a private detective. I want to talk to you."

He didn't say anything. The dark face just watched me.

"How'd you hear so fast? One of Dierdorf's men call you?"

"I told you to get the fuck out of here."

I began to wonder what I was doing out here. Stone-sober, the man was mean and volatile, but in a highly emotional condition and drunk, he would be totally unpredictable. But I also knew that if he was ever going to let anything out, it would have to explode out, like lava from an erupting volcano. "I was there at the river, Merritt. She didn't die easy. And all because you told her about the deal. She knew about the five grand, didn't she?"

"What five grand?" His voice was fuzzy.

The record finder on the jukebox clicked and moved back and forth, hunting its prearranged selection. The forty-five slid into place and the song blasted from the speaker, something about suicide and a lost love.

"The five grand it took you to buy this place!" I shouted over the music. "The five grand she told me you made by selling SAL MEZZANO FOR PRESIDENT T-shirts! The five grand you were paid to kill Realango!"

"Nobody paid me to kill nobody," he growled.

"No? Then where'd you get the money?" You sure as hell didn't get it from selling these?"

I took the piece of singed cloth from my pocket and dangled it in front of his face. "Burning clothes seems to be a favorite pastime of yours."

He lurched forward in his chair and made a clumsy swipe at it, but his reflexes were glacier-slow.

"Give me that," he said, his voice full of menace.

I ignored the command and slipped the piece of T-shirt back into my pocket. "It was stupid to burn those shirts out back. Real stupid. But then they told me you weren't too bright."

He didn't say anything. I decided to apply more kindling to the fire. "What if I told you your girl friend was murdered?"

His body stiffened. "What the fuck are you talking about?"

I could make out his eyes now. The right one was staring directly at my face, but the left was aimed somewhere over my right shoulder. At least that's where I thought it was aimed. All I could see of it was white. If he had been in the British Army, the Americans on Bunker Hill would have had to reload three

176

times. "Somebody wanted her dead, Merritt. Otherwise why would she go up to that Indian reservation? There's nothing up there, nothing but a nice fall into the Truckee River. Who'd want her dead, Merritt? The person who knew she knew, the person who paid you off."

"Nobody paid me off."

"About three hours before she died, just before Sal sent his bondsman down to bail you out of jail, Pebbles was out at Moonfire."

He remained motionless.

"You know, she was pretty uptight when I talked to her a few days ago. She was talking about splitting—"

"She wouldn't split on me," he cut in angrily.

"—She said the pressure was getting to her. She couldn't understand how sweet, mellow you could blow somebody's heart up like that, in cold blood—"

"She wouldn't leave me," he said, almost as if he were in a trance.

"Her bags were in the car, Merritt. Two suitcases in the back seat. Her clothes were in them."

He stared at me, his eyes glowing like an animal's in the dark.

"She'd need money," I went on. "Where would she be likely to go for it? Who'd give a whore money? It wouldn't be the kind of move you would call a good financial risk. How about a man who could get sent up for first-degree murder if it came out that he'd ordered a hit on Realango? How about good old Sal Mezzano?"

He put the palms of his hands heavily on the table and pushed himself up slowly. The chair made a sickening scraping noise against the wooden floor.

I was immediately sorry I'd decided to test out my volcano-theory on him. He must have stood six-four and weighed in around two-forty. He rocked unsteadily back on his heels and started around the table, cracking his knuckles as if I were a chore he had to do before breakfast.

All sorts of winged things were fluttering around in my stomach and my legs were shaking from the adrenalin that was being pumped into my bloodstream. My body was preparing itself for fight or flight and since I didn't think it could ever adequately prepare itself to do battle with this walleyed monster, I chose flight. I held up my hands and began to back up. "Hold on, Merritt, I don't want to fight—"

I thought I'd been backing toward the door, but I must have become disoriented in the dark because when I glanced over my shoulder, I found the bar behind me. He came at me slowly, smiling, the whiteness of that walleye making him look somehow inhuman. I tried to change direction, but he sidestepped and cut off my path to the door.

"You shoulda left when I told you to," he said. "That way you coulda left in one piece instead of a bunch of little ones."

I figured I was giving away a good four inches in height and sixty pounds in weight. My only hope was that he had drunk enough to seriously impair his timing and coordination, but there wasn't much to that. Most of his famous brawling had been done in his present condition, or close to it.

He threw a wild right that I stepped easily away from, but then charged forward and came across with a left that caught me on the side of the neck. I staggered backward, hitting the bar. He lunged at me and grabbed my coat and I slapped both his ears with my open hands. He yelled and grabbed his ears and I hit him with a right hand flush in the mouth. There was a loud crack and pain instantly shot up to my elbow and I knew I'd broken my hand.

He grabbed my coat again and I slapped his ears again and he yelled and grabbed them again and I hit him in the mouth again, this time with a left. That one didn't break my hand, but it didn't do much to him, either, except take him backward a foot or so. I took the opportunity to slide along the bar and get back out into the open, nearly tripping over a couple of chairs in the process.

The man on the jukebox was still singing about death. I hoped he wasn't clairvoyant. I would have made a run for the door, but I would have had to go through him to get to it and besides, I knew I couldn't make it to my car without him catching up to me. He came at me in a crouch, his fists dangling like wrecking balls at his sides. I kept backing up until I was stopped by something solid. A pool table. I slid around it, figuring I could keep circling until I could make a break for the door. Then I bumped into the rack of cues.

He came around the table fast and I plucked one of the cues from the rack and hit him with the heavy end as he made the corner. The cue splintered and snapped in two and blood spurted like a geyser from the cut that opened above his eyes. He reeled back, holding his eyes and bellowing like an enraged water buffalo.

I dropped the piece of the stick I was still holding and ran for the door. As I went through the kitchen, I could hear him crashing over tables, swearing like a madman over the twang of guitars.

I dashed for my car, opened the door, and started up the engine. I'd slammed it into reverse and my tires were spinning on the snow, trying to find traction, when he came careening out of the back door, still hurling curses. I could tell by the way he was moving that the blood from the cut was half-blinding him. He tried for the car door, but I punched it and fish-tailed out onto the highway before he could get a grip on the handle.

As I looked in my rear view mirror, I could see him standing in the middle of the highway, shaking his fists at me and screaming obscenities. At least I assumed they were obscenities. For all I could hear, he might have been singing along with the music.

19

A message was waiting for me when I got back to the Ponderosa that Susan Mezzano had called and wanted me to call her back whenever I got in.

I got a plastic container of ice from the coffee shop and went up to my room. I made an icy compress out of a hand towel and wrapped my throbbing hand with it. It was painful, but not as bad as I'd first thought. The third knuckle joint was swollen and discolored, probably fractured, but the others seemed all right.

Susan Mezzano's voice sounded drained when she picked up the phone. Before I could get anything out, she asked me if I could come over to her place right away. When I asked her if there was anything wrong, she hesitated, but then said, no, nothing, just come over. I told her I'd be there in twenty minutes.

Sal Mezzano's Eldorado was parked in front of the house, which was ablaze with lights. I parked behind it and was greeted by the customary chorus of Sonny and Cher doing their imitation of Sonny and Cher. They stopped barking when I opened the gates and came up to me with their tails wagging.

Sal Mezzano answered the door. He was dressed in a maroon velvet sports suit and a yellow shirt, open at the collar. He had a drink in his hand and a cigar—lit this time—crammed into his pouchy cheek. He smiled and said: "Hiya doin', sport. Come on in."

I stepped inside and he waved the drink at the towel on my hand. "What's with the hand?"

"I got fresh with a girl," I said. "She slammed her legs shut on me."

"Too bad," he said as if he didn't really think it was. "Come on in and have a drink."

Susan Mezzano looked as if she had aged ten years. She was slumped in a chair by the fireplace, dressed in a quilted bathrobe and slippers, her legs splayed in an attitude of complete exhaustion. Maybe it was just the way she was sitting, but her head seemed to be collapsing into her shoulders and her body looked shriveled, as if it had shrunken under the pressing weight of weariness and sorrow. She looked up at me as I came in and managed a weak, "Hello." Her eyes, normally her most expressive feature, were dead, hollow, with no light in them at all.

"What'll you drink?" Sal Mezzano asked heartily.

"Nothing."

"Sure, come on," he said. "What'll it be?"

"Bourbon on the rocks," I said, just to get rid of him.

I sat down across from her on the couch while he went to fix my drink. "You want to talk to me alone?"

She shook her head slowly, then closed her eyes. "No. It's all right. Sal and I talked it over. We made the decision together."

"What decision?"

Sal came back over with my drink. He handed it to me, then took a folded check out of his pocket. "This decision."

The check was made out to me, in the amount of $750.

"What's this?"

"Severance pay," he said. "You're finished, Asch. That squares what Susan owes you."

I looked sharply at her, but she refused to meet my stare. "I've had it, Jake," she said quietly. "I'm through with it."

In contrast to her, Sal Mezzano's face was animated with energy. As he watched her, his eyes burned with a dark intensity I'd never seen in them before, almost as if he were feeding off her very life-source, draining her vital energies like some psychic vampire.

"What brought all this on?" I asked her.

She sighed and looked up. "I'm old and I'm tired, that's what

181

brought it on. More tired than I've ever been in my life." She looked into the fire and her pale face absorbed the shadows it made.

"I still don't understand."

"That's because you're young," she said. "When you're young, you can make yourself believe in dreams. If you're any good, you might even make one or two of them come true. Maybe in the back of your mind you know that none of it is going to mean a goddamn thing, in the end, but you pretend that it will and you do it. You do it because it's the will to fight that gives it meaning. The will is everything. When the will to fight dies, the dream dies. I don't have the will anymore, Jake. I'm old and I'm tired and I just don't give a goddamn anymore."

"You weren't talking like this a few days ago."

She made a defeated gesture with her hands. "I don't know who I thought I was a few days ago. I know who I am now. I'm a crippled old broad who happens to be very good at running whorehouses. So that's what I'm going to do. I'm going back to Moonfire."

She stared back at the fire. The flames made her face a yellow mask. "Sal and I talked. He swears he didn't have anything to do with it."

"And you believe him?"

She thought about that for awhile. "It doesn't matter whether I do or not. But, yes, I do."

"When are you going back?"

"Tomorrow. In the morning."

Sal Mezzano had been standing the whole time. He sat down in a chair and crossed his legs. He took the cigar out of his mouth and held it with his drink hand. "I'm going away for a couple of weeks. Frisco or someplace. I haven't decided yet. I need a vacation. I've been working too hard lately. Susan's going to take over and run things while I'm gone, just like it used to be."

"Just like it used to be," I said.

He smiled. "That's right."

182

"What about Pebbles? She'll never be like she used to be."

The smile left his lips. "What's she got to do with anything?"

"Why don't you tell me? A couple of hours before she went into the Truckee River, she was out at Moonfire."

"So?"

"Did you talk to her?"

"Yeah, I talked to her."

"About what?"

"She asked me to make a call to Carson City to a house over there to see if they had any openings. She said she couldn't stand the pressure anymore with Gene still in jail and everything. She said her head was all screwed up and the only therapy that did her any good when she got like that was to run away to a whorehouse."

That explained the bags.

"Didn't you tell her Merritt was being bailed out today?"

"Sure I told her. She just said she couldn't take it anymore and she had to get out of town. I told her she could go back to work for me, but she said she had to get away from everything and everybody."

"The Indian Reservation is north," I reminded him. "Carson City is south."

He waved a hand at me belligerently. "Whaddya want me to do about it? I didn't tell her where to drive."

"If you wanted to kill somebody and make it look like an accident, that highway would be a nice place to do it. Very little traffic—"

He pushed his jaw out. "Why would anybody want to kill Pebbles?"

"Pebbles told me Merritt got the down payment for Ma and Pa's by selling SAL MEZZANO FOR PRESIDENT T-shirts." I took the piece of T-shirt from my pocket and handed it to Susan Mezzano. "I was just out at Merritt's saloon in Duncan. This was in a pile of ashes by his back door. He must have gotten out of jail and gone straight to the saloon and set fire to them. That sort of shoots the T-shirt story in the ass. If Pebbles knew Merritt didn't get the five grand from selling T-shirts, she probably knew where he did get it from."

Susan slowly pushed herself out of her chair and took the piece of cloth out of my hand. Thoughts moved across her face as she fingered it, then she shook her head sadly and tossed it into the fire. "Forget it. I'm through with it."

That was my last shot, there was nothing else I could say. By the finality of that act, she had closed the door. In a symbolic way, it was a fitting end. In a way, the case had started by a fire and now it was ending with one. I watched the cloth singe and curl in the flames and Sal Mezzano said: "I told you you'd lose."

The smugness in the voice filled me with hot anger. He was staring at me with a triumphant smile on his lips. "You should've taken the money I offered. You were a sucker, Asch. I told you it would turn out this way."

I stood up and shrugged nonchalantly. Nonchalant was not what I was feeling. I was feeling like taking that cigar and ramming it down his throat. "What I've done, I've gotten paid for, Mezzano. If you hire a plumber to fix a sink and tell him to forget it before he's through, what does he care if the shit backs up later over your bathroom floor, as long as he gets paid for his time? I'm a paid laborer, just like that plumber. Goodbye, Mrs. Mezzano."

"Goodbye."

I turned on my heel and went out. I drove back to the hotel and packed, then called the airport and found out there was a flight to L.A. at seven in the morning. I made a reservation on it and went downstairs.

There were a few couples in the bar. I didn't feel like sitting at the bar, so I took a small table in the back and ordered a double bourbon on the rocks. After that I ordered another one. The drinks didn't calm me down, they just seemed to distort my rage. The tinkling of the glasses, the characterless music of the man at the piano bar, the tapestry of muted conversations, all pressed upon me like a suffocating blanket. I started to feel something rising and spilling over inside me, a seething, boiling urge to pick

184

up the table and heave it over, to give myself over completely to emotion, to make a break with the confining strictures of reason and conventionality for just that split-second. But I held back, knowing that once the thread was broken, it couldn't be regained, at least with whoever was in that bar. Those people would never trust me again as they had, and although I didn't know why that seemed important, it did, so I paid my check and left.

I went out to the casino and sat at a blackjack table. I was not a gambler, I never had been, but I felt confident enough about the simplicity of that game to play it. It cost me a half an hour and three hundred dollars to figure out that I was *trying* to lose the seven-fifty Mezzano had given me.

I had cooled off some by that time and I found my emotionality being tempered by thoughts of poverty. I cashed in and went upstairs and took a hot shower. I called room service and asked them to bring up a bottle of Wild Turkey, then lay down on the bed and stared at the ceiling. I kept reciting what I'd told Mezzano, about the plumber, over and over in my mind, but I still couldn't get rid of the nagging feeling that I'd been cheated. To hell with them, I thought. To hell with them all. I was going to be glad to get out of Reno. Let them all drown in their own excrement—him, her, Carew, Merritt, all of them.

It took forty minutes for the Wild Turkey to arrive. Then all I had to wait for was morning.

20

It was nine days later when the call came through to my apartment, waking me out of a sound Sunday morning slumber. The face on the digital clock on the nightstand said 6:32. I reached over the tangled mass of red hair on the pillow beside me and snatched up the receiver.

"Yeah?"

"Asch?"

The voice sounded vaguely familiar. Someone out of my dark past. All I needed was Ralph Edwards and I'd have it. Since he wasn't immediately available, I said: "Who's this?"

"Sal Mezzano."

It took me a full five seconds for that one to penetrate my sleep-fogged brain. "You know what time it is, Mezzano?"

"I wanted to make sure you weren't out."

"As far as you're concerned, I *am* out."

He plowed ahead as if he hadn't heard that. "I want to hire your services, Asch. How soon can you catch a plane up here?"

Liz was stirring now, but only to turn over. She was not your basic light sleeper.

"You hear me, Asch?"

"I hear you."

"Merritt's taken a powder. I want you to find the cocksucker and bring him in."

I was fully awake now. "What do you mean, he's taken a powder?"

"He's gone. Split. Vanished. Disappeared. That so hard to understand?"

"And your bail becomes forfeit if he doesn't come in for trial."

186

"That's right."

The thought of Mezzano getting stuck for $200,000 appealed to me. So did the urgency in his voice. "I'm sorry, but I'm busy—"

"I'll give you ten grand," he said. "For ten grand, you can get unbusy."

"So get your buddy Battaglia. He's a private detective and you've got him on staff—"

"Not any more," he interrupted. "Susan fired him."

"And you let her get away with it?" I asked, somewhat surprised.

"That was part of the agreement we had when she came back," he said in a timid voice. "Besides, Joe's all right if you want somebody's bedroom bugged, but he ain't no bloodhound."

"What makes you think I am?"

"I told you before, I did some checking on you. And I spent half the fucking night doing some more."

I stalled a couple of seconds, thinking it over. "The usual fee for bounty hunting is thirty percent of the total bond, IF the man is brought in, nothing if he isn't. That would come to $60,000 —minus expenses, of course."

"Sixty grand?!" he screamed. "You're out of your fucking mind!"

"Don't pretend to get all excited, Mezzano. You already checked that out, otherwise you wouldn't be calling me. You figured I'd do the job cheaper, that's why you're calling me. Well, you figured right. I'll take your ten grand."

He started to say something, but I cut him off. "Under certain conditions. Your bail doesn't become forfeit for a year. That means I have a year to bring Merritt in. I want half up front— non-refundable—and half if and when I do find him. I want expenses. If I have to hire some people, I want to have the authority to do it. And I'll want all that in writing."

There was a pause. "You don't need it in writing. You got my word."

"I'll still want it in writing."

"You're a prick, you know that, Asch?"

"Yeah," I said. "I know that."

I hung up the phone and sat up. All that had been too much for even Liz to sleep through. She propped herself up on one elbow, rubbed her eyes with two freckled fists and blinked. "What was that all about?"

" 'I Can't Get Over A Girl Like You, So You're Going To Have To Get Up And Answer The Phone Yourself.' Remember that song?"

She yawned and nodded. "Ranks right up there with 'I've Got You, Anthony Quinn.' "

"How about: 'Abbe Lane, Let's Take a Holiday On Abbe Lane.' "

"Let Me Go, Let Me Go, Let Me Go, I'm Your Mother."

"Nothing's So Disturbing As To Wake Up Next To Irving In The Moooorning."

She sat up and her huge breasts rolled over the top of the sheets. The nipples were hard and pointed, but then they usually were. Liz always said she liked to think that her bra kept her tits *down*. "Really, what was that all about?"

"On your way home to feed Derek breakfast, you can drop me at the airport."

She pulled the sheet up to her neck and said: "Why? Where are you going?"

"Reno."

"Again? Why?"

"Ten thousand dollars."

She raised her eyebrows. "That's a pretty good reason, as far as reasons go."

"I have a few others," I said. "But I think you're right. I think that one's about the best one I've got."

188

21

She was standing to one side of the disembarking gates when I came out. It was the dark-haired girl who had been hanging on Mezzano's arm at the bail hearing. She was wearing a short belted brown leather coat this time, and if she had anything on underneath it, I couldn't see it. Neither could any of the twenty other men standing around in her general vicinity, and they were trying.

I stopped in front of her and stared, but she ignored me and kept searching the faces of the passengers filing down the ramp behind me. Finally, her eyes flicked over and she said in an irritated tone: "You want something?"

"No. I think you do. Me. My name is Asch."

"Oh," she said, smiling. "I'm Dawn."

"Glad to meet you, Dawn."

"I got the car outside."

As we walked through the terminal, she said: "Sal asked me if I remembered what you looked like and I said yeah. I guess I was remembering someone else, cause I don't remember you." Her voice was soft and kitteny and had behind it all the intelligence of an after-dinner mint. "I'm lucky you remembered me. You must have a super-good memory."

"I have to in my line of work."

"Really? What do you do?"

"Sal didn't tell you?"

Her black eyes widened and she shook her head. "No."

"I'm a skin diver for Roto-Rooter."

She wrinkled up her nose and fixed me with a puzzled stare. "Why would you have to have a good memory for that?"

"Well, hell," I said, shrugging. "If you can't remember the

189

route, you can wind up in some pretty deep shit."

"Yeah," she said, the light of·understanding dawning in her face. "I guess that's true."

They sure had a lot of bright girls working at Moonfire.

Three hundred and twenty teeth greeted me as I came through the front doors of Moonfire, but that number went down to four when Dawn followed me in.

Afternoon trade looked good. The bar was packed with paunchy, middle-aged men, who were sopping up booze and chatting with the girls. Dawn motioned me through an open doorway on her left that led into the kitchen.

The kitchen was all spotless enamel and tile and stainless steel. Two black women nervously busied themselves over pots on the stove, sprinkling and stirring, trying to ignore the tantrum Susan Mezzano was throwing. The tantrum was being directed at a mousy-haired girl seated at a table in the middle of the room. On the table in front of the girl was a large cashbox and a long white chart. Susan Mezzano slammed a hand down on the chart and said: "I've told that bitch twice now and I'm not going to—oh. Hello, Jake."

She looked as if she were on the road to recovery, or at least started down it. She had dropped more weight and she was leaning heavily on her cane, but her eyes were alive again. "Sorry I couldn't pick you up at the airport myself," she said, "but I've really been strapped here. I had to fire one girl last week and then another bitch quit two days ago, just walked out without giving any notice, and there's a Moose convention in town and we're really short-handed. As a matter of fact, Sal's interviewing a new girl right now. She just drove down from Sacramento."

A slender young girl with a short, boyish haircut came into the kitchen with a twenty and a ten in her hands. "French," she said and handed the mousy-haired girl the bills. She picked up one of the ballpoint pens on the table, glanced at the clock on the wall, logged in 1:43 and $30 on two columns on the chart, and walked back out.

Susan Mezzano pointed to a doorway on the other side of the

kitchen and said: "Sal's expecting you. Second door on the right. Dawn will show you. We'll talk later."

"Are you the reason I'm up here?" I asked. "Did you tell Sal to hire me?"

Her smile turned sly and she winked. "Now you know as well as I do, honey, you don't ever *tell* Sal to do anything. He's his own boss. He decided you were the man to take care of the problem."

I winked back and told her I'd see her later and left the kitchen with Dawn. As we went through the doorway, Mrs. Mezzano resumed her yelling at the girl at the table. "She's been like that ever since she came back," Dawn whispered worriedly.

"Like what?"

"She goes into these rages and yells and everything. She's fired three girls in the past two weeks, and all for little things, like not logging in and out right. Jeez, it's got so none of us knows if we're gonna be next."

I had no idea why the girl chose me upon whom to bestow this confidence. Maybe I had a sympathetic face. Or maybe she thought the "problem" I was here to take care of was the source of Susan Mezzano's irritation and that I was going to get into my little flippers and wet-suit and clear it all up. Whatever her motives, she dropped the matter there and we went down the carpeted hallway in silence.

Alfredo sat in a chair in front of the second door, casually working on his nails with a steel file. He stood up and looked at us darkly.

"Sal in there?" Dawn asked.

He nodded. "Jes. But he with girl."

"It's all right," she said and knocked on the door. "Come in," sounded behind it and she opened the door.

Mezzano was sitting in a high-backed swivel chair behind a large mahogany desk. His head was thrown back, his mouth was open and his eyes were tightly shut. For a moment, he was very, very still, and then a sound came out of his mouth like the expiring breath of a dying man. "AAaaaaaaaaahhhh."

He stayed that way for a long time, not moving, then he opened his eyes and blinked as if he were just becoming aware of his surroundings. He stood up and casually zipped up his fly. "Hello, Asch."

There was a stirring behind the desk and a cute, freckled blond girl who looked as if she could have been the daughter of any of those Middle American Moose conventioners out front, stood up and wiped her mouth with the back of her hand. She looked expectantly at Mezzano and said: "Was that all right, Mr. Mezzano?"

"A little toothy," he said. "Work on that."

Her eyes lit up. "Does that mean I'm hired?"

"Dawn here will give you a room. Dawn, honey, this is Janet. Show her around and get her settled."

The two girls went out and closed the door behind them. "Siddown," Mezzano said.

His office was like his house—plush and tacky. It had yellow walls, an orange carpet, plenty of overstuffed chairs of various colors (all loud) and several of the ubiquitous canvases of the nude female form.

Mezzano opened a humidor on the desk and picked out a cigar, then offered me one. When I declined he lit his and leaned back and exhaled a cloud of blue smoke. He seemed inordinately calm for a man who just had two hundred grand walk away from him. Maybe it was just a temporary tranquilizing effect of the head-job.

He ran the story by me. Merritt had been staying at Moonfire for the past nine days. He had been in a state of depression since Pebbles' death and had been drinking heavily. Some of the girls had tried to snap him out of it to no avail, so everybody had finally decided just to let him alone. Three days ago, he had come to Susan and told her he was going to Duncan to pick up some things and that he would be back later that night. When he didn't return nobody thought much of it, figuring he'd just spent the night there. When he didn't come back the next night, though, Susan sent a maintenance man over to look for him. Merritt wasn't there, neither was his car, neither were his clothes. He'd apparently cleared everything out of his closets and split.

Sal Mezzano had been in San Francisco when all this went down and when Susan called him and told him about it, he took the first flight back and started making calls. The last one he made was to me.

When he finished the story, I asked: "You didn't have anybody watching him?"

He tossed a hand in the air. "Who'd figure he'd jump bail? My fucking attorney told him he was a cinch to get off. It was justifiable homicide, clear as hell." He shook his head sadly. "I still can't believe it. All I done for the prick and he goes and fucks me like this."

"Maybe he got scared you were going to sell him down the river. That stuff in the papers about Candy—"

"I told you that was Frank's fault," he said, scowling. "I don't play things that way. You can ask anybody. Sal Mezzano sticks by his friends."

I shrugged. "Maybe. But I imagine there's a point where a friend can become more of a burden than he's worth."

He glowered at me darkly. "I told you, I don't play things that way."

My neck was stiff from the night before. Liz was a bed-hog and I had awakened during the night to discover I was occupying a one-foot strip on the edge of the bed with my neck dangling over the edge. I rubbed it and said: "Does Merritt have any friends or relatives around here?"

"Not that I know of."

"Where's he from?"

"Waco."

"I'll find out the name of a good agency near there. They'll put a surveillance on Merritt's people there."

He gave me a worried look. "How much is that going to cost?"

"That depends on how long they have to sit there. I can guarantee you one thing: it won't cost two hundred grand."

"Thanks," he said sarcastically.

"Have you talked to Dierdorf about it?"

"Sure."

193

"Does he know I'm coming in on it?"

He took the cigar out of his mouth and spit a piece of tobacco out onto the carpet. "I told him to give you anything you need."

"One thing I'll need is a car—"

"I got half a dozen cars out on the parking lot. You can use any one of 'em."

I took the folded duplicate copies of the contracts I'd drawn up out of my pocket and smoothed them out on the desk. I handed him one. "Oh. I forgot to mention it on the phone, but there's one more condition I have that isn't in the contract. But I won't work unless it's met."

He gave me a sidelong glance. "What condition?"

"I want some questions answered."

"What kind of questions?"

"We might start with where Merritt got the $5,000 to buy Ma and Pa's?"

He grasped the leather arms of the chair with his hairy hands and stared at me. "Fuck off."

I shrugged and picked the contracts off the desk and stood up. "See you," I said and started for the door.

"Wait a minute," he called after me. I turned around. He watched me silently, then shouted: "Alfredo!"

Alfredo came through the door. His lizard-eyes looked questioningly at his master, then at me. Mezzano waved a hand at me and said: "Frisk him."

Alfredo stepped forward and I said: "I don't like being touched."

"I'm not asking you to like it," Mezzano said. "I spent three years in the fucking slammer for getting loose. You get loose and you get ripped off."

I submitted reluctantly to the search and when Alfredo found nothing ominous, Mezzano waved him out. He relit his cigar, which had gone out, and said: "The only reason I'm gonna answer your questions, Asch, is because I've heard from people I trust that you can keep your mouth shut. I want your word that's what you're gonna do. None of what I tell you leaves this room."

194

I nodded. "All right."

"I gave Merritt the five grand," he said. "I felt sorry for the guy." He looked away and shook his head. "When he first came to me with those fucking T-shirts and asked if I'd sell them here, I figured what the hell, and bought a hundred off him. I think we sold four in a week. I still figured what the hell so I'm out a few hundred bucks. But then Merritt comes to me and asks if I want some more, and I have to tell him, 'Sorry Gene, they're not moving.' I get the shock of my life then. The bastard breaks down and cries. I swear to God, like a fucking baby he's crying, about how everything he's ever done has turned to shit on him. That's when he lays it on me that he's got *two thousand* of the fucking things ordered. I felt so bad for the guy, I'd never seen him break down like that, I said, 'Jesus Christ, I'll loan you the five grand already,' and I gave him the bread out of my pocket, right there. I thought he was going to kiss my goddamn foot. He told me he'd give me the T-shirts, maybe I could sell 'em, but I told him I don't want the fucking T-shirts, I want my money back."

"Did you get an I.O.U.?"

"Naw," he said. "I knew he was good for it. I told him he could pay me back whenever he could, not to worry about it. I told him he could pay me back five bucks at a time if he wanted, I didn't care, but I was giving him the money in cash and I wanted it back in cash."

"Why cash?"

He smiled significantly. "I make a lot of loans in cash. I got the IRS looking up my asshole. Cash makes things easier."

"Why did Pebbles tell me Merritt had gotten the money selling T-shirts?"

"Because she thought he had," he said. "When I loaned Merritt the money, I told him it was just between us, that the fewer people who knew about it, the better. So he told her he got the money selling the shirts." He paused, then went on. "That much was fine, cause I knew that if it came out that I gave Merritt the money, it'd look bad for both of us. I could've made out an I.O.U. and backdated it, but even that would've looked bad. By that time

I didn't want nothing to connect me to that five grand."

"How come your wife didn't know anything about it?"

"Why should she? The money came out of my pocket. What was it her business? Besides, by that time, we weren't talking so much. She was running around everywhere with Realango making an ass out of herself."

"What about the T-shirts?"

He held up his hands. "I'm getting to that. When I went to see Merritt in the joint to tell him to keep buttoned-up about the money, he says he's still got the shirts. He says, 'Listen, you take the shirts and make out a slip like you bought 'em.' It takes me twenty minutes to explain to him that the figures for last month are already at the accountant and they don't show no purchase of no T-shirts. I tell him it's better to just get rid of the shirts and say that he sold them to different people, he don't remember who they were. They'd never be able to prove different. I didn't know the asshole would get drunk and burn the fucking things outside his back door."

I sat trying to digest it all. It sounded crazy enough to be true. The best laid plans of mice and men.

"What about the gun in Realango's boot?"

He slapped the top of the desk. "I don't know nothing about the gun," he said emphatically. "I swear to God I don't. I haven't seen it around here in months."

Despite the vehemence of his protest, I was not altogether convinced he was telling the truth. However great his trust in my ability to keep a secret, I doubted he would admit to felonious tampering with evidence in a murder case. I decided to let it go, at least for now. "It's possible Realango took it and kept it hidden," I said. "It wouldn't be altogether out of character for him, from what I've heard. After I left here two weeks ago, I did some checking with some friends of mine in boxing circles. Everything you told me about Realango was true. He wasn't the most popular figure in the sport."

"What did you think, I was lying?"

"I didn't think much of anything at the time." I stared at him

196

levely. "Who made the phone calls to San Diego?"

He cleared his throat. "Merritt."

"On whose orders?"

He waited before answering. "Mine."

"Why?"

"Because I knew what that bastard had in mind, to take over Moonfire. I wanted to let him know he wasn't gonna get away with it."

"What about the phone call to your wife?"

He stirred uncomfortably in his seat. "I don't know," he said in a subdued voice. "I just—it just bugged me, that's all, her falling for that slimy sonofabitch. It was stupid. I would never hurt her." His face flushed as if he were embarrassed by the admission and he looked away. "I have a big ego, Asch. Sometimes *I* can't even control it. But I didn't have Realango hit and I didn't call him at the Ponderosa and that's the honest-to-God truth."

There was something almost boyish in the embarrassment of his confession that compelled belief. For an instant he was almost likeable.

I pointed to the contract. "Read it and sign both copies. You keep one, I'll keep one. By the way, I'll take my five thousand by check, please. No cash."

His coloring returned to normal. He tapped the ash of his cigar into a ceramic ashtray on the desk, then he tilted his chin downward, so that he was looking up at me with his eyes. "One thing, Asch. When I pay a man, he's *my* man. I expect loyalty from him. You get what I mean?"

He said it roughly, trying to regain some of the advantage he felt he'd lost by his confessions. "I'll need somebody to show me which car to take," I said.

He frowned, irritated that I did not answer his question, but he apparently wasn't willing to press the point. "I'll show you myself," he muttered. "Where are your bags?"

"I only have one," I said. "It's in your car."

"You can take one of the back rooms."

"How about the room Merritt and Pebbles slept in the night of the shooting? Is that one empty?"

"Yeah, why?"

"I'll stay there."

"Why?"

"Vibes," I said meaningfully.

"Huh?"

"Vibrations," I explained. "Maybe I'll pick up something."

He squinted in astonishment. "You gotta be kiddin'!"

"Shit, no," I said. "If Peter Hurkos can do it, I can do it." I looked at him seriously. "Don't you know, Mezzano, we *all* have extrasensory powers? They're just latent, that's all."

He didn't know whether I was putting him on or not. He grunted and pushed himself out of his chair.

"This is the first whorehouse I've ever checked into," I said. "You want me to sign the guest register in the kitchen?"

"Anybody who has five grand of my money can consider himself already checked-in."

"What about Merritt?"

He glared at me. "What about him?"

I smiled. "He's got two hundred and five thousand dollars of your money and he checked *out.*"

22

The sky was nearly dark, by the time I pulled up behind Ma and Pa's. I grabbed the flashlight I'd borrowed from Mezzano from the front seat of the Granada and stepped out. I decided to start with the upstairs.

The lock on the door had been broken and it gave when I pushed. I flicked on the lights.

The room looked even shabbier than I remembered it, perhaps because of the absence of Pebbles' perfume collection. The drawers of the bureau were all pulled out and empty. The closet was completely naked, too, except for a dozen or so wire hangers dangling from the metal rod that ran its width. Even the T-shirt Pebbles had picked up from the floor was gone.

The spread was missing from the bed. I looked between the two blankets and under them, but found nothing, and there was nothing under the bed either.

The bathroom had been similarly cleaned out. Not cleaned, but cleaned-out. I don't think it had been cleaned in a year. There was nothing in the medicine cabinet, a few pieces of makeup-smeared Kleenex in the wastebasket. Wherever Merritt had gone, it didn't look as if he planned to come back for awhile. A long while.

I turned off the bathroom light and stepped back into the bedroom. I stared for a few seconds at the bed and something stirred uncomfortably in the back of my mind. I turned off the light and closed the door and went down the shaky staircase.

The kitchen door had been forced open, too, just as Mezzano had assured me. Dierdorf's great work. I stepped inside and felt the wall for the light switch. The switch didn't work. I flicked on the flashlight and let the beam wander around the kitchen, slowly.

Two empty fifth bottles of cheap bourbon stood on the drain-board, along with a clouded glass. A pile of dirty dishes stood in the sink, a few more alongside it. There were some clean plates and pots and pans and other cooking utensils in the cupboards above the ancient gas stove. It would have really bothered me if he'd taken those. I was bothered enough as it was.

I made my way into the saloon. Just inside the doorway, I stopped and listened. The silence that filled the room was thick, heavy. The slot machines in the corner still maintained their marathon vigil, but the jukebox was dark. Unplugged, probably.

I swept the room with the flash. The beam glinted off two more empty fifth bottles standing by the bar, the same brand of cheap bourbon. It looked like Merritt had done some serious drinking before cutting out.

Two pieces of crumpled paper lay on the floor behind the bar. I bent down and uncrumpled them. There were some numbers on them, short columns of figures added up, but nothing that looked as if it would mean anything. I put them in my pocket anyway.

I went across the room and tried the fluorescent fixture sus-pended above the pool table. The tubes flickered weakly, then lit. Balls were scattered randomly across the torn felt. A cue leaned against one side of the table. I looked around for pieces of the cue I'd broken on Merritt's face, but couldn't see any. I was still looking when something moved in the darkness, making my feet freeze and my heart jump. I took a quick sidestep out of the circle of light and at the same time swung the flash toward the direction of the sound. A fat gray rat stood up on its hind legs beneath the slot machines, wriggling its whiskers and blinking into the blind-ing glare. I moved the beam away and released, it scurried off softly.

I stood there, waiting for the pounding of my heart to subside, listening to the darkness. Without the deafening music jamming my hearing, my other senses began to pick up things from the room I hadn't noticed last trip. The damp chill of the place, the stale smells of old wood and dust and smoke and eighty years' accumulated spillings of whiskey and gin and beer. There was another smell there, too, hovering over the others, a heavy, oily smell, like turpentine or paint thinner.

My nose led me away from the bar. I moved the beam of the flashlight slowly over the floor, searching for the source of the smell. I found it in front of the jukebox, a round discoloration in the wood, maybe a foot and a half in diameter. I bent down for a closer look.

It might have been blood, but it would probably be impossible to determine now, even by a lab test. I swung the flashlight up to the wall. Whoever had done the clean-up job had missed a few drops. I couldn't blame them, really. They'd probably been in a hurry. There were four or five small teardrops on the wall behind the jukebox and two more a few yards away, on the floor. Those a lab man would be able to do something with. Maybe not type them, but at least determine whether they'd belonged to a human being or an animal.

I went back through the kitchen and out the back door. Underneath the wooden staircase was a battered trashcan. I poked the flash down into it and began rummaging through the contents. No rags, but the empty two-gallon can of paint thinner was there.

I took a pen out of my pocket and slipped it through the metal handle on the top of the can and pulled it out. I locked it in the trunk of the Granada, then turned the car around and killed the engine and put the headlights on low-beam.

It hadn't snowed in a week, which was in my favor, but the ground was hard from frost. I started away from the car, sweeping the beam of the flashlight over the ground in careful, tight arcs.

About ten yards from the foot of the stairs were several faint sets of tire tracks. It was hard to tell how many sets or even how many different cars they belonged to, as parts of them were superimposed on each other, but one of the sets intrigued me. It ran in an opposite direction from the others, away from the highway, toward a barely discernible trail that headed into the foothills.

My mind chewed that one over and I stood up. As I did, my eye was caught by something on a patch of snow no more than a yard away. The brown filter tip of a cigarette butt. I took a closer look.

It was a common brand. A lot of people smoked them. It could have been flipped there a day or a week or a year ago. Unless that patch of snow was one of the patches that fell a week ago.

I left the cigarette butt there and went back to the Granada. I probably wouldn't have done it if it was my own car, but since I didn't feel like walking and the car belonged to Mezzano, I barely hesitated. I shoved it into low and started up the trail.

It was more of a series of beaten-down bushes than a trail. It was badly rutted and cross-washed and I had to creep along at an agonizingly slow pace, my engine racing as the tires slipped and spun on patches of snow. After a hundred yards or so, the trail turned into a dirt wash that ran between two rocky outcrops. Gradually the walls of the wash began to steepen and two-tenths of a mile later, the wash had turned into a canyon and the dirt had turned to rock. The Granada was having difficulty with some of the rocks, and when I scraped my oil pan on a nasty-looking pointed one, I killed the engine and got out.

An icy knife of a breeze whispered down the canyon bringing with it the sweet smells of pine and manzanita. A coyote yipped somewhere in the night. Behind the mountain, the moon was threatening to rise, diffusing the sky with an anemic light. I clicked on the flashlight and started up the canyon on foot.

The ground was too rocky for tracks here, but there were tread marks in the plots of snow, which were becoming more plentiful the farther I went up the canyon. After what seemed to be at least a mile, but was probably no more than a quarter of one, the canyon widened into a small, flat basin, walled-in on all sides by the steep ascent of the mountains. In the middle of the basin stood the falling-down remnants of two old miners' shacks. Above the shacks, the entrance to a mine stared like an empty Cyclopean eye-socket out of the sheer rock face of the mountains.

I listened. There was only the soft, eerie echo of the winds playing tag in the canyons. I went toward the shacks.

The Bronco was parked behind the second one. It was empty. The doors weren't locked. I opened the driver's side and poked my flash in. There was nothing in the front seat or underneath it. There were a few dark stains in the back, by the window.

I got out of the car and looked into the two shacks through their empty windows. A few rusted cans, a torn mattress with its stuffing coming out, that was all. I went back to the car.

The dirt behind the Bronco looked disturbed, as if someone had tried to cover up his tracks by smoothing it over with his foot. I followed the trail to a rusted, narrow-gauge rail track that ran fifty feet up the mountain into the mouth of the mine.

I started up the steep incline. I stopped at the entrance to the tunnel and shone my flash in. The light poked an insignificant hole in the blackness. My face was covered with a clammy film of sweat and not all of it was from the hike up here. My hand felt greasy on the flashlight. I wiped it on my pants and took a deep breath and stepped in.

The height of the hole was a good foot shorter than my six feet and I had to stoop to get through, but inside the rock ceiling lifted enough for me to walk erect. The timber supports that ran down each side of the tunnel looked rotten and I was careful not to bump them, sticking to the middle of the two tracks. The darkness swallowed my light and I could only see a few yards ahead. Then the light found a pair of huge yellow eyes and there was a high-pitched screech and I dropped the flash and ducked as the eyes came rushing at me. The wings of the barn owl beat the air frantically as it flew past me and out into the night.

I tried to regain control of my thrashing pulse, then realized I was completely in the dark. I went into a mild panic and dropped to all fours and began groping around on the ground. My hand wrapped around the metal cylinder and I picked it up and shook it. The light came on, temporarily abating my panic.

I started forward again, but I didn't intend to go much farther. I didn't trust the light anymore and I had visions of trying to feel my way out of here in the dark and wandering down the wrong tunnel until I fell down some bottomless black hole. It turned out that I didn't have to go much farther. A few more steps and the faint, loathsome odor of putrefying flesh beckoned to me from the darkness. I started breathing through my mouth.

Up on the right wall of the tunnel, a wooden siding had been placed as a precaution over the bottom half of the ventilation shaft. I went to it.

The shaft dropped to a lower tunnel about twenty feet down. He was at the bottom of it, his gray, puffy face staring at me open-mounted. Merritt didn't have to worry about getting a life sentence anymore. He didn't have to worry about anything.

The blood-soaked bedspread had fallen off the body and lay underneath him, providing a bizarre resting place. His legs were bent under him at tortured angles they could never have achieved in life, his arms were flung away from the body as if he was trying to explain something to me. His clothes were all around him, scattered in casual patterns over the rock floor.

I made my way quickly out of the mine. The air outside was sweet and clean, like mountain water, and I took long, luxurious draughts of it, but the smell clung to me, like a whore demanding her pay.

The moon peeped over the rim of the mountain, a corrupt yellow smile, mocking me. I went down the trail at a trot.

23

When Dierdorf came through the door, Harris and I were staring at each other like two tom-cats meeting in an alley for the first time. We'd been like that for half an hour.

Dierdorf stopped in front of me and frowned. He was wearing a white Stetson hat, his green zippered jacket with the fur collar, and a pair of fancy, hand-tooled cowboy boots. "You want to see me?"

"I'm sorry for disturbing you at home—"

"Don't worry about it," he snapped. "I only live a couple of blocks from here."

I felt like asking him why the hell it took him half an hour to get here, then. Instead, I said: "Can we talk in your office?"

He stepped back and invited me in with a wave of his hand.

I sat in the same chair I'd occupied last time and he moved past me and sat behind his desk. He took off his hat and put it on the desk and smoothed down his gray hair. He didn't bother to unzip his jacket. I guess he didn't expect to be here long.

"You don't look too happy to see me, Sheriff."

"Maybe that's because I'm not."

"Why is that?"

He rested his elbows on the arms of the chair, clasped his hands in front of him, and leaned forward. "Because I think you're a troublemaker, if you really want to know. And because I think Sal is wasting his time and money hiring you. But that's Sal's business, not mine."

"You don't think I can bring Merritt in?"

"No," he said. "I don't."

I shook my head sadly. "I'm sorry you feel that way. Actually, that's one of the reasons I wanted to talk to you. I realize our relations have been kind of strained in the past, Sheriff, but I was hoping that now that we're both playing on the same side of the net, so to speak, we might be able to get some teamwork going."

I smiled at him. That went over like a fart in a spacesuit. "Let's get down to it, Asch. What do you want?"

"Several things, Sheriff," I said. "First, I'd like to know what you've done so far to find Merritt."

"I've put out an APB on his car to every county and state law enforcement agency between here and Texas. I called the Waco police department and alerted them that he might be headed that way."

"That's all?"

"That'll bring him in faster than you will, Asch."

"Have you been out to Ma and Pa's?"

"Sure," he said, irritation rising in his voice. "What the hell do you think?"

"What did you find?"

"Find?" He leaned further forward. "Not a fucking thing, that's what I found. That's what you usually find when somebody cleans out all their belongings and splits."

"No clues, though, where he might be headed?"

He leaned back and waved a hand at the wall behind him. "Why don't you go out there and sift through the garbage cans, Sherlock? You'll probably be able to tell us. My men already did it, but hell, we're just a bunch of bungling, incompetent, sap-happy morons. What do we know? You can probably do better. I mean, you're a master at all this tricky detective shit."

"Sometimes it's not a matter of being a master of anything," I said in my most tutorial tone. "Sometimes it's just a matter of cognition. Reality isn't necessarily as we perceive it. All that raw data out there is filtered and molded by us according to the way we're taught to see it. For instance, you or I may look out that window and see snow. But an Eskimo doesn't see just snow. He sees one of thirty-two different kinds of snow because that's how many words there are for it in his language."

He pointed a finger at me and snarled: "You want something, Asch, ask it, otherwise get out of here. I didn't come down here to listen to your smart-mouthed bullshit."

I shook my head, trying to simulate a wide-eyed innocence. "I'm not trying to smart-mouth, Sheriff. I'm only trying to make the point that you're a cop. As a cop, you mold reality according to the way a cop is taught he should see it. You expect people to behave in a certain way because that's the way you're used to seeing them behave—"

"What do you *want*, Asch?"

"I want to look at your file on the Realango murder."

He shook his head. "That's confidential."

"I realize that. But there might be something in there that will help me find Merritt."

His eyes were like pieces of pale, shiny flint. "What, for instance?"

"I can't tell until I take a look. That's what I was trying to explain to you. You might look at all that data and see one thing, I might see another—"

"No," he said, shaking his head firmly.

"I won't take it out of the building," I said. "You can stay with me, or one of your men. I'll look at it right here—"

"No."

"What are you afraid I'll find in it?"

"I'm not afraid you'll find anything," he sneered. "That file is police business. It's going to stay police business. So if that's what you came all the way out here for, you've wasted a trip."

I slapped my knees. "Okay, Sheriff. If that's the way you feel about it. I'm sorry I bothered you." I pointed to the phone. "Before I go, may I make a call?"

He waved a long, slender palm at the instrument on the desk. I picked it up and dialed Moonfire and asked for Sal Mezzano. While I waited for him to get on the line, I sat smiling at Dierdorf.

Mezzano's voice said: "Yeah?"

"This is Asch. Listen, I'm with Sheriff Dierdorf. I've been out to Merritt's place and I picked up a couple of pretty good leads where he might have gone, but I'm going to need to look through the Sheriff's file on the Realango murder to put them together."

There was a pause. "So?"

I glanced over at Dierdorf. "So, Dierdorf doesn't want to show it to me. He says it's classified top secret police business."

"What'd you find at Merritt's place?" Mezzano asked anxiously.

"I'll tell you when I see you."

"You're sure it's good?"

"If I find in the file what I think I might, Merritt might be brought in tonight. Tomorrow at the latest."

"Put Frank on the phone."

I handed the receiver to Dierdorf. Whatever Mezzano told him, it must have been good, because Dierdorf's face was instantly stained crimson and white. He didn't say anything for a full twenty seconds, tried a couple of "Buts", then fell silent for another ten. Finally, he said: "Yeah. I understand. Okay, Sal. Sure."

He slammed the phone down and glowered at me. The muscles in his jaw were a line of knots under the skin. "You think you're a real smart sonofabitch, don't you?"

I let him have that one for nothing. He kept his eyes on me and shouted: "Harris!"

Harris opened the door and stepped into the room.

"Get me the Realango murder book."

Harris looked at him, then at me. "But—"

"GET IT!"

Harris hurried out and returned with a gray looseleaf binder. He set it down on the desk and hovered there, giving me hostile looks. "You can shut the door on the way out," Dierdorf told him.

He followed his instructions faithfully and I picked up the notebook. It was a three-ring binder, neatly separated into sections by colored tabs. The first section was all the coroner's reports, the second, the reports of the investigating officers—photographs of the body, summaries of interviews of witnesses at the scene, etc., the third, the homicide detectives' reports of their follow-up interrogations of the more important witnesses, and so on. In the back of that section was a ten-page transcript of a sworn statement that had been made by Battaglia five days after the shooting. I glanced through the entire notebook, to get the basic structure of it, then went back to the beginning.

"Very nicely done," I said earnestly. "L.A. just started this system a little while ago. It's really a good way to organize data."

He brushed the compliment aside. "How long is this going to take?"

"Twenty minutes maybe. Not long."

It took twenty-two. When I closed the cover and looked up, Dierdorf was drumming his fingertips nervously on the desk as if he had to go to the bathroom. If he'd been peeing in his pants, there would have been no way he would have left me alone with that book. "You wouldn't have the original notes those reports were made from, would you?"

"No."

I put my hand on the cover and patted it. "There's a lot of conflicting testimony in there."

"Like what?"

"For one thing, a couple of details in Battaglia's sworn statement don't match up with what he first told your men at the scene."

He lowered his eyelids. "What details?"

"Right after the shooting, he said he'd heard *two* shots. Five days later, he said there'd only been one."

"Moonfire is sitting in a valley between two mountain ranges, in case you hadn't noticed. There's a nice echo out there. I already tested it out."

"Battaglia's been around guns a lot. You don't think he'd know an echo from a gunshot?"

"Under those circumstances, probably not." His tone was irascible. "Read the other reports. Nobody else heard two shots."

"He was the only one outside," I countered. "Everybody else was inside. Another thing. In the sworn statement, Battaglia said

209

Realango was bent over when he got it. In the first report, he has him standing up." I flipped the book open and turned to the page. "Right here. 'Witness says Realango bent over, then straightened back up and looked at him, then two shots rang out very close together, and the victim fell dead.' "

Dierdorf sighed. He looked like a man whose sister had just died and who had just been handed the responsibility of caring for her twelve-year-old retarded son. "Mister, you ever see an animal get hit with a 30.06? That slug would straighten you up pretty damn fast."

"That doesn't explain—"

"Bullets travel faster than the speed of sound. It *sounded* like the shot came after he got hit, that's all."

"At least four other witnesses interviewed by your men said Realango was standing up when he was hit."

"It'd surprise me if they didn't," he said, making a grandiose gesture with his hands. "It surprises me that one or two of them didn't swear he'd been crawling away from the car on all fours. Eyewitness testimony sucks, Asch. Someday it'll be banned from trials altogether. You talk about your 'cognition' and your 'filtered reality,' that's your prime example. Ask two people who witnessed the same goddamn crime what the suspect looked like and nine times out of ten, one of them will tell you the guy was short and blond and the other will say he was a tall, black man. Why?" He leaned forward and tapped his temple with an index finger. "Because the mind abhors a vacuum, Asch, and if it doesn't remember so well what happened at such-and-such a time at such-and-such a place, it fills in the details from what it does remember from other times and other places. Contrary to popular myth, circumstantial evidence is much more reliable than eyewitness testimony. And in this case, the circumstantial evidence says Realango *had* to have been in a crouch when he was shot."

"*If* he was shot from the kitchen," I added.

"What the hell is that supposed to mean?"

"Maybe he wasn't shot from the kitchen."

He stuck his lower lip out and nodded, as if that was a thought.

"That's right. Maybe he wasn't. Maybe he was shot from the roof of Harold's Club. Or maybe he was shot from a passing satellite. Only Merritt wasn't on the roof of Harold's Club or in a satellite. *He was standing in the goddamn fucking door of the kitchen.*"

I watched him calmly. "Did Merritt ever actually confess to the killing?"

"Sure he confessed."

"To whom?"

He poked himself in the chest with a thumb. "To me. To Sal. To his own goddamn attorney."

I took a deep breath and let it out slowly. "I guess that's how it was then. It just made me curious, is all. But I guess you're right." I paused. "One more question. You think there could be any connection between Merritt's jumping bail and his girl friend's death?"

He squinted at me. "What connection?"

"I don't know. It's just that I called Leland Carew today. He says it's not conclusive, but there is some evidence that the throttle on the girl's car had been tampered with."

"I don't know anything about it," he said flatly.

I nodded and slapped my knees and stood up. "Well, thanks a lot for opening the file for me. It was a big help."

A bitter sneer spread across his thin lips. "You got all your 'hot leads' put together now?"

"Pretty much."

"Let me know if you're going to bring in Merritt tonight. I'd like to be there when it happens."

"I'll make sure you're there," I assured him.

He snorted and waved a hand at me. "Merritt is five states away from here by now."

"Maybe," I said, smiling. "Goodnight, Sheriff."

I went out, closing the door quietly behind me.

24

The delegation from the Moose Convention had picked up in numbers and volume when I came through the front door. I didn't break stride and the girls were still haphazardly trying to fall into line as I walked past them, and down the hallway to my room.

I opened the door with a key and went in. The room was tiny and it took four steps to get around the double bed to the window. I parted the mini-blinds and peered out.

The window looked out onto a barren cement courtyard. Twenty yards away, on the other side of the courtyard, sat two large metal garbage bins on wheels. The back of the courtyard was enclosed by the fortress-like wall that encircled the entire place, except for two large wrought-iron gates in back of the garbage bins.

The gun towers weren't visible from the room. This wing of the building slanted away from the central part of the courtyard and the angle was wrong.

I was lost in thought, staring silently at the gates when Mezzano came through the door behind me.

"Battaglia's on his way over," he said testily. "What the hell's this all about, anyway?"

I pointed out the window. "Are those gates ever open?"

"What gates?" He moved over to the window and looked out. "Oh, the garbage gates. Yeah, sure. We'll open them about four o'clock for the garbage guys. They gotta drive the truck in there."

"They're open from four until when?"

"Depends on when they come to dump the bins. Sometimes

they show up at five, sometimes six, sometimes even seven. Depends on how busy they get."

"They come every day?"

"Yeah, sure." His tone was petulant. "Why? What the hell's the big deal with the gates? Never mind about the fucking gates. What's this shit about having a check ready for another five grand?"

"That was the agreement," I said. "Five in front, five when Merritt was brought in."

"You brought him in?" he said excitedly.

"*I* can't bring him in," I said. "It'll take quite a few men to bring him in. He's at the bottom of a mine shaft in the mountains, about half a mile behind Ma and Pa's."

"At the bottom . . ." his voice faded.

"He's dead, Mezzano. Somebody killed him and dumped him there. Whoever did it had it figured pretty good. We'd all be running around like assholes, looking for Merritt the bail jumper, and all the time, Merritt's body would be rotting down there in the mine, crumbling into dust. If the animals didn't get to it first—"

He blinked at me in astonishment.

"You realize this looks pretty bad for you, Mezzano," I went on. "First, you loan Merritt $5,000 in cash, about which you say nothing to anybody. Then, on your instruction, Merritt starts making long distance death threats on the phone. Four weeks later, the person he's been threatening is dead and so is he. And Pebbles. We can't forget about Pebbles. She was Merritt's old lady. They would be likely to talk. They'd tell each other things. Things that a person who'd paid for a hit wouldn't want to get around."

"I didn't pay for no hit," he said, his voice rising.

"I know you didn't," I said. "You loaned him the money, just like you said. The only thing is, Merritt was the only one who could verify that story and Merritt's dead. I'm just telling you how bad it looks." I leaned forward and searched his face. "You do understand it *does* look bad?"

He nodded dumbly and sat down on the bed. Thoughts moved mechanically behind his eyes. "Did you tell Dierdorf about Merritt?"

"No. I wanted to talk to you first."

"Good," he said. "Maybe we should keep it quiet. Maybe we shouldn't tell anybody—"

"You can't do that."

"Why not?" his voice was petulant again. "Who else knows about it?"

"Nobody yet. But I'm not covering it up. Also, are you forgetting about your $200,000?"

That one stopped him. "As a matter of fact, I was," he said. He put his fist into his mouth and bit down on one finger. He jumped off the bed and began pacing in tight circles. "I still don't get it. Who the hell would want to kill Merritt?"

"That's what I want to talk to Battaglia about," I said. "You say he's on his way over?"

He stopped pacing and nodded. "I called him right after you called me and told him to get his butt over here. He should have been here by now."

"Where is he coming from?"

"Sparks. He's renting a house over there until Susan cools down. I thought she'd have cooled down by now, but she still raises hell whenever I bring up his name." He squinted at me, hard, and said: "Does Joe know something about all this?"

"It's not what he knows that I want to talk to him about," I said. "It's what he thinks he doesn't know that I'm interested in."

His eyebrows knitted in confusion. "Huh?"

One of the girls from the line stuck her head in the door and said: "Joe's out front looking for you, Sal. He said you want to see him."

Mezzano nodded and we went out. Susan Mezzano stood blocking the end of the hallway. She looked as if she was made of cast iron. Her body leaned rigidly on her cane, her features were tightened in rage. When we got near her, I could hear her breath whistling heavily in her chest. "I told you I don't want to see that

214

sonofabitch's face around this fucking joint as long as I'm here."

"I'm the one who asked for him to be here," I told her.

Her eyes flashed angrily on me. "You? Why?"

"I'll explain it all in a little while. I can't right now, though."

She started to say something, but I stopped her. "You trusted me before. Trust me again. He'll be gone within twenty minutes, I guarantee it."

Not all the hostility had drained from her face, but she stepped out of the way and let us pass.

Battaglia was standing by the front doors in a sheepskin coat, nervously pulling on his Pancho Villa mustache. His baggy eyes looked past us, as if searching for some sign of the pack of rabid wolves that had been tracking him since sundown yesterday. "I thought you said she'd be over it in a week," he said in an agitated voice. "It's been almost two and it doesn't look like she's getting over it to me. I thought she was going to take my head off with that cane of hers—"

"Don't worry about it," Mezzano said. "She'll cool down. Just hold on—"

"I've *been* holding on," Battaglia said. "I been living in that shitbox rental for ten days, waiting for a call. Nobody's called. I gotta know what I'm gonna do, Sal. If I'm not gonna go back to work right away, I can file for unemployment—"

"I *said* don't sweat it," Mezzano snapped at him. "It'll work itself out. I didn't call you to talk about that crap. We got other problems right now, more important than your collecting fucking unemployment. You remember Asch here?"

His eyes bounced off me, then back to Mezzano. "Yeah, sure, I remember him."

"He wants to ask you a few questions," Mezzano said.

"What about?"

"The shooting," I said.

Battaglia glanced an unspoken question at Mezzano, who said: "It's okay. He's on our side now. Tell him whatever he wants to know. Don't hold nothing back."

Battaglia shrugged. "Okay."

215

I motioned to the door. "Let's talk outside."

"Why outside?" Battaglia protested. "Why can't we talk in the office?"

"Cause he wants to talk outside," Mezzano said.

"It's colder than a witch's tit out there—"

"So big fucking deal," Mezzano snarled. "You got a coat on, for chrissakes. Look at me. I ain't even got a coat. I swear to God, Joe, lately you're turning into a fucking pansy or something."

Battaglia's eyes had a hurt look in them as he turned and went through the door. Sal was starting out after him when the dark-haired girl who had come to the room came hustling over. "Sal, Susan wants to see you."

He waved a hand at her. "Tell her I'm busy—"

"She says it's important."

He heaved a bothered sigh. "All right, all right. I'll be right there," he said to her, then to me: "I'll be out in a second."

Battaglia stood shivering outside the front door as I came out, his hands thrust stiffly in the pockets of his coat. "I've about had it with that shit," he complained bitterly.

"What shit?"

He jerked his hand out of his pocket and flipped it at the door. "*That* shit. I'm not used to being treated like a dog. He's got no reason to go calling me a pansy. Ever since the shooting, he's been jumping down my throat for every goddamn little thing. I don't have to take it. I still got my license. I can go into business again."

There was something weak and posturing about his threat and I knew he would never voice it to Sal.

"He's been under a strain lately," I said, then realized how ridiculous it sounded, me making excuses for Mezzano.

"You think *I* haven't been under a strain?" he said, his mouth working angrily under his mustache. "*I'm* the one who's the material witness in this thing. *I'm* the one who's gotta appear before the fucking federal grand jury next week—"

"Anybody ever find out what that's all about?" I asked, trying to divert the energy he was working up for his self-pitying tirade.

He put his hands back into his pockets and began chewing his mustache. "I know what it's all about. It's about the shooting. Maybe they're not saying but that's what it is. The Feds have been waiting for something like this to happen, just so they'd have an excuse to come down on Sal. They've got it now and they're gonna come down heavy—with both feet. And the first thing they're gonna land on is me."

The sound of his own words seemed to have frightened him. He looked nervously out at the gates, as if he'd just heard the howling of the wolves in the distance.

"That's what I want to talk to you about," I said. "I want you to show me what happened that morning." I led him over to the front gate. "Where was Realango when you got out here?"

He pointed to a spot on the other side of the gate. "There."

"How about you?"

He took a stance about a foot to my right. "About here."

"What did you say to him?"

"I asked him what he was doing out here."

"What did he say?"

"Just a lot of crazy garbage about someone calling him at the hotel and telling him Sal wanted to see him right away. The story smelled, cause I knew Sal was asleep, so I told him he'd better get in his car and get the hell out of here before Sal *did* wake up. Otherwise he might get hurt."

"What did he say then?"

"That's when he started getting squirrely. He kept asking, 'Why Sal no like me?' over and over like some kind of broken record. What the fuck was I gonna say? He knew why Sal didn't like him. So I kept telling him to get lost and pretty soon we started having some words and he started getting real wild. Told me to step outside the gate and he'd break my face. I wasn't about to step out there. I wasn't no match for him. Besides he had to be a major whacko, coming out here after everything that had been going on. So I parted my coat so he could see the .357 I had tucked in my belt, just so he'd know the score and told him I was gonna tell him once more and that was it. He just looked at me square in the eye and said, 'I no afraid of you,' and went to his

217

car. You shoulda seen the look in his eyes. I'm telling you, the guy was whacko."

"What happened then?"

"He opened the door of the car and bent down and then Merritt yelled, 'Freeze!' and shot him."

"Did it look like he was going for the gun in his boot?"

He rolled his shoulders. "Who knows? All I know is that the gun was there. He might've been bending down to scratch his ankle for all I know. I'm just goddamn glad I didn't get a chance to find out." He paused and shook his head reflectively. "That's what I can't understand about Merritt splitting like that. He had the best mouthpiece on the Coast, he had it knocked for a justifiable homicide plea. Now, forget it. The D.A. will ream him a new asshole when they bring him in."

When they bring him in, I thought, he won't even need the one he has. I opened the gate and he followed me out.

Two sets of headlights split the grove of birch trees and swung onto the lot, parking side-by-side. The doors of both cars were flung open simultaneously and eight drunken conventioners piled out, whooping and hollering. They swept past us to the gate where they stood baying like wolves, waiting for it to open. Maybe this was the pack that Battaglia had heard.

Sal was at the front door to greet the new arrivals with his best smile. While he did that, I walked out to where I remembered Realango's Mustang to have been. "Would you say this is about where he was standing when he was shot?" I asked Battaglia.

He nodded. "Yeah, about there."

"What position was he in?"

He stood by my side and turned around to face the gate, then crouched over. "Like this."

"You told the deputy at the scene that he'd bent down then stood back up again before he got hit."

He made an exasperated face. "Look, it all went down so fast, I can't say for sure how he was standing. He might have been straightening up. I can't say for sure."

Mezzano came through the gate and over to where we were

standing. He got there right when I said: "You also said you heard two shots."

"That's what it seemed like at the time," Battaglia said, nodding uncomfortably. "I thought I heard two shots, but there was only one. It must have been an echo."

"Who helped you with that conclusion—Dierdorf?"

"Nobody helped me," he said resentfully.

"You mean between the time you said you'd heard two shots and your sworn statement, he didn't discuss the second shot with you at all?"

"Sure we discussed it," he said. "But he didn't *help* me. We decided together that was what it had to be."

"Why?"

He looked at me as if I were imbecilic. "Because Merritt only fired one shot, that's why."

I nodded. "At the time, what direction did it seem to you like that second shot came from?"

"The rear guntower," he said, pointing. "I remember, cause after I went out to check on Realango, I looked up there. That's when I saw Merritt standing in the door of the kitchen. I remember I was surprised to see him there, cause I thought for sure he'd been in the tower."

I looked up at the tower. Only the glass cage was spotlighted. It floated disembodied above the roof, menacing, almost surreal.

"How much time elapsed between the shots and the time you looked up there?"

"I don't know," he said. "Two, three minutes maybe. When I heard the shot, I drew out my gun and hit the dirt. I stayed crouched down by the gate there for a couple of minutes until I could see Realango wasn't gonna get up. Then I went out to see how bad he was hit."

"Did you see anybody in the tower?"

"No."

I turned to Mezzano, who looked thoroughly bewildered. "Are guns kept in both towers all the time?"

"Not any more," he said. "Frank took 'em all."

"But there were at the time of the shooting?"

"Yeah, sure."

"Both 30.06's?"

"Yeah. Why?"

I brushed the question aside temporarily, even though I knew he wouldn't like it, and turned back to Battaglia. "When I first saw Merritt's picture in the paper, I wondered how that eye of his would effect his marksmanship. Did you ever see him shoot?"

"Sure," Battaglia said. "We used to go out target shooting every once in awhile. Tin cans and stuff. He wouldn't go out with me after awhile cause I always used to kid him about what a lousy shot he was."

"With a rifle?"

He snorted and waved a hand in disgust. "Rifles, handguns, it didn't matter. He couldn't hit the broad side of a barn at twenty feet."

"But he hit Realango's heart at fifty yards," I said.

"So he got lucky," Mezzano cut in impatiently. "What's the big deal?"

"I don't think he did get lucky," I said, looking down on him. "I don't think Realango was shot from the door of the kitchen. I think he was shot from that rear guntower. And I think that whoever was up there also killed Pebbles and Merritt."

"Killed Merritt?" Battaglia blurted out, his eyes snapping toward Mezzano. "What's he talking about?"

Mezzano ignored him and grabbed my arm. "Wait a minute. Merritt *told* me he shot Realango—"

"Because he thought he had," I said. "He had no reason to think he hadn't. That was the way it appeared to everybody, including himself, so nobody had any reason to doubt it. Once that basic assumption of guilt was made, a new reality was born to fit it. Realango had to have been in a crouch because the autopsy said he had to have been in a crouch. There'd been no second shot because Merritt had only fired once. Battaglia was the only one who'd heard the second shot anyway, so the reality was just that much easier to distort. So one eyewitness heard an echo, so what?"

Mezzano shook his head as if he were coming out of a dream. "Who?"

"That's the question, isn't it? Who?"

Battaglia tugged on the sleeve of Sal's cashmere sweater. "Merritt's dead?"

Mezzano turned and stabbed a finger at him viciously. "You don't know nothing. Just keep your mouth shut. You been talking too goddamn much lately."

Battaglia threw out the palms of his hands imploringly. "I haven't said anything to anybody. Who've I been talking to, Sal? Who?"

"It doesn't matter," I said. "It'll all be out by tomorrow anyway."

Mezzano's head jerked around.

"What's today, Wednesday? I'm going to call Dierdorf now. I'll have to show him where the body is, but I'd like you along to make sure he doesn't try to hold me all night for questioning. He'd just love to do that to me if he got the chance, and I've got to get some sleep. I've got to catch an early flight out of here tomorrow—"

"Early flight to where?!" Mezzano shouted, throwing up his hands excitedly. "You can't leave now—"

"I think I can clear all this up by tomorrow night," I said, stifling his outburst. "But it'll cost you another twenty-five hundred. That's in addition to the five thousand you already owe me for bringing Merritt in, of course."

His mouth dropped open as if it was being controlled by an invisible ventriloquist. For a few seconds, no sound emerged. Then he said: "That's fucking burglary. You're trying to put the squeeze on me—"

"Look," I said, "you're getting off cheap and you know it, so stop bitching. You know what you'd wind up paying a lawyer to take all this off your back? Four times that much."

He didn't say anything.

"Well?" I asked. "What'll it be? Joe here named the tune before you came out, Mezzano. You've got a pack of hyenas circling around, just waiting for you to go lame so they can move in for the kill. Take a look around. It's already started."

He stared at me. His eyes were dark and glossy, like the eyes of a snake. I didn't mind that. I was rather fond of snakes. I'd even had a pet boa once. "I'll take the twenty-five hundred when I deliver. The balance of the ten for Merritt, I'll take when we go inside."

"You know what, Asch?" he said, after studying me for what seemed to be a long time.

"Yeah, I know what," I said. "I'm a real prick."

"Yeah," he said, his thick mouth turning down in a hard frown. "Only this time you'd better be a real *right* prick."

25

The first prelim was already over by the time we reached the Olympic and the house lights were up. The place was filled with people and smoke and the smells of beer and sweat. It looked as if half the Mexican population of L.A. was packed into the auditorium, waiting to see what their boy Bobby Torres, the pride of Lincoln Heights, looked like now that he had moved up a division.

Liz and I moved down the aisle, our feet sticking on the drying puddles of spilled soft drinks and beer, and slipped into the two vacant ringside seats. An immaculately dressed black man with an eight-carat diamond on his right pinkie, leaned across Liz and said: "Where you been hiding, Jake? I haven't seen you in a couple of weeks."

"I've been working for a change," I said. "Liz Patterson, Clifton Rougely."

Clifton smiled. "Glad to meet you, Liz," he said, then motioned to a platinum blonde on his left whose chest rivaled Liz's. "This is Sylvia Armacost. Jake Asch, Liz Patterson."

Sylvia Armacost smiled unintelligently. "Hello."

"What was the first prelim like?" I asked.

"Nothing," he said, making a face. "A real smell-o. Here, have a program."

"Thanks," I said and took the program from him. While I looked it over, Liz leaned over and whispered: "Who's he?"

"Bail bondsman," I said.

She nodded.

The next event was a six-rounder between two featherweights, Stuart Solomon, a flashy young black who was in the stable of ex-heavyweight champ Don Frazer, and an Ecuadorian named

223

Velasquez, whom I knew nothing about. While waiting for it to begin, I tried to pick Schwartz's face out of the ringside seats, but couldn't see him.

A cheer went up from the crowd as Solomon came prancing down the aisle like a frisky colt, smiling. He wore a white silk robe and his taped hands rested on the shoulders of his trainer who trotted ahead of him. As he passed the third row, someone shouted: "Whaddya know? A blind fighter!"

Solomon was in the ring shadow-boxing when the Ecuadorian, a short stocky kid with a bull-neck and hair like a Brillo pad, climbed through the ropes and took off his robe.

Clifton leaned over and said: "Watch the Ecuadorian. I've seen him fight. He's tough."

The lights went out and the bell rang and the two fighters met in the middle of the ring. Solomon turned it on the first round, landing on the Ecuadorian with every conceivable kind of punch —jabs, lightning-fast left-right combinations, hooks, crosses, and uppercuts—stepping easily away from the shorter man's wild hooks and stopping every once in awhile to do his version of the Ali Shuffle. The crowd ate it up.

"Come on, Stu! You coo'! You ain't no foo'!"

"Get whitey!"

"Squeeze a blackhead!" a Velasquez fan countered.

The second round was more of the same, except when Solomon slipped and the referee counted it as a knockdown. The crowd voiced its disapproval by booing loudly. The Ecuadorian kept wading in, trying to counter the wicked shots he was taking, but not having too much success. His mouthpiece didn't fit quite right and it made him look as if he were enjoying the punishment he was taking.

"Why is he smiling?" a woman's voice called out of the crowd.

"I think he's probably queer!" the answer came back.

By the fifth round, Solomon was starting to look worried. He had delivered his best shots right on the button, but the Ecuadorian had not seemed to have noticed, and was still wading in, flailing away. Solomon was able to tie him up before anything major landed but he appeared arm-weary and now just seemed to be trying to defend himself more than mount any kind of an offense. At one point, the fighters were clinched in a corner and a drunk one row back stood up and began singing loudly: "I could have danced all night, I could have danced all night . . ."

"Not at your age, you couldn't!" the man next to him yelled. "Siddown!"

In the final round, both fighters came out slugging and for most of the three minutes, they stood toe-to-toe, ring center, banging away. When the bell sounded, the crowd came to its feet and began showering the ring with coins. The handlers of the two fighters were still scrambling around the canvas, picking quarters and dimes off the mat when the announcer awarded a unanimous decision to Solomon.

I leaned forward and asked Clifton: "You have any money on the Ecuadorian?"

He looked startled. "Me? Sheeit. I'd never bet against my own people. I saw 'Roots,' man."

Someone tapped me on the shoulder and I turned around and stared into a leering, lopsided face that looked as if it were being pulled up on one side by fishhooks. The face went with a head of hair that looked like it had been styled in a wind tunnel, a pair of ripped Levis and a faded T-shirt that said MARATHON MAN on it. "Jake," the face said. "Who do you like in the main?"

"I'll have to go with Torres."

"How much?"

"What are the odds?"

"Nine to five, Torres."

"Thirty-six to twenty?"

"You're on," he said. "Moreno is going to steal the fight, I'm telling you." Although the leer never changed, it seemed to have a lascivious light in it when it turned on Liz. "Lovely lady, Jake."

"Igor, this is Liz."

Igor kissed Liz's hand with a lopsided flourish: "Charmed." He straightened up and said: "Gotta take some more money. I'll see you after the fight, Jake."

225

When he moved off into the crowd, Liz said disbelievingly: "Igor?"

"His real name is Marty Gelson," I acknowledged. "Everybody calls him Igor because of his face."

"He doesn't mind?"

"I think he gets off on it, really. Gives him an identity."

"What happened to him?"

"He had a brain tumor," I said. "When the doctor removed it, his scalpel slipped and he wound up with that face and a hell of a malpractice settlement. He used to sell furniture at the Sofa Supermart. Now all he does is go to the fights and the races and make bets. He says it's the best thing that ever happened to him."

"I'd rather have a normal face."

"That's because yours isn't half bad to start with," I said. "Igor claims he gets more ass now than he did before. He says the girls go crazy over him. See, he claims that when the doctor's knife slipped, it also severed some vital nerve that connected his brains to his balls, and now he can go all night long without reaching an orgasm."

"There's no such nerve," she said skeptically.

"Don't tell that to Igor. He'll just argue with you all night long about there not being any basis in western medicine for acupuncture, either."

"That's what the 'Marathon Man' T-shirt is all about?"

I nodded.

"Jesus Christ," she said, shaking her head. "You sure know some lulus."

The crowd had already begun to shift nervously in their seats in anticipation of the main fight, and within five minutes, the tension had spread until it almost seemed that there was some heavy-breathing beast in the auditorium, waiting for a sign, a scent on the wind. Then, there was a ripple at the back of the room and a thunderous ovation broke out as Bobby Torres and his entourage trotted down the aisle.

He was young and darkly handsome and obviously conscious of the fact. He wore a red velvet robe with gold cuffs and his black hair was carefully styled and sprayed to make sure it didn't become mussed in the heat of battle.

He'd won his last two outings as a lightweight fighting bums, but before that, as a featherweight, he'd been soundly beaten by two mediocre fighters. You never would have known that by the reaction of the crowd, though. The chant had already begun to shake the auditorium: "TOR-RES! TOR-RES! TOR-RES! TOR-RES!"

Torres flashed a smile and waved at his cheering fans and I spotted Schwartz behind him in the entourage. He was with the fat man I'd seen him with in the Main Street Gym. When they reached the ring apron, Schwartz patted the fat man on the back, gave Torres the "victory" sign, and sat down in an empty ringside seat. I gave Liz a knowing nod and stood up.

Schwartz smiled warmly when he saw me. "Jake. Glad you could make it."

"Are you kidding? I wouldn't miss this." I turned to the pale, wide-faced man in the chair next to Schwartz's and said: "See that redhead over there with the big tits?"

The man squinted across the ring as if he were nearsighted. "Yeah?"

"She told me she finds you terribly attractive. She asked me to ask you to come over."

The man looked up skeptically.

"I'm serious," I said emphatically. "I was batting zero with her and she pointed you out and said, 'Now, *that's* my type.'"

Liz was waving at the man now to come over. He cleared his throat and stood up. "Well, now, maybe I'll just go on over and check this out."

"That's the stuff," I said admiringly and took his seat.

Schwartz jabbed a thumb after the man. "Was that for real?"

"Naw," I said. "My girlfriend loves a put-on. I just thought I'd sit over here and get a professional's view of this thing."

There was a scant smattering of polite applause as Moreno, Torres' opponent, parted the ropes and stepped into the ring.

"There's a lot of talk about this being a handcuff job," I said.

"The talk is that the promoters aren't taking any chances blowing that shot at Escobedo, and that Moreno has been told not to unload any bombs."

"I wish it was a handcuff job," he said, picking a package of Rolaids out of his pocket. "Maybe I wouldn't need these."

The fighters were loosening up now, shaking their arms, rolling their heads around on their necks. The bell rang and they went to their corners and the announcer took the microphone that was lowered over the center of the ring and made the introductions. When he announced Torres' name, the place went crazy and the chant began all over again: "TOR-RES! TOR-RES! TOR-RES!"

While the fighters were receiving their instructions from the referee, I asked Schwartz: "How do you think it'll go?"

"KO in seven, maybe. Sooner, I hope. The better Bobby looks, the better the Escobedo deal looks."

"It isn't finalized yet?"

He shook his head. "They're waiting to see how this comes out."

The fighters went back to their corners and the tension mounted as the crowd waited for the bell. Before it rang, I said: "I've really got to give you credit for pulling it off, Jack."

"It isn't pulled off yet," he said cautiously. "Not until I get everybody's name on a piece of paper."

"I don't mean this," I said, waving a hand at the ring. "I mean Reno."

The bell clanged and the lights over the audience blacked out, and the two fighters charged out into the middle of the ring. Torres threw the first punch, a left jab that Moreno slipped and countered with an ineffective right. I watched the two figures moving above me, but I could feel Schwartz's eyes on me. "What do you mean, about Reno?"

"You know," I said, turning to him and winking. "I've got to give you credit. If it hadn't been for a couple of little mistakes you probably would've gotten away with it. Jesus Christ, here I thought you were just a soft, pudgy little guy, but there must be

228

some muscle behind that fat somewhere. It must have been some job dragging Merritt up that hill."

Moreno swung with a looping right hand that caught Torres behind the ear and backed him up. Moreno pressed Torres against the ropes and leaned on him, trying to work inside.

"En la banza!"

"Eso! Eso! Eso!"

"Get out of there Torres!"

Schwartz was staring at the ring, but his eyes were not following the action. "I don't know what you're talking about."

I took two Xeroxed sheets out of my pocket and handed them to him. He unfolded them and his lips tightened when he saw what they were.

"Those are copies of the receipts for the cars you rented when you were up in Reno. Notice the dates."

He didn't say anything.

"What tipped me off to that was when I checked airline reservations and found out there had been no Jack Schwartz on any flights to Reno on the day *after* Carlos was shot. That was the day you supposedly arrived, if you remember. I couldn't find any reservation on the day you were supposed to have left, either. That was simple enough to arrange. Anybody can make a plane reservation under a phony name. All he has to do is pay in cash. But when you want to rent a car, that's a different story. They want a driver's license. So I went around to all the rental agencies and found out you'd rented cars on all the right days. The day Carlos was shot, the day Pebbles went into the river, the day Merritt disappeared. You can keep those, by the way. I've got other copies."

Torres was catching Moreno with some good, stiff jabs now, snapping his head back, and the crowd was loving it, but then Moreno head-feinted and dropped his left hand. Torres took the bait and unloaded a right and Moreno sidestepped it and came over with a left hook that staggered the kid. The crowd came to

229

its feet around us, but Schwartz didn't move. He kept staring at the papers.

Moreno had Torres backed into the corner above us, pummeling him with punches, when the bell rang. The crowd sat back down, buzzing excitedly at the unexpected turn of events, while Torres' handlers wiped his face down with Vaseline and held a cold compress against the back of his neck. The fighter's head snapped back as he got a whiff of the ammonia inhaler his trainer had jammed up his nose.

"It had to be somebody with motive and opportunity and somebody who knew the layout of Moonfire," I said quietly. "That narrowed it down some. Then, when I remembered you telling me you used to hunt with a 30.06, that really got me to wondering. Then you left a few telltale signs at Merritt's saloon, like a cigarette butt."

He tried to sound insulted. "You're fucking nuts, Asch. I still don't know what you're talking about."

"Okay," I said, standing up. "I'll go and talk to somebody who does." I pointed at the ring. "Better look after your boy. It looks like he's having some trouble."

I walked away, but he called my name and hurried after me. He grabbed my arm and said: "Have you told anybody about this?"

"Not yet," I said. "I was hoping we might be able to work out some sort of a deal first. But you're obviously not interested."

I started away again, but he took two quick steps and grabbed my arm again. "Wait a minute, wait a minute," he said, his face flushed with color. His mouth was working furiously on the Rolaid. "Let's go someplace and talk about this."

I pointed up the aisle. "How about the snack bar?"

"I was thinking of someplace more private."

"I've seen the results of some of your private conversations, Schwartz. I'd rather talk at the snack bar."

"Okay," he said, licking his lips. "We'll talk at the snack bar."

I waved him ahead and he started up the aisle. Liz had seen me get up and was watching me carefully. I gave her a surreptitious hand signal and she excused herself to the sexpot I'd exchanged seats with and went up the other aisle to the ladies' room.

The bell for the second round rang and the place went dark as we reached the snack bar. The chant swelled through the crowd, "TOR-RES! TOR-RES!" as the fans desperately tried to focus their collective energy and transmit it to their flagging fighter.

Schwartz moved away from a cluster of beer-swilling Torres rooters and I stood close to him. "How much?" he asked.

"That'll depend on some of the answers I get."

His eyes scoured my face. "What answers?"

"Pebbles saw you walking across the courtyard, didn't she?"

He nodded. Sweat stood out in little droplets all over his face. His voice was low and controlled, but he talked rapidly as if he'd been ready with the speech for a long time and was relieved his cue had finally come. "Yeah. I turned around and there she was, staring at me. I didn't know she was Merritt's girlfriend at the time. I'd never seen her before. But I couldn't take the chance that she could identify me. So I went up to the window and told her that the cops were outside and that I couldn't get caught in there cause my wife would divorce me if she found out. I slipped her a hundred bucks and told her I'd be out to give her some more later if she'd keep quiet about seeing me."

"And you called her a few days later and arranged to have her meet you by the river," I said.

He nodded. "She still didn't think anything of it, even then. She was convinced Merritt had shot Carlos."

"Then why'd you kill her?"

His eyes implored for understanding. "I was already in so deep," he said. "People around her knew me. If she ever found out who I was, it would've started her thinking."

"So you sapped her and fixed the throttle on her car so she'd go over the edge," I said. He didn't answer. "Why Merritt?"

"She told him about me," he said. "He knew what I looked like. I couldn't take the chance he'd put two and two together and match me up to her description."

231

The crowd screamed, jerking my attention to the ring. The two fighters were in Moreno's corner, exchanging furiously. I turned back to Schwartz and asked, "How did you know Merritt would come outside with a gun?"

He shook his head. "I didn't. It worked out better than I thought. I thought everybody's attention would be directed out front and that I'd probably be able to get away, but it wasn't something I planned out. When Susan called me and told me she was going to Reno, something in me just snapped and I said to myself, 'Fuck it. I'm going to go up there and blow that asshole's head off,' and I went. I figured if I ever had a chance to get away with it, this was going to be it."

"But *why?*" I asked. "Why'd you want to kill Realango?"

He leaned toward me, his face hot and angry. "*Why?* Do you know what Carlos did to me? Do you have any idea? He fucking *ruined* me. *Nine* years I spent with him. Nine years of getting ripped off. I'd work my ass off getting a good match for him somewhere and he'd take front money from the promoters and split town. I'm the one who'd always be left holding the bag. I used to put good matches together, big money matches. Now I'm lucky to put together this shit fight." He waved a hand at the arena. "Nobody trusts me anymore, Asch, and all because of good old Carlos."

"So why did you keep booking matches for him? Why didn't you just get away from him?"

He blinked, as if astonished by my stupidity. "*Why?* Because he was *white.* He was a heavyweight and he was *white.* You know what that means in this business, Asch, to find a white heavyweight who can stand up and bang with the best of them? It's like the Devil, tempting you with gold all the time, waving it in front of your face. Pretty soon, your resistance gets low and you grab for it. I should've known when he ripped Sal off for that five grand in Reno. I had to pay Sal back personally. *Me.* Carlos just laughed when I asked him for the money back. I was going to bail out then, but then the Devil popped up with that gold again and I grabbed for it one last time. I had that TV shot with Foster just about worked out. Then I saw how Carlos looked against Majors and I knew—I *knew*—he wasn't ever going to get in shape, that he was just jacking me around, and that the Foster fight would never come off. Carlos wasn't interested in fighting anymore. He had his eye on Moonfire. That's when I decided I'd had it. I'd taken his shit for nine years and I wasn't going to take any more."

"I've heard about enough," I said. "I don't think I need any more."

The audience was on its feet again, stomping and screaming as Torres had his opponent against the ropes, battering him with a vicious series of combinations. Moreno's head was being snapped back by lefts and rights and then his knees buckled and he slumped to the canvas. The place became a madhouse of whistling and screaming and the walls vibrated with: "TOR-RES! TOR-RES! TOR-RES! TOR-RES!"

When the referee counted Moreno out, Torres' manager ran into the ring and embraced his fighter.

"Congratulations," I said to Schwartz. "Your man won big. Second round KO. You've finally got your title match."

His plump hand fluttered on my sleeve. "How much do you want?" he asked.

"Nothing," I said. "No sale."

His body tensed. His face twisted in anger. "Whaddya mean, no sale?"

"Just what I said! No sale." I turned and started away from him. He charged after me and grabbed me by the arm and spun me around. Every part of his face seemed to be working furiously. His eyes were filled with desperation and fear. "What are you going to do?"

I twisted his hand off my sleeve and walked away quickly without answering. He started after me again, but froze, his eyes wide in panic, as he saw Mezzano coming toward me, flanked by Alberto and Battaglia.

Alberto stepped in front of Mezzano and scowled at Schwartz menacingly, while I untucked my shirt and stripped off the recorder taped to my stomach. I handed the recorder to Mezzano

233

and he put it in his pocket, and I turned to face Schwartz.

We stood there, surrounded by the chaotic, ear-shattering, foot-stomping frenzy, staring at each other, and then the light seemed to go out in his eyes. His face went slack and his shoulders slumped and he seemed to wilt under our combined gaze. After a few seconds, he turned slowly and started down the aisle and disappeared into the chanting crowd.